Chiapas Ritual

The Chipotle Saga

David Greenwalt

LORO BOOKS

Rialto, California

Published by Loro Books
A division of Vision Plus Recovery Publishers
Rialto, California

This book is a work of fiction. Names, characters, businesses, organization, places, events, and incidents either are the product of the author's imagination or are used fictitiously. Any resemblance to actual persons, living or dead, events, or locales is entirely coincidental.

Cover design by Kenneth W. Edwards

Library of Congress Control Number: 2011929717

ISBN 978-1-61364-311-2

Printed in the United States of America

This book is lovingly dedicated to my daughter,
Lisa Anne,
who taught me much about the value of a name.

Acknowledgements

I owe a debt of gratitude to the wonderful people listed below. Without their advice, technical assistance and continuous encouragement, this book would never have been written. My sincere thanks...

to my mother for her unfailing support and encouragement through good times and bad.

to my wife, Meche, the very first person to earn a university degree in library science in the State of Chiapas, Mexico, who loved me in spite of my incarceration, supported my writing, and assumed the role of chief researcher.

to my brother, Galen, and his wife, Sondra, who let me share their home and put up with me while I completed my parole term and finish my book.

to my sister-in-law, Julie, who tirelessly proofread and edited my drafts and was never afraid to give her honest critique.

to Hayden and Lee McClung, who inspired me, both in and out of class, and who taught me to love literature and writing.

to my nephew, Steven, a professional truck driver, who provided me with invaluable information about the business of trucking by text messaging from just about every corner of the United States.

to my students in Chiapas, Mexico, who asked me to write an adventure story with a difficulty level appropriate for them, and placed in a geographical and historical setting to which they could relate.

to my fellow inmates who tolerated my readings and provided instant feedback regarding every aspect of the book—the plot, the characters, the setting, sensory detail, pacing, etc., and were brutally honest in letting me know when the story was interesting and when it was not. An aspiring writer can have no greater teacher or sounding board than this. You got my respect!

No doubt I have failed to mention numbers of people who helped me complete this book, and I apologize for not giving due credit. Writing a book is not a solitary effort. To all of you, my heartfelt thanks.

PREFACE

New Year's Day, 1994. Chiapas, the southernmost state of Mexico, exploded into the spotlight of world attention. A revolutionary movement known as the Zapatista Army of National Liberation (*EZLN*) took control of the city of San Cristóbal de Las Casas and its neighboring towns in the Chiapas highlands. Under the leadership of a mysterious *Latino* called *Subcomandante* Marcos, the *Zapatistas* mustered an estimated 3,000 indigenous peasants. Dressed in homespun clothing, handmade sandals, and hooded in black wool ski masks called *pasamontañas*, they occupied government administrative offices and boldly declared war on Mexico.

This was no spontaneous outbreak of rebellion. The guerilla *soldados* in this ragtag army—many with fake, wooden rifles—were eager volunteers from the various tribal groups, all descendants of Mayan Indians who had patiently trained for months for this occasion. Perceived government indifference to their conditions of extreme poverty and prejudicial treatment was the catalyst that sparked the attack.

Local police and military contingents were apparently sleeping off their New Year's Eve fiestas and they initially offered little resistance to the insurgents. When the reaction forces were finally organized, the confrontation was chaotic and bloody.

Police, military, bureaucrats, and politicians at all levels were shocked, outraged, and embarrassed. On this precise date the North American Free Trade Agreement (NAFTA) officially came into effect; throughout the country, speeches had been planned to proclaim solidarity and predict prosperity. The eruption of civil strife, however, cast serious doubt on Mexico's ability to maintain order and control within its borders. Investors, both foreign and domestic, would now think twice before doing business in Mexico.

Thousands of poorly trained and ill-equipped army and air force personnel were thrown into Chiapas; virtually none had combat experience. Hundreds were ordered to establish roadblocks and checkpoints along paved highways and dirt roadways, effectively shutting down the state. Meanwhile, the rebels, using classical guerilla tactics, retreated and disappeared into their mountainous, forested sanctuaries. With ground firepower and aerial bombing, governmental authorities gradually reoccupied their captured communities.

The years following were unstable and often brutally violent. While a blue ribbon committee of grandstanding politicians was flown in to negotiate with an anonymous council of tribal leaders, the countryside was raided and plundered by paramilitary commando squads, killing at will, apparently with government backing, protection, and immunity.

On December 22, 1997, in the village of Acteal, forty-five Mayan members of a Pentecostal-type Protestant congregation—all unarmed civilians—were massacred as they met for a prayer service. No one was ever convicted for these murders. Many other, similar incidents were never even reported in mainstream media sources.

It was my fate to reside, work, and travel in Chiapas during those turbulent times, living under virtual martial law, experiencing the checkpoints, witnessing the destruction and atrocities of war, and hearing eye-witness accounts of indescribable loss and suffering. This fictional story is set in those aftermath years when political and social chaos gripped Chiapas.

PROLOGUE

C hip Oatley sat facing the two most important men in his life. From the perspective of a twelve-year-old boy, one of the men was old and the other was very old.

The younger of the two men, Mr. Ollie Krahn, was 36, a close family friend, a Mayan linguist, and a teacher who had taken Chip under his tutelage. Not only had he taught Chip much about the language, history and culture of the indigenous Mayans here in the Lacondon Jungle, he had tutored Chip in German and French. German was Ollie's mother tongue.

The older man was Matthew Oatley, missionary and founder of the Lacondon Baptist Mission Station. Reverend Oatley was 58 years old, a kindly minister who had become enchanted with the jungles of Chiapas on his first trip as a college freshman. As best he could, he had introduced Chip to Biblical Hebrew, classical Greek and Latin. Missionary Matt was Chip's grandfather.

"To the best of my knowledge," Ollie said, "I am the only non-Mayan who has ever observed the rite of passage in which adolescent boys are initiated into adult manhood. Mayan boys go through this ceremony in their thirteenth year.

"I was twenty-six when I was invited to attend. I was blindfolded and taken to a cave, but once inside, the blindfold was removed and I was led by torchlight through narrow tunnels that descended deep into the bowels of the underworld until we finally came to an immense chamber, lighted only by four torches. Before my eyes were fully adjusted to the dim light, I was pulled to the stone floor and seated with the seven elders who presided. The air was damp and there was an acrid—but sweet—taste in the air. Later I learned that this distinctive odor was the smell of burning blood.

"Since I took a vow of secrecy that I will not violate, I cannot tell you everything I witnessed in those three days, but I will give you an idea of what to expect if you should ever see such ritual practices for yourself."

Placing his hand on Chip's shoulder and looking at the missionary, Ollie hesitated, and then continued, "Matt, I believe your grandson is mature enough to understand the significance of that ritual, but I will say no more without your permission. Shall I go on?"

The missionary placed his hand on Chip's other shoulder and said, "Chip, you are almost the same age as those lads in the cave. You may not fully understand the mysteries and symbolism of the rituals now, but I know from your questions that you have a curious mind and soul, and you will not rest until you have made sense of the world around you. I have heard you ask your mother about the meanings of baptism and the communion service we call 'the Lord's Supper.' You have reached the age when your body is changing and your mind is expanding. I encourage you to explore your new feeling and consciousness and experience the fullness of life in God's great universe. I think it would be good for you to know how our tribal brothers have attempted to pass down their communal heritage from one generation to the next. Listen to what Ollie has to say, tuck it away in your mind and heart, and maybe one day you will see how it compares and contrasts to your world views."

Matt looked at Ollie and said, "Tell Chip as much as you think you can. He's ready."

Chip nodded his head in agreement, not knowing what it was he was supposed to be ready for.

Ollie looked into Chip's eyes and began to describe the ritual. "One of the elders read from a book made from thin slices of bark and hinged together like an accordion. I was close enough to see that the writing was like the glyphs we see on the walls of the ruins at places like Palenque, Bonampak, and Yaxchilan. And the language was strange to my ears. I understood some of the words, but many I guessed were from an ancient form of the language that is no longer used. There were symbols painted on the walls of the cave, and each one of these symbols was explained by the elders. I was shocked to hear stories and explanations that included temptation by beautiful serpents, blood sacrifice, cleansing by water baptism, sacrificial death on a cross—variations on the themes of death, burial, and resurrection. I asked myself if these were universal themes that found expression in every culture from earliest times. I found myself mentally finding Christian parallels to their stories.

"There were certain aspects of the ceremony that have no equivalent in Christianity. At one point, the boys, who had been without food or sleep for almost three days, were required to sit close to an old woman wrapped in rags. It was no accident that her wrinkled skin and rumpled, purple cloth made her look like a giant chipotle chili pepper. She spoke to the boys with the shrill, raspy voice of an ancient conjurer and barely audible incantations which hypnotized the boys. Her eyes flashed and their eyes bulged with fear. Then suddenly she took a thin rope to which sharp barbs were attached at six-inch intervals. The rope end was tipped with a well sharpened bone. She dipped the bone in a bowl of chipotle paste and then opened her mouth and stuck out her tongue.

"Holding the tip of her tongue with one hand, she pierced the bone through her tongue, reached under and pulled the bone and rope downward. The boys instinctively closed their mouths. Quickly the old woman jerked the four-foot length of rope through her tongue and her blood dripped heavily into a ceramic bowl at her feet. Old rags in the bowl soaked up the blood. When the bowl was full and the rags would soak no more, the woman closed her mouth and began to swallow until the bleeding stopped.

"One of the elders brought a torch and lit the rags, causing curls of smoke to rise from the bowl. The old woman commanded the boys to inhale the smoke—the smoke that writhed like a snake. She assured them that they would now see the 'vision serpent.' Their bodily movements and their moans and groans gave evidence that they were having wild visions. Even though I was just a spectator, I shared their visions.

"That's all I can tell you, Chip. After that the boys were subjected to a tortuous body modification that hurts me to think about. I hope you never see—or experience—that part of the ritual."

Chip was quiet for a moment as the various symbols—the blood, the serpent, the cross—flashed and swirled in his mind, then fixed on one. He asked curiously, "Why is the chipotle chili such an important symbol in Mayan culture?"

"As you know, most chili peppers go bad—they rot—within a few days in our hot, humid climate; chipotles last for weeks, sometimes months. In Mayan myths and legends there are stories of a great migration when the gods brought the tribe into this land. Along the way, there were periods of drought and starvation when the chipotles they carried were their only source of food. Understandably, the chipotle took on sacred symbolism as the food sent from God."

"Like manna from heaven," the old missionary commented.

"That makes a lot of sense," Chip said, "but some things I really don't understand—like why some snakes are good and some snakes are bad. I'll have to think about that."

****

Later that evening, Chip went into the mission compound dining room looking for a chipotle chili pepper. Before he reached the kitchen he came across his mother, Laurel Oatley, sitting at the timeworn, solid mahogany dining table that doubled as her desk in the late evenings after all the feeding was done for the day. Noticing that she was crying, Chip sat beside her, not knowing why tears filled her eyes and her hands trembled as she shuffled a stack of yellowed envelopes. She wiped her nose, cleared her throat, and spoke softly, choosing her words.

"These are love letters from your father. They're the letters he sent to me from Vietnam."

Before she could continue, Chip interrupted. "How did he die, Mom?"

"The Army told me that he was eating dinner with some friends on a floating restaurant in the Saigon River when the boat exploded. Everyone was killed."

Chip was startled by a hand on his shoulder. He hadn't heard his grandmother walk up behind him. In a soft, dreamy voice she said, "But he didn't die instantly. Wounded and bleeding, he suffered a lot before he died."

Chip's mother turned and gave her an angry glare, but the old woman would not be hushed.

"How do you know that, Grandma?" Chip asked.

"Because he talked to me. He called out to me and I heard him. He said he wanted me to give him some water. All he wanted was some water to drink before he died. I looked at the clock on the wall. I know the exact time that he died. Your mother thinks I'm crazy, but I'm not. I know what I heard." She turned and walked out of the room.

Chip's mother continued as though she hadn't been interrupted. "You were only two-years old and I was pregnant with your sister Gina. Do you remember when they brought his body home and we had a military funeral? That's when they gave us the flag."

"I don't remember any of that, Mom. I don't even remember moving here to live with Grandma and Grandpa at the Mission Station." He paused a moment, then asked, "What Dad say in those letters? Are they sad? Why were you crying, Mom?"

"I was crying, just thinking about the good times I shared with your father. About how much we loved each other."

"Tell me about my dad. What was he like?"

"He was a lot like you, Chip. He was a poet, a dreamer, an adventurer, a risk-taker, and a romantic. He could learn anything he set his mind to, but he didn't have a lick of common sense. The worst part about him was his stubbornness. He was as hardheaded as a Missouri mule."

Chip was silent for a moment, then asked, "Am I really like that?'

"More so than I want to believe."

"Does that mean I'll end up like Dad?"

"I hope not, Chip. But you've got a lot to learn about life and how easy it is sometimes to make bad choices." She couldn't bring herself to speak aloud her fears that he would be hurt along the way. *I just hope he gets through it without too many scars*, she thought.

"Next year you're going to go live in the United States," she said. "You'll be going to real schools and getting a worldly education. You'll have to be tough inside to endure. Growing up here in the jungle hasn't been easy, but you've learned to survive. The city is another kind of jungle and you've got to be just as careful." Again she stopped herself from voicing her fears.

"Who am I going to go to in America when I get in trouble?"

"Don't worry about that now, Chip. Dr. Lambert, the one you call Uncle Bert, will be there if you need help. He was your father's best friend. Just think of him as being part of the family."

CHAPTER ONE

The campus of Sooner Institute of Biblical Studies, known as SIBS, had a reputation as being a great place to pursue an academic career with a minimum of worldly distractions. *That's just another way of saying that SIBS is a dull place in the small, quiet town of Tecumseh, Oklahoma,* Professor Charles Evan Oatley thought as he walked the eight blocks from his house to the academic dean's office without encountering a single soul or even a passing car.

On campus, Chip was known as something of a maverick with a roguish style. He sometimes went so far as to sign his memos "C.E.O." At this moment, however, waiting outside the office of the academic dean, he harbored no illusions of grandeur. A summons to report to the dean during normal work hours would not have been unusual, but this late evening call, however, raised a red flag.

His anxiety wasn't calmed when the dean's secretary, an aging matron of institutional memory, sidled up beside him and whispered, "Go on in. He's expecting you." She smiled as she slapped him softly on the butt. "I hope you have something left here when he gets through with you."

"Thanks, Gretchen. You really know how to bolster a man's courage." *There's a reason we call you 'Princess,'* Chip mused under his breath.

Before she could follow up with an inappropriate pinch, he sucked in a deep breath and strode into the office. He stood casually in front of the expansive, executive desk, striving to appear unruffled, as if he were used to meeting the dean for a late evening chitchat. Running his fingers through his shock of straight black hair, he said, "Got your message. What's up?" Even to his own ears, his attempt to sound self-assured came out forced.

Without looking up from the thick folder on his desk, Dean Lambert acknowledged Chip's presence only by lifting a pudgy index finger and motioning him to sit on the wooden armchair at the side of the desk, to the dean's left. After a lengthy silence, the dean mumbled into his papers, "I'll be with you in a moment, Chipper."

The dean had a well-earned reputation for making his subordinates squirm and sweat. His methods were working well tonight. The silent anticipation aggravated Chip's suspicion that he was in hot water. Recollections of waiting for the imprint of the vice principal's oversized Ping-Pong paddle emerged in his mind.

Sitting beside the boss's desk could well be considered a sign of intimacy, not having the desk as a physical and symbolic barrier. *Not so with Bert*, thought Chip. *Proximity brings the heretic's feet closer to the fire.*

Chip allowed his suspicions free reign. *Why am I at the left of the dean? Is there a sinister significance here? The Latin word for 'left' also connotes evil, unlucky, or a bad omen. What could be more sinister than this chair?* The stark chair conjured up morbid images of electric chairs where many a condemned prisoner had met his death. Chip imagined his wrists being strapped and buckled to this hard, barren perch. *No wonder they call it the 'hot seat.'* The anticipation of the inquisitor's torture, interrogation, and execution sent a chill through his body.

To extract himself from the imaginary, Chip focused his attention on the reality of his surroundings. There was nothing new here. He had seen it all before. Every item of wood furniture and furnishings, down to the picture frames, the dean had told him, had been hand-crafted from the same caoba mahogany tree in the Lacandon Jungle of Chiapas.

His gaze lingered on a faded, enlarged, black-and-white photograph on the wall. He had seen the original snapshot in his mother's scrapbook many times. From under a giant caoba three college friends hugged each other and smiled. On one side stood Chip's dad, Merle Oatley, a tall, skinny youth. On the other side was young Bert Lambert, a muscular athlete in his prime. Between them was Chip's mother, then a petite, raven-haired, pigtailed, Oklahoma tomboy.

The persistent question returned to haunt Chip. *What if Dad hadn't died?* But before the question gelled and lumped in his throat, the dean coughed several times into his cupped hand— his signal that he was ready to conduct business.

Bertrand Russell Lambert, PhD, tenured professor of historical linguistics, and chairperson of the Language Department at Sooner Institute of Biblical Studies, expected his subordinates' undivided attention when he addressed them. Chip straightened in his chair, looked the dean in the eye, and braced himself for a browbeating.

When the dean turned to face Chip, the swivel chair squeaked in protest. Light from a gooseneck desk lamp revealed thick, maroon bags under green, bloodshot eyes. Chip saw an old, tired, body, but inside a spirit burned with fire. Digging his elbows into his leather blotter pad, the dean said, "Sorry to have you come in so late. It's been one of those days filled with faculty meetings, budget committees, doctoral orals, and now a grant proposal that could bring in megabucks. I love what I do, but there are days when I wish I were back in the classroom, or even back in the jungle with your mom and dad, recording and analyzing languages." The dean's tone was deceptively cordial.

"You are an extraordinary teacher, Bert," Chip said, "but you took the right career path. You've done more for this department and this school than anyone else could have. You've streamlined the program, scraped in a bigger piece of the money pie, and recruited the best scholars in the field. You can take credit for putting us on the map and giving this place world-class status."

"I am very much concerned with the reputation of this institution, Chipper, and that is directly related to what I want to talk to you about." The dean's tone changed. "I'm going to say some things you may not want to hear. I'm going to give you a professional reprimand, and at the same time I'm going to scold you, swat your childish butt and give you some strong, fatherly advice.

"Your mom and dad were my best friends, even before you were born. Your dad made me promise that if anything ever happened to him, I'd take care of you, to help you grow up. You know— like a godfather. I've tried to keep that promise. I sent money to your mom. I paid for your boarding school and college expenses. I opened doors and greased a lot of skids for you. And you were doing so well. You were way ahead of the competition, a rising star on the fast track, getting your master's at an age when all the others were getting their bachelor's degrees. And you were so close to getting your doctorate.

"I was so proud of you. As you know, my ambition is to be the chancellor of this institution, and you also know that I was grooming you to take my spot as head of the department."

There was a pause, but Chip's only response was to bobble his Adam's apple as he swallowed hard.

The dean continued. "Then something went wrong, Chipper. You started shooting yourself in the foot—over and over, in fact. Your hormonal system must have gone berserk and you and Marlene thought you just had to get married. And she just happened to be the daughter of a prominent Baptist minister. Neither one of you was ready for marriage. Now she's running around with super jocks from O.U. and deadbeat rodeo cowboys while you're out seducing hot, young undergrad coeds. You both think you're slick. The reality is that you've become a laughingstock, an embarrassment to the campus.

"Maybe no one really cares if Marlene has gained a reputation as a honky tonk angel, but there are dozens of people who get their dander up when you go out, get drunk, and come hung over and late for class.

"And neither one of you seems to remember that you have a daughter. Are you spending you weekends with Honey Bee? She's only eight years old, but sometimes I think she's the only responsible adult in the family.

"By the way, changing the subject, what kind of progress are you making on your dissertation? The clock is running out. If you put your mind to it, you could wrap it up in no time."

"Look, Bert, we've been over this before. I've hit some rough patches and done some stupid things that I'm not proud of. And I'm trying to get focused again on my dissertation. I'm sorry if I embarrassed you. You've been good to me, and I appreciate everything you've done for me. How can I make you understand that I'm happy just being a teacher? I don't want your job. I don't want your responsibilities, your headaches. I don't know any other way to phrase it, Uncle Bert, but I don't want to be you."

The dean pretended to ignore Chip's last remark. "We're straying from the main point, Chipper. What you do with your personal life has consequences beyond you and me. The school's reputation is at stake, and there are some folks here who seem to think that you've smudged the institution's good name. They believe that your continued presence here is a liability."

Chip's black eyes flashed. "Cut to the chase, Bert. If you're trying to tell me that I'm fired, or that my contract won't be renewed in the fall, just say so. It doesn't come as a surprise. I'm not totally catatonic. I see how people avoid me and conversations hush when I walk into a room. I'm a social leper. And we all know why. We've gone over my personal imperfections. While we're at it, why don't we recount my professional failure? I was one of the young Turks who led the attack on the old guard of Mayan language studies. They said the carvings and paintings were nothing more than pictographs. We showed them there are phonetic elements encoded in the glyphs. Those ruins are screaming at us to read them aloud. But the old boys have been too proud to admit they were wrong. So I've been blackballed. Suddenly my papers don't get published in the prestigious journals. I don't get invited to speak at the major conferences. Two research grants are mysteriously 'put on hold' pending emergency budget revisions. Can you think of a better way to cripple an academic career?

"It sounds like you think I'm excess baggage for this institution. What's one more, bitter pill to swallow? Go ahead. Give me my walking papers and get this academic funeral over with. Forget the condolences." Then, with an abrupt change of tone he whispered, "Sorry to unload on you like this, Bert. I guess I'm just taking advantage of our relationship. I don't seem to have too many friends left these days."

The dean pushed back his chair and stood up. "Oh, come on, now! I've been listening to your sad story because you are my friend, Chipper. You're like a son to me. Now shut up, stop whining, and listen to me. I did not say you were being fired. I distinctly said that your continued presence here might be a liability. Being interpreted, that means you should disappear for a spell."

"Still sounds like I'm getting the ax."

"Fine, I'll spell it out for you. Take a group of students down to Chiapas and spend the summer giving linguistic seminars. Out of sight, out of mind."

"Sounds tempting, but I don't have the resources," Chip shot back. "Besides, I can't run away from my problems. If I'm going to salvage my reputation at all, I've got to stay here and fight. And just how would I be able to spend my weekends with Honey Bee if I were in Chiapas?"

Dean Lambert sighed. He didn't feel like arguing.

"Well, Chipper, go home and think about it. You know the situation now, and you know where I stand. I hope you change your mind. I think a change of scenery, a shift in focus, would be good for you. And a summer at the Mission Station wouldn't hurt Honey Bee."

"I'll give it some thought." Chip promised.

Both men realized that it served no purpose to continue this discussion. Each could see fatigue in the other's face. Chip stood up and walked around the desk to where Bert was waiting with arms spread wide. They gave each other a firm hug and several slaps on the back in a warm Mexican *abrazo*.

"Good night, Princess," Chip whispered to Gretchen on his way out.

CHAPTER TWO

In the boardroom of the Rainwater Building, all the chairs around the long, oval, conference table were empty, except for two at the power end where Brandon Wesley, the Chief Operating Officer, normally held court. Today, "Wes" was holding a private audience with Ted Cravens, Senior Field Representative for Mexico. Rather than assume his place at the head of the table, Wes put his subordinate at ease by sitting directly across the table. Wes believed that face-to-face huddles proved more productive than cold directives from "on high." Besides, these get-togethers didn't leave paper trails.

"Rainwater Pharms is carving out a bigger niche in the drug business, Ted. And as the company expands, new positions open up. I've been going over your file and I like what I see. If you can prove your worth by scooping the competition on these herbal cures from the voodoo witchdoctors down in the Lacandon Jungle, you'd have a good shot at the V.P. slot for Latin American projects. It would definitely move you up to the big leagues."

"Sounds great, but what are my parameters, Wes? Obtaining the secrets of traditional medicines is a tricky business. Doing business in a war zone is bad enough.

Taking on the wackos who scream that we're some kind of ruthless bio-pirates could create some nasty international press."

"We know that, Ted. That's why we've picked you for the job. You know the country. You know the language. You know the culture. Do what you have to do, as quickly and as quietly as possible. Most of your operating budget is somewhat flexible, but there are limits. I'll keep you supplied with cash—both greenbacks and pesos. Spread them out where they do the most good. But I won't tell you how to do your job. For the most part, you'll be on your own, flying by the seat of your pants."

"Understood. Like operating behind enemy lines. Can I contact you if I need to be extracted?"

"I'm afraid not, Ted. The company is going to need credible deniability. Still want the mission?"

"This is my kind of job, Wes. When should I pack my bags and fly south?" Ted responded without hesitation.

"The clock is ticking. We want you on the ground in Chiapas within two weeks. Get back with me in three days to brief me on your strategy and your tactical approach. We're counting on you."

Both men stood up, shook hands, turned, and marched in virtual lockstep out of the conference room. If anyone had been observing, Ted's expression revealed that he was already forming a plan.

CHAPTER THREE

C hip looked out his kitchen window as he waited for the international operator to connect him with Ollie Krahn, director of the research center called La CIMA, located in the heart of San Cristóbal de Las Casas, a quaint colonial city in the highlands of Chiapas, Mexico.

After it became clear that he and Marlene could no longer live together, Chip rented this house because it had a panoramic view of Crystal Lake Park, the pride of the town. But now the new Language Department Building obstructed his view.

An ugly, concrete structure, the Language Building had been inexplicably modeled after the Leaning Tower of Pisa, but few people saw the resemblance. More than one puzzled resident wondered if this was where the Student Union sold pizza. That nickname was lost, however, as the offices began to fill with linguists from all over the world and foreign conversations echoed through the corridors; the more descriptive label "Tower of Babel" caught on quickly and stuck.

Chip had been one of the first to move his office into the Tower and had become its worst critic. "It's functional, but cold, crowded, and uncomfortable, much like a prison," he lamented to his colleagues. Over time, he stopped using his office. Between classes he mingled and counseled students at the rowdy tables in the Student Union cafeteria. And he was much more comfortable grading papers, preparing lessons, and drafting research notes at his kitchen table.

Without Marlene and Honey Bee around, it was lonely, but there was something about being at a table that reminded him of the Mission Station dining room where Mom and Grandma had gone over his lessons. Grandma was like the old story tellers, never using a book, passing her knowledge down orally from one generation to the next. *I sure do miss Grandma,* Chip thought. *They just don't make 'em like her anymore.*

Chip muttered impatiently when the telephone line went dead, but he decided to wait a few minutes before trying again.

The session with the dean had made Chip realize that he needed to call and see how his friends and family were doing in Chiapas. Ollie was his main source of information. The field investigators from the *Centro de Investigaciones de Meso-America* (La CIMA) kept Ollie updated on every aspect of activity, rumor, and idle gossip as it occurred in Maya-land. *If the government had known what Ollie knew,* Chip thought, *there wouldn't have been such a surprise when Marcos and his followers pulled the covers on New Year's Day of 1994.*

Ollie did not look the part of a spymaster, nor did he think of himself in that role. He did not blend in with the crowd; he didn't even look like a Mexican. The grandson of German missionaries, son of unsuccessful coffee growers in northern Guatemala, he had come to Chiapas as an unknown linguist who had failed to earn his doctorate at UNAM, the National Autonomous University of Mexico. In spite of that, he proved himself to be a true scholar, writing "the book" on Mayan languages; he was distinguished and quoted in every journal and textbook in the field.

Never married, Ollie was practically a hermit, at home in the jungle, living like a native. Not at ease in the urban office of La CIMA, he used any excuse to have his driver take him to "the field." His only pleasure in San Cristóbal was sampling the cosmopolitan restaurants that catered to European tourists. His ever-widening girth was evidence of his favorite pastime.

Chip was only a boy when he met Ollie, but the two had become instant friends, sharing an understanding and affinity for language far beyond the norm for most humans. Age was not a factor. They saw each other as colleagues, as equals. Their minds ran parallel and both at lightning speed.

Chip tried again to put a call through and was rewarded when Ollie was heard on the other end. They greeted each other first in Spanish, then German, and finally English. Ollie always wanted to practice his English. His vocabulary and grammar were close to perfect, but his speech pattern and rhythm were usually sluggish. But Chip didn't mind. He was patient with his old friend.

Chip was almost startled when Ollie began to rush his words, creating some unnatural contractions, and quickly substituting Spanish when he couldn't immediately think of the English. It almost sounded like the "Spanglish" one finds along the U.S.-Mexico border.

"*Que pasa, mi amigo?*" Chip asked. "What's happening? Something is wrong. I can hear it in your voice. What is it?"

"I had a meeting with my field investigators this morning, Chip. They are very excited. No, 'agitated' is a better word. They are worried that the Zapatistas and the government paramilitaries are going to have a big, big battle in the jungle near the Mission Station. I have great fear that your family could be in much danger. Rumors are very strong. Many indigenous families are leaving as fast as they can."

"Have you had any contact with the Mission Station, with my family?" Chip asked. "Have any of your investigators heard any news from the Mission Station?"

"Nothing, Chip. So I think I need to go out there and warn them. I don't want anything to happen to your mother, your sister, or your grandfather. And there is another problem to worry about. There is a nurse working in the clinic. Her name is Teresa. She is the niece of the state governor. If anything happens to her, I don't want to think about what the governor will do."

"Is the situation really that bad, Ollie? I've heard about raids in the Lacondon all my life, but nothing's ever happened to bring danger to the Mission Station."

"I don't know why, Chip, but I think there may be some truth in the gossip of the jungle. It's just a feeling I have. So, I must go and warn them."

"My grandfather has always said that if God wants him in the Lacandon, He will protect him."

"You grandfather is courageous to the point of foolishness, Chip. I hope he is not tempting God."

"Well, you go tell him of the danger, Ollie. If you can convince him to leave the Mission Station, you have greater powers of persuasion than I do. And when you go, tell Chete, your driver, to sharpen his machete."

Ollie missed Chip's sarcasm. "He always keeps a razor-sharp one under the seat. He has never depended on his gods for protection."

"*Vaya con dios*, Ollie."

"*Igualmente*, Chip. Likewise."

CHAPTER FOUR

Dean Lambert was not amused when Gretchen bellowed from her desk, "There's an idiot on line two who refuses to believe that you are busy. Would you please take the call and get him off my back?"

The dean tolerated these flagrant displays of disrespect and insubordination from his administrative assistant only because of her professional efficiency. She could accomplish an office miracle under a short suspense. Now, as usual, he did not respond orally, but he did honor her request. "This is Lambert. How can I help you?" he asked, his voice irritated and curt.

A hesitant male voice on the line said, "Thank you for taking my call, Dean Lambert. This is Ted Cravens with Rainwater Pharms. That's Pharms spelled with *p-h*. I apologize for not sending an advance packet of literature about the company and a letter introducing myself before contacting you like this."

"Mr. Cravens," the dean cut in, "I'm very busy and my agenda is rather full today. If you are promoting agricultural goods and services, I'm afraid you'll be disappointed to learn that we do not have an 'aggie' department here at Sooner Institute of Biblical Studies. The nature of our institute is narrowly restricted to

Biblical studies and linguistic research, mainly used for Biblical translations. Are you following me?" The dean's tone was noticeably sarcastic.

There were a few seconds of silence. The dean was impatient and ready to hang up. When Mr. Cravens spoke again, there was considerably more confidence in his voice.

"I assure you, Dr. Lambert, that I am not a manure salesman, even though there are fortunes to be made in that line of work, and we here at Rainwater Pharms do have an entire division dedicated to the research, development, production, marketing and sales of fertilizers.

"And believe me, sir, I am well aware of the nature of your institution. That is precisely why I would like to propose a sizable financial grant to your prestigious linguistics department in return for research services for our international pharmaceutical division. The connection may not be immediately obvious, but there is a link that I would like to discuss with you, and I am confident that we can work out a mutually beneficial relationship. Are you following me?" The mocking sarcasm was not lost on the dean.

The dean was fully alert. His tone became professional. "Mr. Cravens, I must apologize. I did not mean to insult your company. If, perchance, you are not indisposed, I can clear my agenda and meet with you personally. Where are you?"

"As we speak, I'm at the corporate offices in Chicago. Momentarily, I'll be aboard a private jet en route to Mexico City, with several stops on the way. I'll touch down in Dallas, Texas early this afternoon. Would it inconvenience you too much to meet me there for a late lunch?"

"I'll clear my calendar and find a puddle jumper to get me there," Dean Lambert assured him. If I have to, I'll commandeer a crop duster."

"If you like barbeque, you'll love the baby back ribs at a place called Chili's. May I suggest that we meet at their original Dallas location? About 3 o'clock would be convenient for me."

"I never turn down tasty Texas barbeque, Mr. Cravens. I'll be there waiting for you."

"Fine, Dr. Lambert. Bring a generic grant proposal with you. If we can reach an agreement, we can pencil in some tentative facts and figures. I'm sure you won't be disappointed."

"I like the way you do business, Mr. Cravens."

"*Igualmente*, Dr. Lambert."

CHAPTER FIVE

Dean Lambert flew into Love Field, rented a car, and had no trouble finding the Chili's restaurant. Although the lunch rush had subsided, business was still brisk. It wasn't long before the dean was able to park near the entrance. He was twenty minutes early, so he sat and watched the restaurant's clientele come and go. He noticed that only a few of the customers ordered their meals "to go." Even though this was "fast food" territory, Chili's was a bit upscale.

Acting on curious impulse, the dean went inside, found the assistant manager. As he suspected, Ted Cravens had already called in a sizable order.

"We always look forward to having Mr. Cravens in town," the young woman said. "He always orders enough food for the entire aircraft crew and his personal staff. We go out of our way to make sure he is well taken care of."

The dean thanked her for being helpful, gave her one of his business cards, and took a seat near a window where he could see Ted when he arrived. He didn't have to wait long, but in those brief moments, he indulged his imagination.

Dr. Bertrand Russell Lambert was ambitious. He had been proud of himself when he became a fully-tenured professor of historical linguistics at the University of Oklahoma. He was even prouder when he was named Chairperson of the Linguistics Department at SIBS, Sooner Institute of Biblical Studies, at Tecumseh, Oklahoma. But his goal was still higher. The dream had taken shape when he was a freshman at Harvard. He had attended a seminar by a Mayan scholar from SIBS and had been so captivated that he had signed up for a summer session in Mayan Studies in Chiapas, Mexico. Before the summer was over, he had decided that one day he was going to be the chancellor of SIBS. If everything went well on this now much-brighter-than-expected afternoon, he would be another step closer to fulfilling his dream.

Dean Lambert mentally reviewed his credentials. He had been able to climb the ladder and accumulate power within the walls and halls of academia for a variety of reasons. First, he had mastered the art of manipulating bureaucracy. He knew all the rules and regulations, every form and every file folder, and every box and job description in the organizational chart. And he instinctively knew the difference between the chain-of-command and the chain-of-influence.

The most significant qualification in his career arsenal, though, was that he had made himself the undisputed heavyweight champion of grant acquisition. He had raised more financial support for the school and his department than all the other staff members combined, including the vice-chancellor for endowment and development. Another grant today would be another feather in his mortarboard war bonnet.

When Mr. Cravens arrived late, Dean Lambert made a mental note to determine whether Ted was making a power statement or just proving not to be a punctual person. Either way, the dean was not about to let petty personality traits derail a money train.

The two greeted each other like old friends and both quickly insisted on using first names. Bert stepped back, expecting a hostess to lead the way to a table, but Ted had made other arrangements. "I hope you don't mind—I called-in a 'to go' order. Thought we'd could eat and discuss business in the corporate limo at my disposal. It will provide a bit of luxury and privacy in one small package."

"I don't mind at all," Bert responded.

Ted turned to the restaurant manager who was busy checking the order. In fluent Spanish, Ted made small talk with her and checked to see that she had included a generous tip in the prepaid account on his corporate credit card. They chatted like old friends while a baby-faced kitchen helper carried the food bags out in cardboard boxes. When the boy returned, Ted slipped a twenty-dollar bill into his shirt pocket. Turning back to the manager, Ted excused himself and ushered Bert out to the waiting limo. A moment later they were headed toward a quiet, shady spot in a nearby park.

Dean Lambert had observed Ted's interaction with some of the restaurant staff.

"Your Spanish is native-fluent, Ted."

"There's a good reason for that, Bert. Allow me to begin our conversation by telling you a little about myself," Ted suggested. "It'll help explain why I'm bilingual.

Bert nodded agreement as Ted continued.

"I was born in Mexico City. My father was an oilman from Houston, Texas. He married my mother—she was Mexican—six months after I was born. He stalled out as a middle management supervisor for Standard Oil. His salary was in dollars, so we lived well. When I was nine years old, the Mexican President Cardenas nationalized the petroleum industry and told the American oil companies to go home. My father stayed on as a 'consultant,' but on a reduced salary, and he was then paid in pesos, which, as you know, devalued every day. My father wanted to go back to Texas, but my mother didn't speak much English and refused to leave her family. They both started drinking, so I started running the streets. I was totally bilingual by that time and I found it easy to hustle the English-speaking tourists. Supplying them with marijuana and other recreational drugs was no problem in those days.

"When I was eighteen, my folks were killed in a car wreck. They left me just enough insurance to get me through a couple of years of college in Illinois. In order to finish, I had to find work, so I started selling cosmetics to independent drug stores. On my rounds, I met lots of pharmaceutical representatives and it didn't take long to find out that their commissions were a lot more than mine. After graduation, I heard about an opening at Rainwater Pharms and I was lucky enough to get in on the ground floor.

"Rainwater started as a food processing company to help supply the troops in World War II. After the war they managed to escape a number of hostile takeover attempts. Post-war business was so good that they began to buy up the farms that had been supplying their fruits and vegetables. Then they discovered Mexico's cheap labor and began to establish mega-farms. Almost by accident, while pioneering in bio-engineered plants, they got into pharmaceuticals. It was like a license to print money. Now they are a transnational conglomerate. I've been fortunate enough to ride the crest of the wave."

Indicating that he had finished his brief *curriculum vitae*, Cravens picked up the juicy rack of baby back ribs with his fingers and bit a mouthful of barbeque pork meat cleanly off the bone, then licked the sauce from his fingers and lips.

"Would you like to know who I am?" Lambert asked.

"I know who you are," Ted cut him off. "I've taken the liberty to dig into your past, Bert. Your record is spotless and you have a reputation for being a man of your word. And I was impressed to learn of your ability to memorize scripture. Is it true that you won a Bible-quoting contest?"

"You really have done your homework," Lambert said, recovering quickly from his surprise. "Yes, when I was sixteen I won a contest by quoting from memory the entire first four books of the New Testament according to the King James Version. That seems like a long time ago."

"Yes, but that accomplishment points to an intellect I admire, Bert. And from what I hear, you're the power plant, financially speaking, that runs your school. If you don't mind, I'd like to hear how you describe Sooner Institute. In five-hundred words or less, tell me about SIBS."

"Sure," the dean said, and helped himself to several generous dips of guacamole smothered with salsa. From the quantity he was putting away, it was clear that his taste buds found the food delightful.

"Let me begin by putting SIBS in context. Oklahoma, the 'Sooner State,' takes great pride in its various institutions of higher learning. Its large, state supported college and university system is nationally renowned for its perennial production of athletic powerhouses. Of more importance, but much less well-known, is its assemblage of internationally recognized scholars who research and publish on every aspect of ethno-culture, especially

Native-American cultures. Most of their studies are published at the Norman campus of O.U.

"Forty miles down the road southeast of Oklahoma City, in the small town of Shawnee, is the campus of a private, religious-affiliated school called Oklahoma Baptist University. There is probably as much truth as humor in the saying that this fine institution accepts an inordinate number of unsophisticated farm boys and girls, and somehow transforms them into well-informed, educated preacher-boys and missionaries who go on to the seminary and become fine Southern Baptist leaders, not only in the religious realm, but also in the business community.

"Sooner Institute of Biblical Studies is located just seven miles from O.B.U. We are a private, non-denominational school, practically unknown to most Americans. We attract the best-of-the-best scholars from the fields of Biblical Studies and Linguistics. Besides producing Biblical scholars, translators, interpreters, and missionary candidates of the highest quality, Sooner Institute supplies many prestigious universities with their annual quota of profane linguists, language instructors, anthropologists, sociologists, and archaeologists.

"Not surprisingly, recruiters from the U.S. State Department and the CIA are among our greatest fans. They purchase every one of our cultural publications and study them with intense interest. Reliable sources tell me that their field agents and bureaucrats alike have more faith in our studies than they do in some of their own intelligence reports and analyses, perhaps because we have a distinct advantage; we don't have to be politically correct.

"That, Ted, is a very brief overview of SIBS. I have deliberately avoided boring you with statistical, historical, or financial details. If you have any interest in such minutiae, I can recite them to you *ad nauseam*."

"Thank you for sparing me, Bert. In my office I have a report that fills five hundred and eighty-six pages to say what you just told me in five minutes. And since we are being concise, I'll briefly explain why Rainwater wants a SIBS scholar for our research services.

"The process of developing and testing pharmaceuticals in the laboratory has become cost-prohibitive. Searching for alternative methods has turned up some viable options. We have found that there is a hidden gold mine in the traditional cures that are used by indigenous peoples in 'underdeveloped' regions of the world. The effectiveness of these 'folk medicines' has been attested to for thousands of years. We save millions of dollars by focusing on these herbs and plants in our labs, identifying and analyzing the curative chemical ingredients, and reproducing them in marketable form.

"For admittedly financial motives, we have become 'tree huggers.' Most of the world's pristine forests are being destroyed by loggers, and with them the tribal peoples who know and use herbs for medicine are being exterminated, displaced, and brainwashed into the twenty-first century. Their ancient knowledge is being irretrievably lost.

"At the same time, the *curanderos*, the healers, are becoming less cooperative. Some folks are trying to convince them that we are bio-pirates. What we need is a first-rate Maya scholar who can do two things. First, convince the medicine men that the world needs their knowledge. Second, research the old manuscripts, letters, diaries, and papers that make reference to medicinal plant remedies. If the plant can be identified and located, we can take it from there."

Bert cut in. "Just for starters, Ted, can you finance a year's research in the Chiapas highlands?"

"I can commit to that. If the research proves productive, you're looking at sizable endowments for SIBS. Roughly speaking, we're talking about a cool million the first year and the royalties will continue to flow for about seven years."

"You're in luck, Ted," Bert grinned. "I have a Maya scholar who can be in Chiapas within two weeks. He grew up on a Baptist Mission Station down there. They don't come any better qualified."

"Fine, I'll contact you tomorrow to get his complete dossier." Ted said and returned Bert's grin, then suddenly asked, "Do you still like the way I do business?"

Bert chuckled and said, "Not bad for a manure salesman."

CHAPTER SIX

The first rays of golden sunshine pierced through the triple canopy of dense jungle and began their daily chore of burning off the early morning mist. This sacred ritual of nature was incorporated into this morning's celebration of a sunrise service in its most mythic sense.

Long before the introduction of Christianity, the ancient civilizations of this land had found religious significance in the cycles of night and day, of death and life, of burial and resurrection. The solemn, but joyful ritual of springtime renewal was being repeated today in the Easter Sunrise Service at the Baptist Mission Station in the heart of the Lacadon Jungle.

The Mission Chapel was often used by individuals needing a quiet place to meditate and pray for the healing and recuperation of a sick, injured, or dying family member or friend. Sunday worship services, however, were normally held on the lawn, under the trees, beside the Chapel building, unless the rain was strong enough to drive the worshipers inside.

This morning there was no rain, but there was a slight chill in the air as the old missionary, Matthew Oatley, greeted his flock with a warm smile. Patients from the infirmary, who could safely be moved had been carried out to join the service, some stoically tolerating their aches and pains. The missionary's daughter and granddaughter had organized the arrangement of sickbed pallets on the ground. Although Reverend Oakley's wife had been dead for seven years, he could still picture her banging on the old, upright piano, badly out of tune, for every Easter service at the Mission Station for forty years. The old piano sat dormant in the chapel this morning.

Without being prompted, an old woman began to strum a guitar that was probably older than she was. The congregation came to life, first humming the melody, then mouthing the words to an ancient incantation that echoed back to the earliest days of Mayan culture. The theology behind the song was not Christian, and the lyrics were not Spanish or any other "modern" language.

These people had not forsaken their gods; they had incorporated Jesus into their god-family. But Pastor Matt had never felt the need to burn the temples of the ancient deities. That strategy had failed the Spanish *conquistadores*, as well as the parade of Catholic and Protestant missionaries who came after them. Total immersion by Southern Baptists hadn't been any more successful in stamping out the old beliefs. The old missionary held on to the hope that bringing some degree of relief to suffering through kindness and medical attention, much like Jesus had done, would produce results. Maybe he would never save their souls, but his own soul was in no danger.

The ancient psalm was nearing a crescendo when the guitar suddenly stopped and most of the voices became silent. The air was filled with the banging sound of an unmuffled internal combustion engine. A 1969 Dodge pickup truck roared into the rutted entrance of the mission compound and skidded to a stop at the edge of the chapel celebrants. Everyone froze in fearful anticipation.

Five guerillas fighters materialized from the truck. The driver, a passenger from the cab, and three others from the truck bed jumped out and ran to the front of the audience that had been seated on wooden folding chairs, but was now cautiously rising, ready to run into the jungle. The driver, wearing a ragged, olive-drab fatigue uniform, began to bark orders. The others, all dressed in half-military uniforms, reacted reluctantly, but obediently. Waving machetes and pistols, they stormed into the crowd. *"Todos al suelo!"* they shouted and fired shots into the air. "Everybody get down!"

Disbelief hung in the air as the majority of the congregation scrambled to the earthen floor. Pastor Oakley, however, showed no signs of panic. With a pleasant smile he casually walked up to the leader of the intruders and, in perfect Spanish, calmly said, "Gentlemen, if you care to join us in our worship service, please remove your hats and sit down. We would be honored to have you as our guests. And you are welcome to stay for lunch."

The leader's face turned scarlet. *"Callete, gringo loco!"* he screamed. *"Cerra la boca!"* But the crazy white man wouldn't shut his mouth.

The jungle soldier shook his fists and turned his back on the missionary. In anger and disgust, he started to walk away, then suddenly turned, pulled a pistol from his belt, and fired three shots into the missionary's body. Rev. Matt Oakley crumpled to the ground, blood flowing from his wounds.

The other *soldados* spread through the stunned gathering of worshipers looking for specific individuals. Within minutes they had three women hostages. But they had not counted on the fierce resistance of the *gringas*, so it took the slapping of fists and several blows from pistol butts to gain the unwilling cooperation of the female victims. Semiconscious, the women were bound, hands behind their backs.

Chip's mother, Laurel Oakley, and his sister Gina were roughly hauled into the back of the pickup. Teresa, the summer-intern nurse, was pushed into the middle of the cab.

As quickly as it had come, the raiding party drove back out of the compound and was swallowed up by the thick foliage of the jungle.

As the attackers departed, a cluster of angry and anguished followers crowded around the bleeding missionary. They held his hand, mopped his brow, and prayed for his soul.

Matt Oakley felt no pain. He was only aware of serenity in the faith that his prayers were being answered. God was taking him home. He was about to be reunited with his departed wife. He hadn't expected his death to happen in this manner, but who was he to question the mysterious ways of God? There was a peaceful smile on his face.

CHAPTER SEVEN

"So tell me about your wonder boy Chip Oatley," Ted Cravens said.

"Professor Charles Oatley is more than my protégé," the dean began. "I am more than a mentor to him; he is like a son to me. I met his parents, Merle and Laurel, in the late sixties when we participated in a summer seminar in Chiapas. They became my best friends. In fact I was best man at their wedding, and when Chip was born, I was honored when they asked me to be their child's godfather. None of us ever suspected that I'd ever have to fulfill that role, but Merle enlisted in the Army. In 1972, when the war was supposed to be over, he got sent to Vietnam, where he was killed. Chip was two years old and Laurel was pregnant. Merle never saw his daughter, Gina, who was born two months after his death. Laurel, who was living in post housing at Fort Benning, Georgia, packed up what she could, and moved to the Lacandon Baptist Mission Station in Chiapas where her parents were the resident missionaries.

"As the *padrino*, the godfather, I was able to send them some money, clothes, medicines, books, and toys for their birthdays and Christmas to make their lives a little more comfortable. They wrote to me every month and often sent pictures. At least once a year I visited the Mission Station to see how they were doing.

"It was clear to everyone that Chip was a gifted, precocious child. I've yet to meet anyone who has a greater natural ability for learning languages. His mother home-schooled him in English and Spanish, while his grandfather tutored him in Hebrew, Greek, and Latin. Ollie Krahn, a frequent visitor from the La CIMA research Center in San Cristóbal, helped him with the basics of German and French. But the amazing thing is that he picked up about five indigenous Mayan dialects simply by playing with the kids who came with their mothers to the mission clinic. By the time he was ten years old, Chip was the mission translator and interpreter.

"When Chip was thirteen, I talked his mother into letting me enroll him in "Uni-Hi," the high school for gifted students from around the University of Illinois, where I was an assistant professor of historical linguistics. Chip breezed through his courses and graduated when he was sixteen. He maxed out the advanced placement exams in math, physics, and chemistry and scored off the scale on the SAT. Every prestigious university in the country tried to recruit him, but he was a stubborn kid with a mind of his own.

"He was a serious student, and since he was younger than most of his classmates, he didn't have many friends, so it was natural for him to turn inward for a while, seeking for some spiritual answer to the mysteries of life. He was active in the church and during one of their periodic revival meetings he felt 'called' to become a missionary like his grandparents.

"When I was enticed to go to the University of Texas, I convinced Chip to enroll there. I thought I could watch over him. I bought a two-story house so he could have his own house upstairs. When he was seventeen I bought him an old pickup. But with that kind of freedom in the midst of puberty, he metamorphosed into a party animal. He discovered rodeo, tobacco, alcohol, cowgirls, and Texas Two-Step dance halls."

"Honky-tonks have always had a way of turning a young man's fancy," Ted commented. "I've been known to close a few of them in my younger days."

"Right after his graduation from college at the ripe age of nineteen, he impregnated the daughter of a prominent Baptist minister from El Paso and was pressured into a hastily arranged shotgun wedding. Unable to shake the idea that he was called to be a missionary, he enrolled in Southwestern Baptist Theological Seminary at Fort Worth. Before long he had a baby daughter to provide for, and a witchy wife who made it clear that she had no intentions of being a missionary's wife. She said she had been through enough hell growing up as a preacher's kid. Chip was sure he could change her mind, but another, totally unexpected roadblock obstructed his path. He had an open, inquiring mind and began to explore an ever-widening range of theological and philosophical ideas, many of which did not jibe with the conservative, fundamentalist prescription of a literal interpretation of the Bible. When he innocently asked his professors about these 'ideas,' he was told, in no uncertain terms, that such unorthodox heresies were of the devil and that whoever had recommended such writings to him was not his friend, nor was that person a Christian, but was going to burn in hell's hottest fires. Chip was warned that any further consideration of such filth would only pollute his mind and soul and cause him to doubt the true beliefs of the 'Baptist Faith and Message.' Totally confused and discouraged, he dropped out of the seminary.

"By that time, I had joined the faculty at Sooner Institute, so I lured him into a combined master's-doctoral program in linguistics at O.U. Since it wasn't far away, once again I thought I could keep an eye on him. When he was awarded his M.A., I got him on as an assistant professor at SIBS. That kept his wife happy. While he was buried in his books, she was sneaking out to the honky-tonks, leaving the baby girl with baby sitters. As time went on, he gradually realized that he was raising his daughter like a single parent. His in-laws hinted that they could take the child and raise her in a 'good, Christian home,' but Chip wouldn't hear of it.

"By the way, almost every summer, during all those years, he returned to Chiapas to be with his family and help around the Mission Station. When I learned that his wife Marlene refused, after her first visit to Chiapas, to ever go back again, I suspected the marriage was doomed to failure. But that didn't stop Chip from taking his daughter on those trips. In fact, Marlene seemed happy to be rid of her for the summer.

"The year he got his M.A. his grandmother died. That affected him deeply and he began to search again for answers to life's big questions. It took awhile, but he bounced back and finally began to live up to the potential we had all seen in him. He got involved in faculty committees and even volunteered to be the faculty sponsor for the school rodeo team. He has become one of the most popular professors on campus and his summer linguistics seminars in Chiapas draw dozens of enthusiastic students."

Dean Lambert hoped Ted wouldn't see through this lie about Chip turning his life around. He desperately wanted Chip to be chosen for this opportunity.

"He sounds almost too good to be true," Ted said. "If he's human, there must be some pages in his bio that he'd rather not discuss. What can you tell me?"

"Well, I don't think I'm breaking any confidences when I say there have been a few problems. A coed has accused him of sexual harassment. That still has to be sorted out by the legal system. Then there's a professional squabble involving some of the venerable scholars of Mayan linguistics. Chip stepped on their toes by pointing out their failure to find phonetic aspects in ancient Mayan glyphs. I'm working right now to smooth a few ruffled feathers. Meanwhile, although he doesn't realize it, his reputation as a leading scholar of contemporary Mayan dialects continues to grow."

Ted Cravens had been listening carefully and was pleased with what he was hearing, but he still had some questions. "Is he still married?"

"Marlene finally divorced him. The court gave her custody, so we all thought she would take Honey Bee back to Texas, but she surprised everybody by moving in with a rodeo clown. At least Chip gets to spend weekends with his daughter."

"Can you spare him for a year?" asked Ted. "And will he want to stay that long?"

"We'll manage without him," the dean replied. "And actually, he won't have any choice in the matter."

"I like the way you do business," Ted said. "Not bad for a Bible thumper."

CHAPTER EIGHT

Ollie arrived at the Lacandon Mission Station one day after the raid. Only a handful of staff members and patients remained on the compound. The walking wounded and those who could be carried away by family and friends had quickly disappeared into the jungle.

Ollie knew it would be a day or two before the authorities arrived to make a report of the attack. He took notes of everything he was told about the raid, but those who remained were unable to tell Ollie exactly what had happened. All they could tell him was that the old missionary had been shot three times and three women had been taken—the missionary's daughter and granddaughter, and the young female nurse. The attackers had started to leave with the three hostages in a pickup, then came back a few minutes later to get the missionary's body. The strange thing was that the missionary's body was gone. No one knew exactly what had happened to Matt Oakley's body, but several witnesses said they had seen an old *curandera* woman hovering over him and tending to his wounds. Maybe they had taken his body to bury in one of their sacred caves. If so, the word would soon spread through the jungle.

Ollie organized a clean-up of the compound, packed up some of the missionaries' earthly possessions and stacked them into his vehicle. What he couldn't take, he locked in the rooms, knowing that the cheap locks were only a temporary delay to anyone wanting to break in.

With only the obligatory *abrazo* for each of the staff members who remained on the mission compound, Ollie Krahn nodded his head gravely as each one whispered, "*Vaya con dios*, go with God." He engulfed them in a massive bear hug and gently patted their backs. There was no sobbing, no tears, nor wails of lamentation, but there was fear in every eye.

There was fear that the hostages had been raped and killed. There was fear that the raiders would return to silence the witnesses. There was fear that any gathering for worship or a memorial service for the old missionary would bring the raiders back again. And there was fear that Ollie would be ambushed on his way back out of the jungle. They were surprised that he had made it in through the jungle without harm.

Ollie Krahn, a tall, obese scholar of German descent, and his driver, Chete, a short, gaunt indigenous Maya, tossed the last of the bags and boxes into the back of a sixteen-passenger minibus that had been gutted of its rear seats to make room for cargo. With a farewell wave, they climbed into the vehicle. Chete perched himself on the thickly padded driver's seat while Ollie stood in the stairwell gripping a horizontal handrail on the dashboard with his left hand. In his right hand he held 12-gauge, double-barreled shotgun.

Chete wasted no time. In less than a minute, the crowded, emerald foliage swallowed the minibus. Ollie slid the plastic wing window open and poked the twin muzzles of the shotgun out into the cool, damp air.

Ollie had never in his life shot a firearm of any kind, but at this moment he was ready and willing to squeeze his finger on the trigger. The realization spread warmly through him that he could—and would—kill another human being to protect himself.

Ollie's driver was also prepared to engage in mortal combat. He had a .38 caliber pistol stuck in his belt and a well-honed machete within reach on the floorboard. He had killed before with this machete. He would not hesitate to use it now. With good reason he had acquired the nickname "Chete."

He said nothing to Ollie, but Chete was expecting an ambush this morning. He pushed the minibus to its limits, bulldozing through overhanging vines and branches until they snapped and scraped along the vehicle as it bounced and splashed along the narrow, muddy, winding trail. His mind raced ahead, trying to guess the most likely spot for an ambush. But there were so many possibilities that he soon gave up and focused his attention on the road immediately in front of him.

The expected ambush did not occur. As the minibus, a veteran of frequent forays into the rainforests, disrupted the morning tranquility, the only humans it encountered were the tribesmen on their morning hunt. Curiosity and annoyance reflected in their eyes as their thin-clad bodies camouflaged perfectly into the olive shadows and morning mist.

Neither Ollie nor Chete felt a need to talk. After working together for more than two decades, they could almost read each other's thoughts. Over time, they had come to believe that in times of danger, it was not good to speak of fear because verbalizing it would make it contagious. Chete's father had taught him that fear is a disease that must not be allowed to spread. "Fear is like sadness," he had admonished. "It is best suffered in solitude. True grief, on the other hand, is something to be shared, but too often we do not know how to share it."

It was midmorning when the La CIMA minibus broke out of the rainforest and found smooth, solid traction on the asphalt road. From here it would be another 125 miles to Palenque. Chete drove a short distance, then cautiously pulled off the pavement and stopped behind a clump of tall shrubs. Both men jumped out and ran into the heavy brush and relieved their bladders. Fear affects men that way.

When they were back in the vehicle, Chete dug a large thermos from behind his seat and poured two mugs of strong, hot coffee. Chete had boiled the *café de olla* in an earthen pot, and flavored it heavily with sugar and cinnamon. Ollie preferred his with a dollop of heavy cream, but he didn't complain as he found a bench seat and sipped the thick, dark liquid, his spirits rising.

When he had finished his coffee, Ollie worked his way back through the minibus, restacking and straightening the boxes and bags onto the seats, opening a passable aisle way. He went back to the bench seat near the front, sat down, leaned his head back and closed his eyes. He was exhausted but could not sleep. Taking a pencil and notebook from his shirt pocket, he scribbled a detailed account of the events of the past few days. He included his thoughts and feelings. Unaware that he was doing so, he wrote in his native German.

Ollie rarely forgot an incident, and could "instant replay" a life scene when he wanted to relive the past. Now he wished he could forget the last three days. *If only I could rip these pages from my journal and erase the video.* But he could not forget. And at last the dam broke. His huge body shook as he buried his face in his hand and wept. He could not remember feeling such intense emotion since 1968, when the student radicals had occupied the university administration buildings and burned his records and the draft of his doctoral dissertation. When Chete stopped for gas, Ollie was relieved that he had regained his composure. Only dry salt remained of his tears.

Seven military checkpoints interrupted the trip to Palenque. Chete's indigenous facial characteristics aroused cautions among the soldiers, but Ollie's European features and his university credentials speeded the process, and after each stop the minibus was waved on. Although the vehicle was covered with caked mud and powdery dust, the logo and the lettering of the university research center was readable. In bold script it proclaimed: La CIMA—Centro de Investigaciones de MesoAmerica, and in smaller letters: UNAM—National Autonomous University of Mexico.

Most readers recognized the significance of "*la cima*," Spanish for "the summit," "the pinnacle," "the highest point." And every educated person was aware that La CIMA researchers were the best-of-the-best scholars in the fields of anthropology, who spent their lives recording and interpreting the history and culture of the Mayans. Oliver Krahn had held the esteemed position of Director of La CIMA for almost two decades. As the minibus sped into Palenque, neither Ollie nor Chete had any thoughts concerning the prestigious reputation of La CIMA; their focus was more mundane.

Nearing *el centro*, the downtown business district around the central plaza, Chete forced himself to concentrate on the narrow streets which had been laid out five centuries before by Spanish conquistadors for horse-drawn carriages. Twentieth-century vehicles had transformed these postcard, picture-perfect, cobblestone pavements into slick skid ways where colorful stands and walking vendors sprawled over narrow sidewalks and out into the lanes of traffic. Pedestrians and vehicles scurried around these obstacles like ants on the jungle floor.

Chete managed to maintain his stoic composure in the steamy jungle air. In contrast, Ollie had never been able to hide his emotions. His discomfort in the extreme heat and humidity, combined with the stress of the recent events, reflected in his expression, his demeanor, and his appearance. His obesity contributed to profuse sweating, leaving his clothes stained and rumpled. His hair was uncombed and his face sprouted a three-day growth of gray beard. And with his bloodshot eyes, he could easily be taken for an alcoholic on a three-day binge. With a stubby pencil he scribbled in his notebook a brief message in English. With sweat dripping from his hand onto the paper, he swore in German when Chete skidded to a stop, causing an illegible word. They had reached the front of the Hotel Maya Plaza.

In near-perfect Spanish, Ollie spoke quickly to Chete. *"Favor de enviar dos telegramas por Western Union a Los Estados Unidos."* He handed Chete a fistful of fifty-peso bills. *"Apurate, por favor,"* he added, but his urging to hurry was not necessary. Chete had already dismounted and disappeared into the dark shadows of the hotel's open-air lobby.

Both telegrams contained the same message: "Mission attacked. Laurel, Gina, and Teri taken hostage. Matt dead. Body missing. Will e-mail ASAP."

Hours before Ollie and Chete arrived back at the La CIMA complex in San Cristóbal, the two telegrams had been delivered to their addressees at Sooner Institute of Biblical Studies in Tecumseh, Oklahoma. One had gone to Dr. Bertrand Lambert; the other went to Professor Charles Oatley.

CHAPTER NINE

Ted Cravens did his homework, finding out, in the short time he had available, everything he could dig up about Charles Evan Oatley's past. Ted had learned to be meticulous and to categorize his information. For Chip, he made a dossier, separating his information into two main sections: "Personal" and "Professional." In addition to the normal data, he created a special subsection, "Analysis," under each of the major sections. After digesting the facts within each of the "Analysis" subsections, he created two additional subheadings: "Strengths" and "Weaknesses."

By the end of his analysis, Cravens was confident that he knew what made Chip Oatley tick. He knew the wants and needs of this scholar of linguistics. He knew his tastes, his desires, his motivations. He knew what pushed his buttons and aroused his emotions. He knew what gave him pleasure and what made him hurt. He knew his passions.

Cravens felt he was ready to put his plan into action. He wasn't totally sure how far he would go to manipulate Chip, but now he possessed the knowledge of where to apply pressure if an "attitude adjustment" became necessary.

While these considerations were fresh in Cravens' mind, his phone began to ring. *I should have disconnected that thing*, he muttered to himself.

Brandon Wesley curtly identified himself and came directly to the point. "The timetable has been moved up, Ted. You've got to move fast and get results."

"I never drag my feet, Wes," Ted said, the irritation rising in his voice. "What's the problem?

"I wouldn't do this if the situation didn't call for it," Wesley explained, but there was no apology in his tone. "Let me make this clear to you, Ted. This mission gets hotter every day. I'm hearing rumors from my sources in Mexico that there is a collection of Mayan writings in Chiapas that includes a compilation of herbal medical cures. I'm not asking you; I'm ordering you to find that bundle of papers before anybody else does. Get them copied and translated into English. If you have any doubts about your ability to accomplish this, you'd better bail out now. My job—and yours—depends on doing this right and doing it fast. Don't screw it up."

Cravens barely refrained from using the profanity on his lips, but he didn't bother to compose a polite response. "Can you be a little more precise about the adjusted timetable, Wes?"

"Cancel whatever you had planned for socializing in Oklahoma City tomorrow. Proceed to Chiapas immediately."

"That's fine with me. I'm ready to leave tonight, but I have to meet our new 'business associate' in San Antonio, Texas. I need to impress upon him the urgency of our project. Then I'll go on to Mexico. Tomorrow's a go."

Wes Brandon had heard what he wanted to hear. He hung up.

CHAPTER TEN

Chip's heart rate increased as he held the printout of the promised e-mail from Ollie. The telegram earlier had worked his imagination overtime. His hands trembled and he fought to control his emotions.

It was apparent that Ollie had chosen his words carefully. Even though German was his mother tongue, Ollie was fluent in English.

Chip read aloud, imagining he was listening to Ollie speak the words:

Dear Chip,

I am the messenger of bad news. With deepest regret and sorrow I must inform you of the sad and tragic events which have occurred here in Chiapas.

Since the Zapatista uprising, there have been many attacks and counterattacks in the regions where there are Mayan communities. The Army does not attack directly. It pays mercenary guerilla bands called "paramilitary" to raid the indigenous villages. One of these groups attacked the Baptist Mission Station in the Lacandon Jungle.

Your grandfather, my dearest friend, Rev. Matthew Oatley, was shot and his body has disappeared. Some people think that a curandera has taken his body to a nearby cave. Your mother, Laurel, and your sister, Regina, and the intern nurse, Teresa Robles, were taken as hostages by the raiders. The women were handled roughly and beaten, but, according to eyewitnesses, they were conscious and able to walk. We are hoping and praying that they have not suffered more and that they are still alive.

Alfredo Olivares, the volunteer doctor from San Antonio, and two other staffers were wounded by machete slashes. They were carried on litters to the paved road and taken by an Army truck to a mobile hospital. I have not been able to locate them yet. The regional military commanders do not respond to my inquiries, and they have not yet honored my requests to investigate the attack on the Mission Station.

Ever since your grandmother died, your grandfather has told me many times that he wished to have his body laid to rest beside his beloved wife in the enclosed garden behind the mission chapel. When his body is returned, we will honor his wish. I know that you would like to be present, but due to the tropical climate, it will be necessary to bury him expeditiously.

Since you were very close to your grandfather, I assume that you will come at your earliest convenience to pay your respects, arrange for a memorial service, and settle the affairs of his estate. Also, I know that you will not rest until you have exhausted every option to insure the safety and return of your mother and sister.

After notifying the Army, I contacted the local and state officials and informed them of the incident. I gave them my official statement about what I saw and heard when I arrived at the Mission Station a few hours after the attack occurred. I helped the mission staffers and patients prepare their statements and I translated the Mayan into Spanish. Then I translated all of them into English. I know that the Baptist Foreign Mission Board *will want copies of every document. When the police and military investigators finally get here, they will not know the Mayan languages, so I will have to serve as an interpreter.*

I have contacted some of my friends in government agencies and in political positions. They are outraged and deeply troubled by what has happened. The governor has called the president. The president is going to order the Regional Army Commander to assume responsibility for the immediate capture and prosecution of anyone involved in this crime. Perhaps you did not know that Teresa is the governor's favorite niece. This relationship has been most favorable for the Mission Station. The governor is infamous for the fury of his anger. Heaven help the man who harms a hair on the head of his niece.

Your grandfather was a humble man, but he had the love, respect, and admiration of many people, some in positions of influence and power. It would be wise to personally invite these people to attend and participate in the memorial service.

Please let me know if there is anything I can do before you arrive. I will make arrangements for your transportation and lodging. You are always welcome to stay in the guestroom at my house here in San Cristóbal. Now that I am connected to the internet, you can e-mail me at any hour. Please let me know your plans as soon as possible. I will keep you informed of any new developments here.

My heart is heavy and I share your grief. Lo siento mucho, amigo mio.
Ollie

When Chip tried to focus on the printout, he saw that it was blotted with salty tears. It took him a moment to assimilate the information he had just read. His mind knew it was true, but his heart refused to accept it. The mixture of shock and disbelief almost kept his emotions in check. He stood up, half expecting a volcanic eruption of rage and anguish to rumble through his guts, but it didn't happen. Numbness settled over him like shell shock.

Only vaguely aware of his movements, Chip reached into his back pocket and pulled out a worn leather billfold. Unsnapping a tab, he opened the section which contained photographs in yellowing plastic protectors. One by one he leafed through this portable family album. When he came to the faded black-and-white portrait of his grandfather, he pulled it out.

Chip's mind eased into a memory of the day he had turned thirteen. His grandfather had taken this photograph of himself and scrawled the words "Know thyself" on the backside with his heirloom Esterbrook fountain pen, then handed the pen to Chip and said, "The fine old pen belongs to you now, Chip. Happy Birthday."

Chip remembered thanking his grandfather, then curiously asking him, "Why should I know myself, Grandpa?"

His grandfather had replied, "If you do not know yourself, you cannot know your weaknesses, your faults, your handicaps, your shortcomings, your sins. But you must also learn your capabilities, your gifts, and your assets. Without knowledge of these, you cannot possibly control or discipline yourself. If you do not control or discipline yourself, you are doomed to be controlled and disciplined by others. You will be at their mercy. If you do not know what causes you pain and suffering, you will never know the meaning of pleasure."

Chip put the photograph back in its protective sleeve and thought aloud. "Maybe I am learning something about myself, Grandpa. Maybe I'm not as smart as I thought I was."

CHAPTER ELEVEN

"Well," said the dean's secretary. "It's Professor Hotshot again. You're getting to be a regular around here. To what do we owe the pleasure of your company this time?"

"No time to flirt with you this morning, Gretchen,"

"Go on in, then," she barked. "He's expecting you."

Chip strode into the dean's office, went straight to the "hot seat" and sat down without waiting for the dean's directive.

This time there was no need to wait for the dean's attention, so he opened the conversation without the usual pleasantries. "You win. I'll go to Chiapas. I'll do the summer linguistics seminar. How soon can I leave?"

"Too late, Chipper," the dean said. "You had the opportunity, but you turned me down. You said you wanted to stay here and solve your own problems."

"Then you're going to have to put me on administrative leave or terminate my contract. I have to go to Chiapas and I have to go now."

"What's the urgency? Have you, by chance, impregnated a coed?"

Chip tossed the e-mail printout onto the desk. The dean picked it up, briefly looked it over, and calmly handed it back to Chip. He sat back in his swivel chair and smiled.

"You already know, don't you?" Chip said.

"Ollie sent me a copy. I've been expecting you," the dean replied, his smile settling into a grin.

"What do you find amusing about this situation? I fail to see the humor. Care to explain?"

"Chipper, my boy, you're the proverbial country bumpkin who falls into a cow patty and comes up smelling like a rose. I'm putting you on a one-year sabbatical. You're going to Chiapas to do some research for a big company and, hopefully, you'll finish up your doctorate.

"You have twenty-four hours to wrap up your classes, turn in your grades, pack your bags, and get out of Dodge."

Stunned, Chip could only ask, "I know better than to doubt your word, Bert. But you've really got me curious. How did you manage to slip this by the faculty senate? I'm not due for a sabbatical."

"I had to call in a few IOUs. I've survived in the academic game only because I learned early-on the value of favor trading."

"You should consider a career in politics," Chip mumbled.

"What do you think this game is all about, Chip? It has little to do with advancing humankind's intellectual database. It has more to do with inflating pedantic egos."

"Just curious," said Chip, looking up, "what Santa Claus is financing my vacation to the warmth of Mexico?"

"Normally, I'd have to shake the money tree pretty hard for a grant, but this one fell right into my lap. Some big conglomerate called Rainwater Pharms—spelled with 'p-h'—has more money than it knows what to do with. I don't know much about it except that it's a family-owned corporation that started out in food processing and expanded by buying up the farms that supplied them. Then they began to buy into the bigger agricultural concerns in northern Mexico. Now they've got their sights on dozens of locations farther south and into Central and South America.

"They've become leaders in biogenetic plant engineering and are grabbing up transnational pharmaceuticals. They must be doing something right because profits have doubled every year for the last seven years."

"So let me guess," said Chip drily. "They want to buy Chiapas. I wonder why. I'm not aware of any mega farms down there. What's their special interest?"

"I don't think it's the farms they're after, at least for now. Their main concern is pressure from the pharmaceutical division which wants to learn everything about traditional medicines. And they think someone like you, who speaks the Mayan dialects, can help them identify the plants – especially the herbs – that have been used for thousands of years and learn their curative secrets.

"Obviously they have no interest in abstract, intellectual monographs about anthropological linguistics. They just want someone who can lead them to cheap, untapped resources. If they're willing to pay your salary and expenses for a year, I'm not going to scrutinize the dentures of the gift horse too closely.

"Anyway, this symbiotic relationship we have with corporate America gets a little complicated at times. They set up a non-profit foundation and get a tax write-off. The foundation gives a grant to the school; the school keeps its financial head above water. The school does the research, which the corporate business uses to develop new products to keep it ahead of the competition and make more profits to keep the shareholders happy. And the cycle repeats itself. That, my boy, is the reality of the corporate-academic complex."

"And little people like me," Chip added, "keep the drug companies floating in black ink by consuming their little antacid pills."

"Is your stomach still bothering you?"

"My stomach is trying to catch up with the burning questions that fill my head."

"What kinds of answers are you looking for now? Are you still trying to solve the mysteries of the universe?"

"Those questions have been crowded out by more mundane problems."

"Like what?"

"Like how I'm going to find Mom and Sis." Chip said. "And right now I've got a big problem."

"What's that?"

"What am I going to do about Honey Bee?"

"If her mother doesn't take care of her, I'll send her down to you in Chiapas when you get settled."

"You think of everything, don't you, Bert." It wasn't a question.

It wasn't until he had left the dean's office, passed through Gretchen's office, and stumbled out onto the front porch that Chip realized that Dean Lambert hadn't said a word about his grandfather's death or the kidnapping of his mother and sister. But right now he had too many more important matters claiming his attention to dwell on than the Dean's apparent lack of concern for Chip's loss.

CHAPTER TWELVE

Professor Oatley was mentally and physically overwhelmed by the news and events of the week. His meetings with the dean, the news of his grandfather's death and the kidnapping of his mother and sister in the attack on the Lacandon Mission Station, the arrangement for a sabbatical, and turning in semester progress reports and grades – all contributed to a whirlwind of activity and anxiety. Pushing himself to his limits, Chip had accomplished more in the last twelve hours than he normally did in two weeks.

When his phone didn't ring, Chip telephoned or e-mailed Ollie every four hours. There were no new developments. The jungle had gone silent. *No news is the worst news*, he thought glumly.

Early in the evening, in spite of his weariness, he drove across town to the house where his ex-wife and daughter lived. He would tell Marlene his travel plans and broach the idea of letting Honey Bee come down to Chiapas for the summer. He didn't expect Marlene to be receptive to the idea, but he thought it might help to plant the seed now. All of that aside, his chief objective was to spend this last evening with his daughter Honey

Bee before heading out to Chiapas. He anticipated an ugly confrontation with Marlene.

As he drove into the gravel driveway in front of Marlene's shabby garage house, he noted the porch light bulb was shattered, the screen door hung half open, and the front door wide open. He could see Marlene and her latest rodeo cowboy sitting at the kitchen table with a near-empty bottle of vodka and a half-pitcher of orange juice. At any moment, Chip half-expected to hear a drunken rendition of "Another Tequila Sunrise."

When Marlene and her woozy cowboy saw him at the door, they remained seated, but slurred a hostile greeting, ordered him in, and insisted on making him a drink. He politely declined and stood stiffly at the kitchen door while the tipsy couple returned to their libations and ignored him.

Honey Bee roused from her sleep on the living room sofa and managed a groggy "Hi, Dad," and rubbed her eyes. Chip saw her start toward him, but when she leaned over and saw that the kitchen cocktail lounge was still open for business, she stiffened and fell back into her makeshift bed. As her eyes widened, Chip sensed her tension. Hoping to calm her, he threw her a kiss before turning back to the kitchen.

"I have to go to Chiapas," he stated flatly. "I'm leaving tomorrow and I'll be gone for quite a while, so if you don't mind, I'd like to have Honey Bee come spend some time with me before I go. I'll bring her back tomorrow morning."

Surprisingly, Marlene agreed without an argument, but failed to disguise her pleasure at having Honey Bee off her hands for the night. She and her cowboy gave each other a knowing look, nodded their heads, and smiled.

Chip observed their not-so-subtle exchange and took advantage of the moment to add casually, "And since I'll be in Chiapas for a while, I'd like to bring Honey Bee down for the whole summer."

"No problem," Marlene said. "Just buy her ticket and I'll put her on the plane."

Chip glanced at Honey Bee and saw a tear roll down her cheek. He walked quickly over, wrapped his arms around her, and whispered, "Get your things together, Bee."

Must be tough for nine-year-old, Chip thought, *to live in a place where she knows she's not wanted. Let's get out of here before the witch changes her mind.*

Honey Bee ran to her room, pulled a small suitcase from under her bed, and quickly filled it with a change of underwear, her pajamas, and her toothbrush. She had done this before and knew the routine. On the way out she grabbed her purple sweat suit. Chip whisked her into his pickup truck and drove away before Marlene could change her mind.

Driving towards his house, Chip several times considered reaching across the bench seat to Honey Bee and pulling her to his side, but decided that she probably needed some space to sort things out, even if she was only nine years old.

From the day she was born, Chip felt a special bond with his daughter, but since the divorce decree had given Marlene custody and only visitation rights for him, Chip was finding it nearly impossible to maintain a close relationship with Bee, and the slowly dissolving bond burned like acid eating away at his heart.

For most of the drive back to Chip's place, Bee stared silently out the side window, but as Chip pulled to a stop in the concrete driveway, she turned to him and said, "Thanks Dad," before opening her door and jumping out.

Once inside the house, Bee deposited her things in the spare bedroom she knew was hers, then hopped into the kitchen where Chip was rummaging through the refrigerator. "Don't worry about fixing anything," she said, "I'm an expert at ordering pizza," she informed him as she picked up the phone.

Waiting for the pizza delivery, Chip attempted to start a conversation. "How are things going at school?" he asked.

"Same as always," she said without looking up from the comic section of the newspaper Chip had left scattered on the coffee table.

"What did you learn this week?" Chip asked, using a prompt that never failed to open her up, but uncharacteristically she replied, "Nothing."

"What's the problem, Honey Bee?" he asked finally.

"Daddy, I don't like my name," she said.

"Your name? What's wrong with your name?"

She rolled her eyes in disgust. "Honey Bee is a kid's name. A *little* kid's name. At school everybody makes fun of my name. They don't know how to pronounce Beatrix, so they call me Trix or Trixie. And Trixie is a dog's name. I don't want a dog's name," she blurted, lowering her head, on the verge of tears.

Chip sat down beside her and kissed the top of her head. He loved the smell of her hair. "What would you like to be called? Have you picked out another name?

"No," she mumbled into her arm. "I just don't want a little kid's name or a dog's name."

"Can I make a suggestion?" Chip volunteered. " I know a beautiful Mexican name. It's really an Aztec name. It's easy to say, but it's hard to spell. The name is Xochitle. It's spelled X-o-c-h-i-t-l-e. You could shorten it to Xochi."

"So-chee," she sounded it out phonetically. "What does it mean? It better not be the name of those hairless dogs the Aztecs used to eat," she responded without lifting her head, but he felt encouraged that at least she sounded interested.

"No, it simply means pretty flower."

"I like that name."

"I thought you might. Honey bees are attracted to pretty flowers."

"Since I'm your daddy, can I still call you Honey Bee if I want to?"

"Just don't call me that when anybody else is around," she insisted.

The moment was broken when the doorbell chimed repeatedly. Chip stood up, took out his wallet, and prepared to pay for the pizza. As he neared the door, he heard a commotion on the porch. Curious and cautious, he opened the door slightly and peered out. A crowd of his students shoved through the door and flowed into the living room and kitchen. All carried grocery bags and six-packs of assorted soft drinks.

"You can't leave without an AMF party," someone yelled above the sudden din of voices.

"What does AMF mean? And how did you know I'm leaving? Chip asked as he elbowed his way back to Honey Bee to reassure her that these were friendly students.

"The nice meaning is *Adios My Friend*," someone near his ear informed him.

One gaggle of students took over the kitchen and soon had an assembly line stacking sandwiches and piles of chips onto paper plates. A longhaired, unshaven graduate student sat down at the piano, pounded out a horrendous rendition of 'chopsticks,' but then wowed everyone with a medley of popular Mexican favorites, with almost everyone singing or humming along, their mouths stuffed with snacks.

Abruptly, a shy-looking co-ed kicked off her shoes and jumped up on the coffee table. As everyone quieted, she took off her glasses and took on a new personality. Smiling broadly as someone handed her a small, gift-wrapped package, she looked right at Chip and said, "We came here to tell you how much we enjoy your classes, and to thank you for always making yourself available when we needed help. As a token of our appreciation, we have a small gift for you."

From its shape, there was no secret about what was in the gift box, but everyone wanted to see it. Chip tore off the wrapping and lifted out an ivory colored stick.

"Oh, it's only a Montblanc. At first I thought it was a fine writing instrument," Chip joked, but then turned serious and said, "With this, I shall always remember you."

"We want you to do better than that," said a student behind him. "You have to promise to come back."

"*Pueden contar conmigo, mis amigos.* You can count on me, my friends."

As quickly as they had come in, the students ushered themselves out of the house, and, to Chip's amazement, the place was actually tidier than when they started the impromptu party.

From across the room a soft voice said, "That pen will go with the Esterbrook pen your grandpa gave you."

He swung around. "No, Xochi. The Esterbrook belongs to you now."

Walking over to her, he pressed the fine, old fountain pen into her hands and again kissed the top of her head. "All I ask is that you use it to write to me once in a while."

"*Puedes contar conmigo,*" she smiled, using the intimate form of the Spanish verb. "You can count on me."

"I guess you heard me tell your mother that I want you to come to Chiapas this summer," Chip said. "I really do want you to come, but I don't know how safe it will be for you. Have you heard about the problems they're having down there? I told your mother about the attack on the Mission Station. Did she tell you?"

"Yeah, she told me the story. She said that's just one more reason why she doesn't want to go there. But I'm not scared, Daddy. If it's safe enough for you to go there, then it's safe enough for me." Her wide eyes and serious expression told him she still had faith in his ability to care for and protect her.

"Well, I'm going to check it out first and see if it's safe. I won't let you come if there's any danger. You understand that don't you?"

"If it isn't safe at the Mission Station, maybe I could stay with Uncle Ollie at the research center in San Cristóbal."

"I'm not sure Ollie is ready for a hyperactive kid like you," Chip said.

"You still think I'm a little kid, don't you, Dad?"

"My, my. Aren't we grown up, now?"

"I have to take care of myself, now," she said. "I fix my own breakfast, get myself dressed, and get to the school bus without waking up Mom in the mornings."

Xochi's words stung Chip like a slap. He realized that neither he nor Marlene had been good parents. And he knew she was being neglected. Before he could stop himself, he said, "You deserve better, Xochi. A kid your age needs some grownups around to take care of you."

"There you go again, Dad, thinking of me as a little kid."

"Well, I know this cute young lady who has a favorite breakfast that starts with blueberry pancakes slathered with sweet butter and smeared with clover honey. And with those pancakes she likes two strips of bacon, and a bowl of honeydew melon cubes with a scoop of pistachio ice cream on top. She tops it off with a mug of hot chocolate with miniature marshmallows floating and melting in the thick, dark, liquid. Would you be too upset if I cooked the bacon in the morning?"

"I just have one question, Dad. What are we going to do with the pizza?"

"I didn't even know it came."

"Uncle Bert paid for it."

"He was here? I didn't see him."

"Just for a minute. He told me to call him if I needed anything while you're gone."

"I'll call you every day. And I want you to call Uncle Bert every day, okay? And if you can't get him, talk to growlin' Gretchen. She acts mean and tough, but she's a softie underneath."

"I don't like Uncle Bert."

"What? Why not?" Chip was startled.

"He called me Trixie."

CHAPTER THIRTEEN

Early the next morning after the promised pancake breakfast, Chip took Xochi back to her mother and fumbled through an awkward goodbye. He returned to his house and loaded his vintage pickup truck with boxes, duffle bags, and suitcases. Even with his tool boxes, ice chest, and sleeping bag, the long bed under an aluminum camper shell was only half-full. There was still enough room to crawl in and stretch out if he felt the need for a siesta on the long, open rural roads of Mexico. He shoved in six boxes of books near the tailgate.

Before checking that the house lights were turned off and the windows were locked, he made one last call to Ollie and heard the same report. There was no change in the situation. He locked the house doors and drove to Bert's office.

This time, Chip's entry to the office was blocked by the massive girth of Gretchen the secretary. "Excuse me," he said politely, but the woman didn't budge.

Extending her bulldog snarl into his face, she growled, "If you ever call me 'Princess' again, I'll have you tortured and thrown into the dungeon." Then her countenance melted into sugar sweetness. Backing away, she said in an artificial drawl, "Now, if you'll just sign these papers and give me your keys, I'll see that you can get on up outta here."

"I just love the way you southern belles talk," Chip drawled back at her. "You just drip with honey."

"Watch your mouth!" she barked, switching back to her natural German accent. And then, changing the subject, added, "I've already got an interested renter for your house."

"Thanks. You really are a princess."

She marched up to him and gave him a smothering bear hug. He felt a sudden fear that she could crush him if she so desired.

"Would you do me one more favor?" he gasped.

"What now?" She released him, rolling her eyes.

"I'd appreciate it if you would check on Honey Bee from time to time. Oh, I almost forgot. She wants to be called Xochi now. She seems to think she's all grown up. Must be having an identity crisis—or some such phase."

"Don't you worry, none, partner," she answered in mimic western. "If any cowhand so much as looks at that girl the wrong way, they'll have me to tangle with. And believe me, sonny, I've been known to bulldog, calf-rope, and brand a few head of cattle in my day. Ain't nobody 'round here gonna mess with me.

"Oh, I almost forgot." She stepped back to her desk and handed him a note that Chip recognized as being in Bert's handwriting. It instructed Chip to meet a Mr. Ted Cravens at the Alamo Hotel in San Antonio, Texas.

When Chip looked up, Princess Gretchen was sitting on her throne, typing at lightning speed. Without looking up, she lifted one hand and waved him out. He turned and left, but not before seeing her swipe quickly at her cheek.

CHAPTER FOURTEEN

El Mapache, the Raccoon, was an experienced and careful trucker. He knew the routes, he knew the roads, he knew the seasons and the weather, and he knew his truck. Like a jockey checking his mount, he gave his twenty-year-old, five-ton, stake-bed truck a thorough inspection before starting a run. Meticulously, he checked the fluids for correct levels and looked for any leakage. He checked the wear and tightness of the belts. He checked the tires for wear and air pressure. He stood in the dirt for a moment listening to the engine. When he was satisfied that all systems were in working order, he checked the trucker's knots securing the canvas tarp over the top of his load.

"All systems go," he said, repeating a phrase he had learned in California years ago. Looking up, he saw that the Chiapas moon was right.

It was midnight when Mapache pulled out of Villaflores, the major agricultural region in the southern lowlands of Chiapas, and drove through the cool night. He enjoyed driving this *tierra caliente*, hot country, at night. He avoided the sweltering heat and there was much less traffic; in the early morning hours just before dawn, the pungent fragrance of the chili pepper plants in the fields on both sides of the road filled his nostrils. He inhaled deeply, savoring the intoxicating aroma. The heady perfume was magnified by the ventilated crates of jalapeno chili peppers stacked in the bed of his truck.

Like many solo truckers, Mapache kept himself company by expressing his thoughts and feelings aloud, talking to his reflection from the windshield. The sound of his voice helped keep him awake. "It's finally paying off," he said. "We're turning chili into money. I hope it lasts. But if it doesn't, *ni modo*, that's the way it is and there's nothing you can do about it."

Seven years ago, Mapache had acted on truck stop rumors and a gut feeling. He had helped his friend, Roberto Camacho, start a small jalapeno farm. It had been a risk, but now it was making a sizable profit. The demand for jalapenos increased every year, especially for foreign export and prices were soaring. The farm was doing so well this year that Roberto was suggesting they buy more land and plant more jalapenos.

Mapache set aside his thoughts of a bigger jalapeno farm when he pulled into the *Central de Abastos*, the large complex of produce and grocery distribution warehouses in Tuxtla Gutierrez, the capital of Chiapas. At the loading docks a swarm of swampers descended upon him, all adolescent boys desperate for work. When he had selected two lean and hungry *muchachos* to offload half of the jalapeno crates, Mapache drank a cup of *atole*, a hot beverage thickened with cornmeal. He chatted with the dock supervisor and the stall owner who bought the chili peppers and learned that a *chilango*, a city slicker from Mexico City, had come around asking a multitude of questions about medicinal herbs and had paid high prices for truckloads of the plants. The story aroused Mapache's interest because his mother was a *curandera*, a medicine woman. He determined to ask her if anyone had approached her. She would remember if any inquisitive strangers were snooping around. For some months Chiapas truckers had been swapping stories about big pharmaceutical companies bio-pirating the traditional herbal cures without compensating the curanderos. Mapache wondered if anyone was trying to 'steal' his mother's ancient knowledge and wisdom. He had no idea how anyone could measure the worth of that knowledge in monetary terms.

His business finished in Tuxtla, Mapache urged his truck up the mountainous road to San Cristóbal de Las Casas, the ancient, Spanish colonial capital of the region, where he quickly sold half of the remaining load of jalapenos. From there he drove directly to Ocosingo, his hometown in the highlands, and sold the rest of his chili pepper to an old friend who had a stall in the *mercado*, the central marketplace. Mapache set aside one crate for his mother. She would share the bounty with her friends and neighbors.

It was late in the afternoon when Mapache arrived at his mother's *choza*. The cabin was rustic, but clean. The old woman sat motionless on a wooden stool under a shady tree near the cabin. Both Mapache and his mother were dirty and sweaty, but neither cared as they embraced and held their foreheads together, looking into each other's eyes, as if reading each other's soul. He knew she had been out collecting plants, flowers, roots, bark, and leaves. Such treks through the woods were becoming difficult for her, and he could see something more. She was not only tired; she was worried.

"What's troubling you, Mother?" he asked in their native Mayan dialect. He cautiously approached the topic that had tormented her for many months, especially since the Zapatistas had declared open hostilities against the government. "Have the bad dreams come to haunt you again?"

"Yes, my son, I am fearful. We are walking into a time of great suffering, and I do not know if we, as a people, will endure. I do not know if we are prepared. The hard times will overwhelm us like a flood of water. How can we be strong enough to survive the coming torrent?"

"Mother, there is always hope. I have read in the Bible, the sacred book of the Jews and Christians, about an ancient family that survived a great flood of water by building a large boat they called an 'ark.' That family, that 'people' survive to this day because they have developed a social ark that bonds them together to overcome hardships and persecutions. They have been able to preserve their culture – their way of life."

"An ark? That's exactly what we need, my son, to keep our culture, and our customs floating above the flood of change that threatens to sweep us out of history. Our people are ignorant of our traditions and the history of our ancestors. And fewer and fewer of our children are keeping our language alive."

"You speak truth, Mother. And it shames me because even I have been guilty of turning away from my Mayan ways. There were times in my youth when I was ashamed to speak our tongue."

"Our tongue and our ways will vanish forever if we don't fight to keep them alive."

"My son, do you remember how your father was always collecting the stories of our people?"

"Why was that so important to him?"

"I think he sensed, as I do, that those stories could help us survive. They tell us the lessons our ancestors have learned.

"It was your father's lifelong project to collect the stories, the knowledge, and wisdom that had been passed down to us. It was his obsession. When he was dying, he asked me to give his papers to you when the time was right. He said you would know what to do with them. My dreams have told me the time is right now."

"I do remember him writing down the stories he heard, and I have wondered what he did with those papers. From what you tell me, Mother, he had enough material to make many books of Maya knowledge. There is a word for such a collection of books. The word is 'encyclopedia.' I do not know if there is such a word in our language."

"One day your father came home repeating a word over and over. The word was 'codex.' Maybe that was what he wanted to write for our people. He said he wanted a codex that the church could not burn. I didn't understand what he was talking about, but I have learned many things since then.

"I have kept your father's papers hidden in a cave not far from here. I went there today and brought them here for you. They are in that box behind you."

"I will take them, Mother, and I will protect them. I will find someone who can turn these papers into a book that will preserve our knowledge. I do not want this codex to be destroyed like most of the others."

"You father was convinced that not all the old books were destroyed. He suspected that the elders hid the books in our sacred caves and on special, ceremonial days, they would meet secretly to read the stories of our origins and perform the ancient rituals. I think your father was writing about those old histories. He wanted us to understand how they are relevant and meaningful to us today."

"Mother, do you think that he has given us a design for an ark? Was he searching for a way to preserve our culture?" Mapache asked hopefully.

"And now I am curious, Mother," he continued. "I have so many questions. Have you read Father's papers?" he asked, then suddenly remembered that she had never been to school and that she could not read. Quickly he asked, "Did he ever explain any of the rituals to you?"

"He read many of the papers to me. Then he did more than explain. He took me to the cave." She paused, then whispered reverently, "We performed the sacred rituals."

For an instant, as her mind flashed back to that experience, both the pain and the pleasure were reflected in her countenance. When she had regained her composure, she said, "Son, promise me that you will read the writings of your father and that one day you will go to the cave. And when you have done that, teach your daughter what you have learned."

"I do not understand what you are asking me to do, Mother, but I will do as you wish."

"I cannot ask more of you. Now, let me give you my blessing."

Standing before him, she placed her hands on his head. "My son, I blessed you before you were born. The gods have placed a heavy responsibility on you. It is a burden you must bear, and it is a curse as much as it is a blessing." She was silent for a moment and then, as her tears fell upon the crown of his bowed head, she chanted her Maya blessing. When she had finished, she slumped to the earth and whispered, "I hear the floodwater lapping in the distance. Take the papers and go. Prepare our people an ark."

CHAPTER FIFTEEN

Professor Chip Oatley checked into the Alamo Hotel in San Antonio, went straight to his room and made three phone calls.

Ollie Krahn was expecting Chip's call. There had been a startling development.

"The police did not tell me. Neither did the military officials. It was the governor, himself. He told me confidentially that reliable informants are saying that the old missionary is still alive. Somehow, perhaps miraculously, he survived the gunshots he received when the mission was attacked. When the raider realized that he was alive, they allowed a *curandera*, a healer-woman, to take him and care for him. No one knows for sure where he has been taken, but most everyone believes the story that he is alive."

"That is wonderful news, Ollie," Chip said, his throat choking with emotion. "That's great news! And what about my mother, my sister, and Teresa? Any word about them? Please tell me they're alive and well, too."

"There are rumors," Ollie said, "that the women are being held in a cave, and that all three of them are alive. But there has been no communication from the kidnappers."

"I'm grateful for what you're doing, Ollie. I can't thank you enough. Now I'm going to drive straight to Chiapas. It'll take a few days to get there, but I'll push my old pickup as fast as she'll go. Keep your ear to the ground and let me know where you think we should look when I get there. Since you and I speak the languages, we will learn more than the police and the military together."

"I know how you must feel, Chip," Ollie said. "But we have a little breathing room now. Get here fast, but you really need to make a quick stop in Mexico City to pay a courtesy visit to the director of the anthropology department at UNAM and pick up the most recent research they have on language extinction."

Chip started to reject the idea, then hesitantly said, "Okay. I'll call you as soon as I get there."

As soon as he and Ollie hung up, Chip called his daughter. Learning that she was alone in the house made him angry, but he was relieved that Xochi could speak freely to him without Marlene's presence putting a damper on the conversation. When Chip told her about his call to Chiapas, she seemed to read his mind.

"Don't worry, Dad. You'll get them back. And when you do, I want to come down there and help you take care of them. I know what it feels like to be kidnapped and taken away from home."

"Xochi," he said, "I'm sorry I let that happen to you."

"I know, Dad. I'm trying to figure out a way for you to kidnap me back."

"I thought about bringing you with me, but that wouldn't have been a good idea. I'll make sure you come down for the summer. I'll call you as often as I can."

After he tore himself away from Xochi's call, Chip dialed the dean, but his phone rang until Gretchen finally answered. She told him not to worry and to go on to Mexico City and check in from there.

Within seconds after hanging up, there was a knock on the door. A bellhop informed Chip that a Mr. Ted Cravens was expecting him in the hotel bar. Chip thanked him with a modest tip, sure that Cravens had already made the errand worthwhile.

Washing his face, but not bothering to change clothes, Chip went to the Alamo Lounge and was greeted by Cravens. They were both startled to see that they resembled each other, enough so, they might even be mistaken for brothers. They were both uncomfortable, but Cravens quickly composed himself and shook Chip's hand firmly and spoke as though they had been intimate friends for years. Although Cravens insisted they use first names, Chip's instincts made him cautious and cool. Because he realized he was harboring an active dislike for Mr. Cravens, he was careful to maintain a surface politeness. He casually declined Ted's urging to join him in ordering the local longneck bottles of Lone Star beer.

Chip's long drive had left him no desire for idle chit-chat. "Dean Lambert wasn't very specific in explaining what you want from me, Mr. Cravens. Can you fill me in?"

"Of course, Professor Oatley. I'm sure Dean Lambert told you about Rainwater Pharms and what we are doing in Chiapas. Our project is turning out to be more complicated than we had anticipated. The problem is that the *curanderos*, the tribal healers, are being less than cooperative. Activists and agitators are convincing them that we are trying to pirate their knowledge of traditional cures. They're calling us 'bio-pirates.'

"We need someone like you, Professor, who speaks their language, who has their respect, to lay the groundwork for our plant collectors, to persuade the curanderos to be cooperative."

"Wait a minute," Chip interjected. "There's something missing here, Mr. Cravens. I'm not a botanist, a biologist, or any type of agriculturalist. I don't have a green thumb. I don't have a garden or even any plants in my office. How do you expect me to be a plant collector?"

"Let us worry about collecting the plants," said Cravens. "Besides being a liaison with the *curanderos*, the only thing we want from you is information about medicinal plants, information that can be gleaned from Mayan writings. We want you to find out everything you can that has been written or passed down orally in Mayan languages concerning plants used in traditional medicinal cures."

"But surely you must know, Mr. Craven, that almost every written Mayan document was destroyed by the colonial Spanish officials, especially the religious ones."

Cravens' friendly façade hardened momentarily. "Please, Professor Oatley, do not insult me. I may not have the academic degrees that you have, but I am not totally ignorant of Mexico's history. Like you, I grew up in Mexico. I know that supposedly there are only four known Mayan codices in the world, but for centuries there have been reports that at least one other codex exists, and there may be others. And they are still consulted in secret by tribal elders in Chiapas. If there really is one, and you are able to locate it, to verify its existence, do you know what that would do for your academic career? I think you do.

"And I am certain that such a codex contains a wealth of traditional medicinal cures that have the potential to make Rainwater Pharms—and your school and you—very wealthy."

Chip's mind reeled with the implications. The prospect of never again having to worry about being published in the most prestigious academic journals held his attention. Whatever reservations Chip may have had about Rainwater Pharms were quickly evaporating, but still he felt compelled to clarify the corporation's motives.

"What part—if any—of the profits do you plan to share with the curanderos, the Mayans, who provide the source knowledge to you?" Chip asked. "Some people equate the source knowledge with intellectual property."

"Professor," said Cravens, slowly measuring his words, "if you're suggesting that we really are bio-pirates, you're mistaken. We are not out to rob anyone of their intellectual knowledge. Whatever knowledge they have preserved needs to be extracted for everyone's good. In fact, you could even call it our social responsibility to seek out that information so that it can be used for the benefit of all mankind."

"That sounds a bit pompous." Chip replied. "What you mean is it should be used for the benefit of Rainwater Pharms."

"If your role in this enterprise places you in a moral dilemma, Professor, it would be best if you disengage now. I understand your misgivings. Believe me, I wouldn't want you to be forced into a compromising position. For the sake of all concerned, it would be best to resolve your questions before continuing any further."

Cravens saw that Chip needed time to consider his position and resign himself to his fate. "Let's drop the business talk," he said quickly. "Let's go out and relax a bit. There's a great German restaurant not far from here. You'll enjoy the food and the music.'

"The music?" Chip asked. "What kind of German music? I'm not in the mood right now for Wagnerian opera."

"Traditional folk music. It's quite a show. German glee clubs, dressed in Bavarian folk costumes, playing polka accordions, get together and have choral competitions. Most are all-male groups and the more beer steins that are emptied, the louder and more raucous the singing becomes."

"Well, I suppose I could use a little diversion. This conversation has been top-heavy on the serious side. Let's go."

They walked out into the warm San Antonio air and followed the Riverwalk for a block.

Curious, Chip asked, "How did you happen to find out about German places?"

"Digging into the history of Chiapas, I discovered that a good number of Germans, disenchanted with nationalistic flag-waving and imperialistic wars, found their way to southern Chiapas and established coffee plantations. There are still pockets of blue-eyed blondes throughout the region. As a sidebar, I discovered communities of Germans through the Americas. Oktoberfest is a big event in New Braunfels, near San Antonio."

"That's true," Chip acknowledged, "but for the most part in Chiapas, German settlers have assimilated into the mainstream of Mexican culture. Few of them have any knowledge of the German folk customs and traditions you see preserved here with singing clubs. Virtually none of the coffee plantation families speak German anymore. And intermarriage has erased many Germanic surnames."

"We must have read the same ethnic studies," Ted commented. "There seems to have been a conscientious effort to shed much of their cultural past. Do you think they have been successful?"

"Losing two wars has contributed to anti-German sentiment on this continent," Chip said. "They don't want to stand out as ready targets for hate mongers."

"True, but do you think down deep there are those who secretly harbor neo-Nazi convictions?"

"There may be some," Chip answered thoughtfully. "And that attitude surfaces in prejudice against the indigenous Maya, whom some see as primitive and sub-human. I see it as much like the anti-Semitism that spread like a cancer in Europe in the 1930s."

"Do you really think that it will reach that level of fervor? Will people become that irrational?"

"I certainly hope not. There are already too many forces at work that are pushing the Mayan culture toward extinction. Something must be done to revive their self-esteem—on a broad, tribal scale."

"Have you ever thought," Cravens suggested, "that it might take the involvement of an outsider—someone like yourself—to light a revival of cultural pride?"

"Mr. Cravens," Chip replied, "I think it is obvious that there is already too much outside involvement in this social upheaval that some people are calling 'the Indian problem.' As for me, the only concern I have is to try to save their languages. But I'm not sure that anything I do will make a difference."

"You've already made a difference."

"How so?"

"You've started me thinking about how Rainwater Pharms can get involved to resolve 'the Indian problem.' "

"That's the last thing they need," Chip said, shaking his head. "Another major player wanting to get involved."

CHAPTER SIXTEEN

Mapache took the soiled wooden box containing his father's papers and buried it under a stack of similar-looking boxes in the bed of his truck. After driving back to the Ocosingo mercado where he had sold some chili peppers that morning, he bought two dozen *costales* of vegetables that had not been grown in chili pepper country, down in *la tierra caliente*, the hot country. He arranged the large burlap bags to hide the boxes, especially the one containing the papers. Satisfied, he drove toward San Cristóbal.

Fearful of attracting the attention of military patrols, Mapache held his speed down. But as much as he tried to concentrate on his driving, his mind drifted from the road to the box of papers. He wished he had time to read them, but more importantly, he felt an urgency to store them safely—and soon.

At the San Cristóbal mercado, he sold half of the costales of fresh vegetables. Except for four, the remaining costales would easily be sold back in Villaflores. Of the four set aside, two were for Roberto and his wife at the chili pepper farm, and two were for the owner of the boardinghouse where Ramona, Mapache's daughter, was staying.

By the time his business at the mercado was done, it was late afternoon. He thought about calling Ramona to let her know he was on his way, but then thought he'd take a chance that she was already off work and try to surprise her. He hoped he wouldn't be too disappointed if she were not home.

Not for the first time, he considered the mixed emotions of fatherhood. On one hand, he found distasteful the idea that she might be out with a passionate young man. *On the other hand,* he thought, *I cannot control her, and I wouldn't want to, even if I could. I want her to be happy. Even if that means love and marriage, then I couldn't—I wouldn't—deny her that.* He smiled then, thinking of the grandchildren he might someday take riding in his truck.

The sun was still high when Mapache drove into San Cristóbal, skirted the busy city streets and brought his truck to an idle at the wrought iron gates of Casa Rodriguez, the boardinghouse where Ramona rented a room. The boardinghouse was, in reality, a complex of residential units. Some boarders rented single rooms; others had houses of various sizes. Along one side were four self-contained houses, sharing adjacent walls in the condominium style common throughout Mexico. At one end, separated from the rest of the structures, stood a well-preserved single unit house, which had been originally designed for the *mayordomo*, the butler in charge of all other servants and hired workers. An adobe wall, one meter wide and four meters high, surrounded all the buildings, which occupied an entire city block.

When he pulled in and parked his truck at the back entrance of the boardinghouse kitchen, Mapache sensed immediately that Ramona would be there. She was frugal, it was dinnertime, and she would not waste money to go out to eat, since the meals were included in the rent payment.

Walking casually into the long dining room, Mapache saw the boarders, most of whom were students, had already finished their meals and left the dining room. He could see a few of them walking leisurely under the arches of the wide, tiled courtyard. Ramona was sitting at the large wooden table in the boardinghouse dining room having coffee with the house owner, an aging widow, whose long, lean body was folded possessively over her brown mug.

Before Mapache could respond to Ramona's effusive hug and an offer of coffee, the house owner interrupted in a flat, yet commanding voice, "*Por favor*, Ramona. Just a cup of coffee? A man needs a full meal after a hard day's work." Her voice softened, and with a coy smile, she cooed, "Please sit down," as she patted the captain's chair at her side. Then with another sudden shift, she returned to the imperious lady role, shouting toward the kitchen, "*Muchachas*! Bring this *hombre* a complete dinner and a stack of hot tortillas. And a pitcher of cold *horchata*."

Taken off guard, Mapache quickly sat in the offered chair. "*Gracias, señora. Muy amable*, you're very kind. I am hot and tired from a long day. A glass of sweet, rice water does sound good."

Ramona moved in to place a clean plate and silverware in front of her father, making belated introductions.

"*Doña* Sabel, this is my father, *señor* Map Ach."

"Please, call me El Mapache," he said modestly.

"And this is *Doña* Sabel, *la duena*, the owner of this *casa de huespedes*, this boardinghouse. She is our 'housemother.' Most of the renters here are young college girls who often need the advice and discipline of an experienced woman to keep them out of trouble."

The landlady reached out and shook Mapache's hand, stretching her full lips in a wide smile. "Isabel Rodriguez, *a sus ordenes*, at your service," she gushed with a not-so-subtle downward glance that ended with her peering up at him from the sides of her eyes. "I am the widow of Señor Ricardo Toledo," she added, making it known that she was not to be considered married.

"*Mucho gusto de conocerle*, pleased to meet you," he said, carefully withdrawing his hand from her soft grip, not wanting to appear rude.

"*El placer es mio.* The pleasure is mine," she cooed.

Two kitchen workers helped Ramona set various dishes in front of Mapache. As he served himself and began to eat, *doña* Sabel scooted closer to him, watching each time he lifted his fork to his mouth. He suspected that she was ravenous, not so much for food, but perhaps for male attention and affection, although he felt no inclination to satisfy her desires.

As he ate, Ramona explained that *doña* Sabel's deceased husband had been the publisher of San Cristóbal's only newspaper for many years and had written several books about the history of the region. *doña* Sabel visibly swelled with pride. Her husband had apparently been an important and highly respected member of the community.

"If you are finished eating, *señor*, I would like to show you my husband's library," the landlady said, leaning closer to Mapache until he was forced to shift away.

"It's much more than a library, Papa," Ramona put in. She seemed oblivious to her housemother's leering grin in her father's direction. "It's a museum. And I remember you telling me how much you enjoy going to museums. Not only is there a collection of rare books, but there are the archives of all the newspapers he published, many manuscripts, court records, and personal letters.

Since I am an archivist, you can imagine how that attracts my interest. And there are many pieces of art and antique furniture. Some of them are hand carved and are more than two hundred years old."

"Please keep your voice down, Ramona," the landlady whispered sharply with a frown and a quick glance around the dining room. "I don't want any of the *sirvientes* to know about the contents of the library. They are never allowed to enter that part of the house. I keep the doors and windows locked."

"It would be a privilege to see your husband's library, *doña* Sabel," Mapache said formally. "I have always been fascinated by the past, and its influence on the present and the future. You do a great service to civilization by preserving our heritage." He honestly wanted to compliment her, but he didn't want to be too lavish in his praise. He wouldn't care to be escorted alone by *doña* Sabel in the library.

Without waiting for the kitchen workers to clear the table, *doña* Sabel stood up, pulling Mapache to his feet. He quickly reached out his hand to Ramona and allowed *doña* Sabel to lead them both to the library. When she was certain that no one had followed them, she unlocked the cavernous series of rooms, ushered them in, and locked the door behind her. Crossing the room, she carefully posited herself in a large, comfortable chair upholstered with dark, soft leather.

"My legs are not working well today," she grimaced, looking up at Mapache for sympathy. "You show your father around, Ramona. I'll sit here and relax awhile."

Relieved, Mapache led Ramona to the far end of the library. Quickly and quietly he told her about the packet of papers he had received from his mother and that he needed a place to keep them safe.

"Father, I am sure they can be hidden right here in this library," Ramona responded. "Your manuscripts would be as safe as all the other books, documents, and papers already here."

"Do you think *doña* Sabel would mind?"

"I suspect there isn't much she wouldn't do for you, Papa, but there's only one way to find out. Let's ask her."

When asked, *doña* Sabel did not hesitate for a second. "I will guard them as though they were my husband's papers."

Mapache wasted no time retrieving the papers from his truck. Doña Sabel showed him a hidden niche behind a book case. He thanked *doña* Sabel and asked her to accept some fresh vegetables. Although she refused graciously, he left them in the kitchen, knowing she would be pleased.

When Mapache asked *doña* Sabel if he could use her telephone for a long distance call, she waved her hand, assuring him the telephone was his to use anytime. When he said that he would leave sufficient funds to cover the cost of the calls, she told him that the vegetables were payment enough. She grabbed his hand and pushed him into her private sitting room to make his call.

A few minutes later, he took leave of Ramona and *doña* Sabel to hurry back to Villaflores. An order for a full load of jalapenos had come in. They were to be delivered to the Rainwater Pharms processing plant near Nuevo Laredo, just south of Laredo, Texas.

Doña Sabel flushed with envy when Ramona kissed her father goodbye.

CHAPTER SEVENTEEN

C hip took his leave of Rainwater Pharms agent Ted Cravens and strolled along the banks of the famous San Antonio Riverwalk that meanders through the heart of the city. He was only partially distracted by the aroma of spicy Mexican foods being hawked by street vendors, interspersed with mariachi bands serenading with their special blend of guitars, violins, trumpets, and rebel-like yells. Although his eyes took in the sights and he heard the sounds, his mind was elsewhere.

Near the historic Alamo, he found a phone booth and again called Xochi. He knew it was late, but he wanted to let her know he was thinking about her and wished he was there to tuck her into bed and tell her goodnight. Xochi was happy he called, but she reminded him that she was a big girl now and she didn't need anyone tucking her into bed anymore. Even though the call was short, Chip felt better after hanging up.

With his spirits lifted, Chip returned to his pickup truck and headed south again. There were few cars on the road and soon he was in the border city of Laredo, Texas, where he planned to find a cheap motel and spend the night. He had not yet decided if he would stay on the U.S. side, or cross over into Nuevo Laredo on the Mexican side.

The short line of cars at the customs checkpoint made the decision for him.

He crossed the border without delays, feeling no obligation to slip a discreet *mordida* into a greedy palm to obtain an official stamp. Although he was familiar with the custom of officials taking "little bites" of currency to make the wheels of bureaucracy turn more expeditiously, he had never been comfortable "greasing the wheels" in that manner. It left him feeling dirty.

Crossing the border into Mexico always fascinated Chip. Being a student of cultural influences on language, he was attuned to differences that extended well beyond the switch from English to Spanish. In every culture, houses and streets are designed and constructed for a specific way of life. Buildings are constructed from available resource materials. The rhythms of life dance to the beat of alien *tambores*. A mixture of Latino and indigenous cultures jump out and prick the sensory receptors. Pungent odors and neon-glowing houses shock the unprepared newcomer.

After the initial assault of obvious differences, Chip reflected, the more discerning observer begins to detect subtle changes that affect both sides of the border when two cultures come into contact. The collision breeds strange hybrids. Spanglish and Tex-Mex cuisines are just the tip of the iceberg. Keeping up with exotic mixtures of customs and traditions keeps sociologists well employed and political analysts pulling their hair out. For a hundred miles on both sides of the border, a new dialect – almost a new language – has come into being that is neither Spanish nor English, but an authentic "creole." *Viva la difference!* thought Chip.

Chip found a quiet-looking motel with a fenced parking lot to secure his pickup. When he had taken his bags to his room, showered and changed his clothes, he walked to a nearby food stand and ate an order of *tacos de lengua*. The delicious tongue meat in blistering salsa tantalized his palate, but unfortunately tortured his stomach. Acid reflux sent fire up his esophagus. He practically ran to the *farmacia* a block away.

Halfway to the drug store, his path was blocked when two men stepped from the shadows. A roundhouse slammed into Chip's midsection and a miniature bat thudded against his skull. A split second of crackling light subsided into total darkness.

CHAPTER EIGHTEEN

The burnt-orange laser rays of the dawning sun accentuated the faded, red-tiled roofs of Nuevo Laredo in the distance when Mapache turned off the highway and took a frontage road to the belching smokestacks of the Rainwater Pharms processing plant. Well before he drove up to the security gate, he smelled the rich aroma of tomatoes, onions, garlic, cilantro, and chili peppers being cooked and processed into *salsa*. A slight breeze brought the pungent aroma of *jalapeños* being smoked and dried into *chili chipotle*.

Backing in to the loading docks, another powerful fragrance vied for his olfactory attention. It wasn't hard to identify the source as *salsa adobo*, the spicy, rich stew into which smoked jalapeños would be marinated.

Before Mapache could climb out of his truck and stretch his legs, the dock foreman assigned a strapping youth to unload the burlap *costales* of jalapeno chili peppers from the truck onto the waiting pushcarts.

While the swamper hauled the bags of chili out of the truck bed, Mapache hand-carried the necessary paperwork through the bureaucratic process. While waiting for the load weight to be verified, he went into a litter-strewn storage room that served as the drivers' lounge. Through a broken window he noticed a group of twelve Chinese businessmen being led on a tour of the plant. He was amused when the group leader spoke to the tour guide in excellent Spanish: "Excuse me, sir. Most of us do not speak Spanish, and I assume that you do not speak Chinese, so if you would be so kind as to speak English, we would appreciate it very much." The tour guide readily agreed.

Mapache had always wanted to tour the plant, so when the group turned and followed the guide, he quickly donned one of the surgical masks and a pair of safety glasses that had been made available for the visitors and tagged along behind, listening to the well-rehearsed speech.

The plant guide's patter was almost monotone, but it became clear that he was knowledgeable about the technicalities of chili pepper processing. "The most popular–and considered by many to be the best–chipotles are processed from ripe, green jalapeno chili peppers. These are called *tipicos* or *chili meco*. Until *Americanos* developed a taste for raw jalapeños, nearly a quarter of the Mexican jalapeño chili harvest was processed into chili chipotle. Now the *gringos* are developing a taste for chipotle chili, both as a dried pepper and as a spicy seasoning for a variety of dishes.

"The market for jalapeño chili and chipotle is growing faster than Mexican farmers can supply the demand. Rainwater Pharms has expanded its production by thousands of acres, but we are still dependent on many small, independent farms to meet our needs."

What he says is true, Mapache thought, *and if these Chinese can market jalapeño chili and chipotle in their global business expansion, jalapeño farming will be even more profitable.*

"When they are picked, jalapeños are dark, shiny green," the guide continued. "They are about three inches long, and an inch wide. They must be eaten or processed within a few days or they will rot. After the smoking process, they normally turn a brownish gray or purple color and shrink until they look like a two-inch chewed-on cigar butt, or perhaps a dried prune."

When a perplexed member of the group asked his fellow businessman about the meaning of "rot," Mapache whispered "spoil." He was immediately embarrassed when several of the men turned to him, bowed slightly, and whispered their appreciation, at the same time nudging him into the middle of their entourage. Turning, the guide flashed him a hostile glare, but stuck to his memorized script.

"Another variety of chipotle is called *morita*, or little blackberry. These are made from cheaper chili peppers, and do not need to be smoked as long as jalapeños, so they cost less to produce. There is a demand for these chipotles, but, as I mentioned, they are considered to be inferior to the *tipicos* made from jalapeños.

"A small portion of the smoked chipotles are wholesaled dry to be retailed in the traditional open markets you find everywhere in Mexico. The majority of these shriveled-up, smoked chilies, however, are marinated in a spicy salsa that starts with a base of tomato sauce, garlic, onions, lemon juice, cumin, oregano, cinnamon and vinegar. The strong aroma you smell now is that sauce in its cooking stage.

"Another interesting fact is that the 'hotness' of a chili pepper is not affected by the chipotle smoking process. Jalapeños are rated between 5,000 and 10,000 Scoville Units. That makes them 'medium hot' compared to other chili peppers. Green bell peppers have a rating of zero, and orange habaneros range from 10,000 to 50,000.

The hottest chilies I know about are the jolokia peppers from India. They have an incredible rating of 1,000,000 Scoville units.

"The chemical element in chili peppers that makes them 'hot' is called capsaicin. Pure capsaicin is rated at 16,000,000 Scoville units. The pepper sprays used by law enforcement agencies, especially prison guards, has two percent capsaicin content."

Without pausing to ask the group if they had any questions, the guide herded the group into a conference room where four tables stood bearing an array of chipotle products. The guide informed the tour members that they were welcome to taste the available samples. Holding up one of the jars, he intoned, "This is a seasoning salt with a chipotle base. It has become quite popular." With a slight bow, he handed it to the leader of the tour group.

Pointing to another table, the guide said, "Here are various chipotle pastes used to prepare meats for grilling and barbequing. On the two remaining tables you will find twelve different kinds of party dips made with chipotle powder. Feel free to taste them with the assortment of chips provided for you. And, of course, there is a bottle of tequila and some mixes to help put out the fire if you should sample anything too hot for your tastes." He cocked one eyebrow and gave them a knowing smile.

In spite of their guide's obvious anticipation of overheated tongues, the businessmen were not hesitant to sample either the chipotle products or the tequila drinks. And he did not have long to wait: as the Scoville Units and the desert heat radiated through the non-air conditioned room, the unaccustomed Chinese began to 'pop sweat' and excitedly shared their reactions with one another. But he was not pleased when they continued to speak English so Mapache would understand. Mapache was pressed to correct them if their grammar or vocabulary was faulty. They quickly gathered around him, showing more intense interest than they had displayed throughout the long monologue of the "official" tour guide. They hushed when Mapache explained how Aztecs and Mayas had perfected the art of chipotle preparation thousands of years ago "They learned that the smoking and drying process kept the fleshy chili peppers from rotting," he told them conversationally. "This preservation principle is the same as drying meat into jerky."

In return, while listening to the businessmen talk, Mapache learned that chipotle was becoming popular in every corner of Asia, and that large orders were expected to be placed for Rainwater Pharms chipotle products. Intrigued, he soon slipped away from the tour group and found a telephone.

Speaking quietly into the mouthpiece, Mapache said, "Find a large farm for more jalapeños, Roberto. I'll make the arrangements to buy the land when I get back to Chiapas. You and your pretty wife Paulina negotiate a good price. And start making plans to plant a crop now."

Before Roberto could ask any questions, Mapache hung up. If the tour guide had been able to see his face at that moment, even he would have noted the signs that Mapache's mind had shifted into high gear.

CHAPTER NINETEEN

It was late afternoon when Dean Lambert and his secretary Gretchen put the finishing touches on the grant proposal packet for Rainwater Pharms. Their exhilaration outweighed their physical exhaustion. Hard work was already paying off. The institutional financial office called to confirm that Rainwater Pharms had deposited the first installment of $250,000 into a special, designated SIBS institutional account.

Dean Lambert popped the cork on a bottle of Dom Perignon champagne and filled two crystal goblets. Gretchen smiled and said, "We really do make a great team, don't we?"

"Here's to you, Princess," Dean Lambert replied.

His intimate little speech was interrupted by the ringing of the telephone. Since officially it was still business hours, he took the call. Ted Cravens was on the line. "Make it fast, Ted," the dean snapped. "I'm busy getting your grant proposal packet—."

Cravens cut him off. "This is urgent, Bert. As your favorite manure peddler, I've got a load to dump on your doorstep.

"I've just come from the police headquarters here in Nuevo Laredo. The Mexican authorities are reporting the death of Charles Oatley, your hotshot linguist. It seems he wasn't such an expert on Mexican customs and courtesies. They tell me he was drinking in one of the less reputable *cantinas*, insulted one of the clientele, and got into a fight. The police took him to the local hoosegow to cool down and sober up and while he was in the drunk tank, someone bashed his head into the concrete block wall. He died before they could find a doctor to work on him."

Shocked, the dean responded slowly, "You say he's dead?" He ignored Gretchen's alarmed stare and turned away from her. "That can't be true. Where is his body now?"

"Well, here's where it gets messy," Cravens said. "They're not real sticklers for keeping a chain of evidence down here. They've lost his body. It just disappeared. They're out in the desert now, looking in the spots where they usually find discarded bodies. Now and then, they're lucky enough to find a cadaver before the coyotes eat it or mutilate it beyond recognition."

"This is incredible," the dean muttered, slumping back in his chair with his hand over his eyes. "I can't believe Chip would get himself killed. I know he likes to have a drink once in a while, and he can be indiscreet, but he was in a hurry to get to Chiapas. He wouldn't think of getting drunk—at least not until he paid his respects at his grandfather's grave." Lambert knew he wasn't making sense, but nothing he'd heard seemed real. He recognized his own denial of the facts, but said anyway, "Wait. You say they don't have his body. Maybe he's not dead."

"Dean, I'm just telling you what I heard from the cops. He may or may not be dead. Regardless, his disappearance creates a problematic situation for us. Our agreement is for you to supply me with a linguist to research the oral and written resources in Chiapas to find plants that are used for medicinal purposes. If, for some reason—like getting himself killed—your wonder boy cannot perform that function, then you'll have to find someone else. If you don't have a ready replacement, Dean Lambert, then you'll have to come down and do the job yourself."

The dean sat up, controlling his anger for the moment. In carefully measured words, he growled, "I strongly suggest that you stay where you are until you confirm Chip's death and personally identify his body. If you can't do that, then I'll come down and find him myself. That boy is like a son to me. If I find out that you had anything to do with letting any harm come to him, I'll personally feed you to the coyotes." The receiver slammed down into its cradle.

CHAPTER TWENTY

After his unofficial tour of the Rainwater processing plant, Mapache inquired about getting an outgoing load. He was rewarded with a load of canned chipotle chili peppers for a distribution warehouse in the industrial city of Monterrey, Nuevo Leon. While the truck was being loaded, he performed his pre-trip inspection ritual. It was late afternoon when he pulled out of the Rainwater Pharms loading docks and headed south.

It didn't take long for the hot, dry desert air to make Mapache's eyelids heavy. Before he had driven two hours, he guided his truck into an open field behind a Pemex gas station, shut down the engine, tilted his head back and was unconscious the instant his eyes closed.

Awakening from his siesta, Mapache saw that darkness had enveloped his world and he felt relieved that the air had begun to cool. Within minutes, he checked his load and was back on the highway feeling rested. He was making good time and felt at peace in the silver moonlight that bathed the desert landscape.

Slowing for a curve in the road, Mapache caught a roadside movement from the corner of his eye. At first he thought it was an animal—perhaps a rabbit or a coyote. But as he shifted down to a lower gear, he saw that the bent-over form was a man staggering toward the road. The figure in the pale light faltered, lost his balance, and toppled face down into the desert sand.

Mapache quickly braked and eased his truck off the pavement onto the soft shoulder, taking care not to bog down his tires in the loose sand. He flicked on the emergency flashers and engaged the emergency brake. Grabbing his flashlight and a canteen of water, he opened the door, swiveled out to the side step, jumped to the ground, and jogged to the groaning figure.

Gently, Mapache brushed blood-soaked sand from the man's battered face. He checked for pulse and breathing, and was relieved that the man was still alive. When he found no bleeding wounds or signs of broken bones, he tried to revive the man into consciousness. Dampening a handkerchief with water from his canteen, he squeezed a few drops onto the man's parched lips.

With dazed and pleading eyes, Chip looked up at the trucker and mumbled, "Xo...chee," then drifted back into another world.

CHAPTER TWENTY-ONE

The Campestre , a roadside restaurant in the middle of nowhere, was subdued when Mapache led a hobbling Chip to a table and sat down. In a smooth, quick motion, El Mapache slapped a corn tortilla between his grease-stained hands. With the fingertips of his right hand, he caught the lower curve of the tortilla, pressed and pushed upward, rolling it into a tight yellowish cigar. Taking it between his thumb and forefinger, he dunked it into the heavy stone *molcajete* brimming with watery red *chile salsa*. The mealy tortilla absorbed the liquid like a dry sponge. Just before the tortilla dissolved, he gingerly withdrew it, allowing a few drops to trickle back into the lava stone bowl. Jutting out his lower jaw, he stuffed the *puro ahogado*, the drowned cigar, into his mouth, managing to chew, swallow, and lick his fingers simultaneously.

From the opposite side of the white plastic game table, Chip sat wide-eyed, deaf and mute, watching the trucker feed himself. Even in his state of semi-shock, his powers of observation were functioning. *Mechanics' hands are the same in any language*, he thought.

Although he had just scrubbed with gasoline and a gob of degreaser, followed by soap and water, Mapache could not erase the dark oily lines, streaks, and smears from his hands and forearms. Nor did the scrub brush remove the half-moons of grime from beneath his fingernails.

Mapache noticed Chip's stare. "*Mugre de uñas,* fingernail crud," he said. "No matter how hard I try, I never get the grease out from under my fingernails."

The trucker's mixture of Spanish and English surprised Chip, but language was not his concern at this moment; his overriding interest was fixed on the red wicker basket and the *molcajete* of salsa. The lidded basket, hand-woven from tiny sugarcane reeds, was about eight inches in diameter and six inches deep. When lined with a *sevilleta bordada,* an embroidered cloth napkin, it had just enough space to hold two dozen tortillas. Steam seeped up from the folds in the cloth, drifted across the table to caress Chip's nostrils, causing his nose to drip and his mouth to water. He swallowed three times, but not in time to prevent a bit of drool from rolling down the corner of his mouth.

"I can look at a man's hands and guess what kind of work a man does," Mapache said, pretending not to notice Chip wiping his chin with both hands.

"Or what kind of work he doesn't do," Chip said, slightly embarrassed that the trucker has caught him staring. He had a sudden, odd sensation that the trucker saw more than the surface of his hands. *He's probably good at reading palms, too,* he thought.

Examining his own hands again, he saw that they were covered with fresh scratch marks and clots of sandy blood. Under the scabbing there were few signs of manual labor; there were some calluses on the palms from gripping a rope, but no scarred knuckles, no grease.

"You can clean yourself up at the sink on the back patio," Mapache suggested. "There's a fifty-five gallon drum of water to wash with, but don't drink it. When you're clean, I'll put some alcohol on those cuts. I've already applied antiseptic cream on those lumps on your head, but you've got scrapes and bruises all over your body. You'll need a primer coat of alcohol, and then you can spread a light coat of fresh axle grease on the rough spots. It works just as well—or maybe better—than *Vitacilina*, the Mexican version of a first-aid kit in a tube."

Chip slowly nodded his head in agreement. The act of standing up, even slowly, shot pain through his ribcage, causing him to dig his fingers into the edge of the table. After a brief hesitation, he shuffled out a side door and followed a brick path to the back patio. He found the leaking water barrel under a naked 40-watt light bulb. Without benefit of a mirror, he ladled water with his hands and washed his exposed flesh, trying to ignore the pain he felt from the slightest touch. The cold water felt abrasive to the sensitive raw skin, but at the same time it refreshed him. Using his outspread fingers, he gently combed his dripping hair, careful to avoid a goose egg knot above his left ear. After checking to see that the wound was not oozing blood, he went back inside.

"*Tienes hambre?*" Mapache asked Chip. "Are you hungry?"

"*Sí, señor*," Chip answered with more desperation than he had intended. Under the table he clamped his hands together to control his trembling. He didn't know how long it had been since he had eaten. He wondered how long he had been in the desert before the trucker found him. *What day was it?*

"Help yourself," Mapache offered as he pushed the tortilla basket across the table. Chip's hand shook as he unfolded the cloth and peeled off a single tortilla. He doubled it twice, dipped it into the salsa, and shoved it whole into his mouth. The presence of food in his mouth caused a spasm in his jaw muscles, and his tongue curled in reaction to the salsa picante, the burning sensation of spicy hot. He pursed his lips and sucked in air, creating a reverse whistle. The mushy meal slid down his throat. Through teary eyes he became aware of the trucker holding a bottle of beer out in front of his nose.

"*Pica*, no? Wash it down with this."

Chips signaled his acceptance by bobbing his head and reaching out with both hands. He pressed the cold, wet bottle against his lips, then sloshed the liquid around inside his mouth, and gargled before swallowing. It brought momentary relief, so he set the bottle down and dug into the basket for another tortilla.

"*Muchas gracias, señor.* Thank you very much," Chip said, watching for a reaction to his own mix of Spanish and English. He grinned when he saw the trucker raise his eyebrows.

A young waitress came to the table carrying two bowls of steaming hot soup.

"I ordered *menudo*," said Mapache. "It will make you strong. It's a soup made from cow stomach. We normally eat it with lots of salsa picante after a night of heavy drinking. It's one of our best cures for *la cruda*, the hangover."

"But I don't have a hangover," Chip said.

"You are suffering from *la cruda* of another kind," Mapache replied.

This guy not only reads palms, Chip thought. *He also reads hearts.*

"I know what menudo is," Chip said, not wanting to address his personal problems, especially not with a stranger. Slurping the savory broth, he began to feel warm inside and wanted to know more about this trucker who had rescued him. The only thing he could think to say was, "Your English is very good."

Mapache smiled and said, "Your Spanish isn't bad."

When the waitress passed the table, she asked if she could bring anything else. Chip reached for his wallet and suddenly realized he had been robbed. He now had no identification, no cash, no credit cards. And his watch and Montblanc fountain pen were gone.

"*No te preocupes*. Don't worry, my friend. "*Te invito.* This is my treat."

"*Por qué?*" Chip asked. "Why are you doing this for me? You don't even know me."

"*Perdóneme*. Please forgive me for not introducing myself," the trucker said, pushing his chair back and standing up. "*Me llaman El Mapache*. I am called 'The Raccoon.' That is my nickname. My parents named me Map Ach, but when I started school, the school master and the village priest told me I had to have a Christian name, so all of my official records say I am Miguel Espinoza. Please call me Mapache." He thrust his muscular hand across the table, palm up, fingers spread wide.

Chip involuntarily flinched. When it dawned on him the trucker wanted to shake hands, he stood up and gripped the open hand. He felt a current of energy pass into his arms and his body. *This guy should have been a faith healer*, he thought. *He's got the 'hot hands' for the calling.*

"*Mucho gusto*. Nice to meet you, Mapache. My name is Charles Oatley. Please call me Chip."

"The pleasure is mine," Mapache said as he loosened his viselike grip and sat down. "If I may ask, why are you called Chip?"

"Because of my tooth," Chip said, raising his upper lip and pointing to his upper front teeth. The left one was an eighth of an inch shorter than the right one. "Happened when I was eight years old. I was running up the pyramids at Palenque when I fell and hit my mouth against a stone step."

Mapache nodded his understanding. "Chip," he said. "Chip Oatley." He repeated the name several times, as though he were trying to remember where he might have heard the name before. Suddenly he grinned and broke into a belly-shaking chuckle.

"Do you think I have a funny name?" Chip asked.

"Chip...Oatley," Mapache said again, separating the two names. Then he slurred them together. "Chipoatley. Do you hear it? It sounds like *chipotle*...chili *chipotle*. That's what I'm going to call you. Mr. Chipotle." He laughed again and ordered two more beers.

After an awkward silence, Chip said, "You didn't answer my question. Why are you doing this for me? I'm a total stranger."

Mapache's jovial expression changed to sober and serious. The sparkle in his eyes clouded and his voice muffled. "Many years ago, I went to California, looking for work. I was a *mojado*, a wetback. I was illegal. I was walking along a field road near Bakersfield. I was so hot, thirsty, and hungry, I thought I was going to die. Then an old man came driving down the road in an old pickup truck. He stopped and gave me a ride. He gave me a drink of cool water from a plastic milk jug. He took me to his farm where his wife fed me and they let me sleep in the barn. He gave me work and paid me well. Over time he taught me how to fix the truck and the farm machinery when they broke down. They were good to me." His voice trailed off as he commented, "I will never forget them." He emptied his bottle.

There was another pause before he continued.

"When I saw you beside the road...when I found you there with your head in the sand...I saw myself in your place. So, I picked you up and brought you here. I don't know what kind of problems you have. Not my business. But I thought about that old man helping me. Maybe this way I can pay back the debt I owe him and his wife."

"Who were they, Mapache? Give them names."

"Wilber and Mae Webster. Out of respect, I called them *don* Wilber and *doña* Mae. I think they liked that. They became my teachers. Even though I had been to school, they taught me many things about life—things they don't teach you in school.

"They were also my English teachers. Don Wilber taught me the names of all the parts in an engine, and how they work together. Doña Mae patiently worked with me to improve my vocabulary and grammar. Every night they read to me. Some nights it was children's books; other nights they read the Bible to me. One night they asked me to read to them. That was a proud day for me."

"I can see that you loved them," Chip said.

"They were good people. They treated me like the son they never had."

"It sounds like they were religious people."

"They were close to their God. They depended on Him to make their crops grow. They prayed to Him to send the rain."

"Were they Baptist?" Chip asked.

"How did you know?"

"They sound like my grandparents. They were Baptist missionaries."

"Then they must be good people, too."

"They don't come any better," Chip said, not yet ready to explain what had happened to them in Chiapas.

CHAPTER TWENTY-TWO

C hip was relieved when Mapache called for the check and paid the waitress. Without a word, Mapache came around the table and helped Chip to his feet. As he stood up, Chip felt the burning sensation creep up from his stomach and inch toward his throat.

As Mapache and Chip made their way to the restaurant door, two truckers came in looking for an empty table. "*Compadre!*" one of them yelled across the room when he'd spotted Mapache. They made their way to where Mapache stood holding Chip's elbow.

Chip stepped back awkwardly and watched as the truckers greeted each other with hearty *abrazos* and backslapping. The new arrivals were not about to let Mapache leave anytime soon and Chip elected not to interfere.

It was not until the three amigos had seated themselves around the table and agreed that a bottle of tequila was in order that the two new truckers seemed to notice that Chip had seated himself with them.

"*Quién es este gringo?*" one of them asked, pointing at Chip.

"This is my new friend *don* Chipotle," Mapache said, but before he could introduce the two truckers, a balding, middle-aged man in a sweaty, white dress shirt rushed up to help clean off the accumulation of dirty dishes and empty bottles. He made a show of wiping the table with a wet rag. Clearly he was more than a bus boy and this group of truckers wanting a bottle of tequila deserved his personal attention. Lifting a finger, he ordered a waitress to bring shot glasses and saucers of sliced *limones*, little green limes, and mounds of salt crystals. Another wave of his arm brought an older woman out of the kitchen with assorted *botanas*, finger snacks. *He must be the owner*, Chip guessed.

When the man produced a liter of Herradura tequila, the taller of the truckers picked up the bottle and gave a slobbery kiss to the large red horseshoe in the middle of its yellow label. He looked in Chip's direction and, in passable English, said, "I always do that for good luck."

Mapache took the bottle, filled the four shot glasses, and distributed them around the table. Taking his own glass in his right hand, he raised it and held it at eye level. He addressed his old friends, "Don Chipotle is very special to me. The angels have brought him to me and made me responsible for him. I now have an obligation, a sacred duty, to take care of him. So, if you are my friends, you will help me to see that no harm comes to this man."

Chip started to object, but a glance from Mapache told him to keep his mouth shut. He felt uncomfortable and slightly embarrassed at being in the spotlight of Mapache's show.

"*Salud!*" Mapache said.

"*Salud!*" echoed Chip and his two new guardians. They clinked their shot glasses together and downed the amber liquid in a single gulp. In unison, they hunched forward and exhaled as though they were blowing out a candle in the middle of the table. Mapache squeezed a piece of lemon onto the back of his left hand. After sprinkling a pinch of salt onto the juice, he licked it clean. Chip and the others followed suit.

Speaking to Chip, Mapache said, "These are my friends," as he gestured to the two truckers. "*Muy buenos amigos*," he stressed. Switching to English, he continued, "The tall one is Tomas; the short one is Gerardo."

"Is this a joke?" Chip asked. "You can't be serious."

"Did I say something funny?

"Like the cartoon cat and mouse—Tom and Jerry?"

Mapache stared at him for a moment, then laughed and said, "I never thought of that."

Chip was surprised when the two truckers joined in with the laughter. They half-stood, leaning over the table to stick out their hands and introduce themselves.

"Me Tom," said the tall one.

"Me Herry," the other said, pronouncing the "J" like a hard "H," as in Spanish.

Mapache smiled at Chip and said, "Don't let their Tarzan-style English fool you. These two *vagabundos*, these highway hobos, speak English better than I do. It's an old game—deeply ingrained in our culture."

"'I'm not following you," Chip said. "What kind of game uses Tex-Mex pidgin English?"

"Yeah," said Tom with a carefully blank face, "*Qué quieres decir*? Just exactly what are you talking about?"

"What I'm trying to say," Mapache went on, "is that this game is not new. It has been evolving here in Mexico for over five hundred years. You can find it in all of us who have some Indian blood in our veins."

"I'm still lost," Chip interrupted.

"It's a *fachada*, a front. It doesn't show you what's inside. Tom and Jerry were playing this game on you, trying to make you think they don't speak English very well. They weren't sure they could trust you."

"What he is trying to say," Jerry put in, "is that we're not as ignorant or stupid as we act. We're just dumb *burros*, stupid jackasses, when it serves our purpose."

"That trick was not invented by Mexican Indians," Chip said. "I suspect it's as old as humanity." Everyone laughed and drained their shot glasses.

With only a small amount of food in his belly, Chip was starting to feel the effects of the alcohol. As Mapache began to pour another round, Chip held his hand palm down over his glass. Mapache smiled and said nothing as Chip sat back and listened to the friendly banter.

Tom and Jerry ordered a tray-load of soft tacos as the men began swapping road stories, trucker jokes, and talked about where they had been recently, and what they had been hauling. They ate, drank, talked, and laughed with gusto. *They deserve an evening of fun, Chip thought. Tomorrow they will be back on the road to who knows where...I wonder where the road of life will take me tomorrow?*

Crunching on a piece of *chicharrón*, crispy, fried pork skin, Chip mentally replayed what Mapache had said. *This trucker has a deeper understanding of language use than most of the sociolinguists I know. Hope I don't have to reveal my academic background or my occupation.* He was wondering why they hadn't already inquired about who he was and what he was doing in Mexico when Tom startled him.

"Where are you going, don Chipotle?"

Without elaboration, Chip said, "It was my plan to go to Mexico City and then to Chiapas."

The three truckers choked on their tequilas. It was far more than surprise he saw in their faces. It was fear.

CHAPTER TWENTY-THREE

C hip woke up in the passenger's seat of Mapache's truck. The throbbing roar of the engine and the whine of the tires drilled through his brain and mixed with the slow, dull pounding at the base of his skull. He sat up and looked around. With some difficulty he forced his eyes to focus.

Warm air streamed into the open windows, stinging his eyes. The sun was already well above the horizon to his left, meaning they were heading south. Out of habit he checked his left wrist, forgetting that he no longer had a watch.

"It's almost nine o'clock," Mapache said, observing Chip out of the corner of his eye.

"The air is already hot," Chip said. "And dry."

"*Agua?*" Mapache asked, handing Chip a cool, one-liter, plastic bottle of water, knowing from experience that the inside of Chip's mouth would be like cotton.

Chip unscrewed the bottle cap and nursed the water while taking inventory of his surroundings. Through the large, rectangular mirror mounted on the side of the door, he saw that a flat truck bed extended back five or six yard. Gray metal "stakes" poked up from the perimeter of the truck bed like a picket fence. A heavy, blue plastic tarp was stretched over the top and was tied down with yellow nylon rope. At four-foot intervals, trucker's knots kept the covering taut.

Looking forward through the pocked windshield, Chip saw that the engine hood was sandblasted to a rough, rusty camouflage. Attached to the front of the cab was a giant grill made from three-inch galvanized pipe, welded to the front bumper.

The cab was roomy. The two oversized bucket seats—one for the driver and one for the passenger—were worn, but they were comfortably padded and the faded upholstery was still intact. Chip guessed that the truck was at least twenty years old. Except for the paint job, the truck appeared to be in good condition.

A large console with a deep tray separated the two seats. In the tray were two more bottles of water, a small plastic bowl of loose coins, and an assortment of dog-eared paperback books. *A trucker who reads*, Chip thought, verifying his first impression that Mapache still held back more about his background than he'd shared so far. *Then again*, Chip thought, *there's a whole lot I haven't told him about myself, either.*

Chip turned his attention to the dashboard and noticed that all the dials and meters on the instrument panel appeared to be working. The speedometer held steady at one hundred kilometers per hour. Chip mentally calculated the conversion to be a little more than sixty miles per hour.

The only exception to a totally functioning cab was an old, combination radio-cassette player bolted to the bottom of the dashboard. Directly below it dangled a bundle of loose wires of various colors, dancing to the rhythm of the moving truck. Chip suspected that this ancient entertainment center had not served its intended purpose for many years.

"How far south are you going?" Chip asked.

"Depende," Mapache said. "I've got a full load of canned chili chipotles in the back that I'm dropping off in Monterrey. If I'm lucky, I'll pick up a load of glassware and head to Guadalajara. If not, then I'll try to get a load of cement and take it wherever it needs to go. And while we're in Monterrey, I'll help you make arrangements to get to Mexico City."

A flat blanket of gray sand stretched out to the horizon in all directions, broken in spots by an outcropping of stony hills. The black asphalt highway shimmered like a shiny serpent and faded in the distance into a pass between two barren hills. Except for a few dry plants, there were no signs of life.

"Beautiful out here," Mapache stated.

"I prefer green," Chip said. "Trees, grass, flowers. Things like that."

"I like those things, too," Mapache said. "But there's a different kind of beauty here. I didn't like it at first, but as they say, after a while it grows on you."

"I take it you've spent some time in this area," Chip said. "More than just driving through, I mean."

"The road of life leads us to some strange and unexpected places."

Another pearl of trucker wisdom, Chip thought, waiting to hear the story behind it, but the trucker seemed to interrupt himself.

"As soon as we get to Monterrey we'll stop and have some breakfast, and then we'll buy you some new clothes. Those bloody rags you've got on will have to be burned."

"A hot shower and a strong cup of coffee would be a good start," Chip said. "Not necessarily in that order."

Keeping his eyes on the road, Mapache leaned forward against the steering wheel, twisted his torso, reached under his seat, and pulled out a thermos bottle. Sitting back, he handed it to Chip.

"Brewed this morning while you were unconscious."

"You think of everything."

"It's strong and black. No cream. No sugar."

"That's the way I like it. How'd you know?"

"Just a good guess. There's a small pack of paper cups under your seat."

As Chip bent over and pulled out the cups, he said, "You take sugar in yours, don't you?"

"Was that a good guess?"

Chip grinned. "I saw the little packets of sugar in the console."

Chip took two cups, unscrewed the thermos lid, and poured the coffee. After a period of silence while they sipped their coffee, Mapache asked directly, "Why are you in Mexico? Why are you going to Chiapas?"

Chip had been waiting for the question, but now that it was asked, he wasn't sure how much to tell and how much to hold back. He covered his hesitation by taking a sip of coffee.

"I'm a professor of linguistics at a small institute in Oklahoma. I've been teaching and working on a doctorate in contemporary Mayan dialects in Mesoamerica. Now I'm going to Chiapas as part of a research project coordinated with UNAM, the National Autonomous University of Mexico. It's being financed by a grant from a giant transnational corporation called Rainwater Pharms."

"I know what Rainwater Pharms is," Mapache said. "I also know what UNAM is. Is that why you're going to Mexico City first?"

"Precisely," Chip said. "I have to make contact with the people in the anthropology department there. They supervise the activities of the research center in Chiapas.

Of course, since it's a bureaucracy, I have to fill out a mountain of forms. And if I have the opportunity while I'm there, I want to look through their departmental library. Their collection of field studies and monographs on anthropological linguistics is one of the best in the world."

From the sudden interest on Mapache's face, Chip could see that something had caught his attention. He hoped it wasn't the academic jargon he was tossing out.

"Sorry if some of this goes over your head. I'm not trying to impress you with big words." Immediately, he could have kicked himself for sounding patronizing.

"I don't mind if you drop a two-dollar word once in a while," Mapache answered without offense. "Just don't try to baffle me with pedantic cow pies."

"Pedantic? Don't accuse me of using two-dollar words," Chip shot back, relieved that the trucker hadn't taken offense. "Sounds like you've been soiled by the crapola we fling from the ivory towers of academia."

"*Bastante!*" Mapache said. "More than I care to remember. Just because I went to *gringolandia* as a 'wetback' doesn't mean I was illiterate. A good number of 'illegal aliens' are well educated."

"I'm aware of that," Chip said. "My mechanic back in Shawnee has a master's degree in mechanical engineering from the National Polytechnic Institute of Mexico. And it's obvious that you've had a bit more schooling than the average trucker."

"Enough to know what anthropological linguistics means," Mapache said with a sideways grin.

"I taught a course in anthropological linguistics last semester." Chip said. "The course title scared off a lot of students, so I changed the name to 'Language and Culture.' Enrollment in the course doubled."

Mapache chuckled politely, then brought the conversation back on track. "You've been to Chiapas before, haven't you?"

"How do you know that?" Chip asked.

"You told me," Mapache said. "You told me some things yesterday, some things last night, and some more things this morning. You didn't know you were telling me. You were talking in your sleep. You were delirious until your fever finally broke. I thought for a while that I was going to have to tie you down."

Chip felt his cheeks burn and sweat beaded on his forehead. "What did I say? Anything I should be ashamed of?" He tried to sound unconcerned, but wasn't sure he pulled it off.

"Not much," Mapache said with another sly sideways grin. "Nothing I could blackmail you with. You said enough to let me know that your heart aches as bad as your body does. You and some woman have had some serious problems. You've stabbed knives into each other's hearts and you're still bleeding."

"Sounds like I had a real nightmare," Chip tried to bluff, laughing unconvincingly. "What else did I say?"

"Your love for your daughter is the only thing that keeps you from going over the edge, isn't it?"

"You're getting too personal," Chip said, his temper beginning to flare. But his heart melted when Mapache said, "Xochitle is a beautiful name."

Chip's lips trembled as he said, "That's what I call my daughter now. She's probably wondering why I haven't called her."

Mapache sensed that the drift of the conversation was making Chip uncomfortable, but he persisted. "Your marriage didn't survive the stress, did it?"

"It most certainly did not," Chip said emphatically. "I need to put some distance between us. But it's not that or my doctoral research that makes it important—and urgent—that I get to Chiapas as soon as possible. The main reason I need to go there—and get there fast, is that the Baptist Mission Station in the Lacondon Jungle has been attacked. My grandfather, the senior missionary, was killed and his body is missing. My mother, my sister, and the staff nurse were taken hostage and hidden somewhere in the jungle. I hope they are still alive.

"Speaking of stress, it's eating my stomach lining away. A steady diet of academic pressure, domestic problems, and international intrigue takes its toll on the digestive system. In fact, my esophagus is on fire now. And, as you might guess, my intake of vitamin T last night did nothing to alleviate the problem."

"Vitamin T? What's that?" asked Mapache, confused.

"T, as in *tacos, tortillas, tomates, tamales, tortas, tostatos, et cetera*," Chip said, stressing the initial consonant with a straight face, but was amused that Mapache had not heard the joke before.

"Don't forget the *tequila*," Mapache said. "The breakfast of *campeones*."

"How could I forget?" Chip said. "The coals in the pit of my stomach were stoked with the distilled fuel of the agave plant. I'm still breathing the acrid fumes." To prove his point, he opened his mouth and effortlessly barked a loud belch.

"*Fuchi.* You're disgusting." Mapache said , wrinkling his nose. "I assume they took your toothbrush, too."

"Besides clothes, I need a full set toiletries and hygiene items."

"Especially deodorant. You're stinking up my truck."

"You're the one who keeps dragging me along for the ride. If I had any sense at all, I'd jump out of the truck and hitchhike back to Oklahoma."

"You know you can't go back now. Except for your daughter, there's nothing to go back for, is there? And you'll be bringing her to Chiapas soon enough."

"You're right, of course. But I really do need to make some phone calls. It's going to take a little time to get a new passport, money, credit cards, and all the other things I'm going to need here in Mexico. I should have called last night. How am I going to explain this to my boss, the American Embassy, and the Mexican *Federales?*"

"Don't worry," Mapache said, shaking his head. "I'm sure this is not the first time a dumb gringo was mugged, robbed, and dumped along the highway south of the border. And it happens to a lot of Mexicans on the other side of the border. Anyway, I called the Border Patrol and gave them your description. I told them that except for some nasty bruises and scratches, you were all right. I told them I patched you up with a first aid kit, but I'd get a doctor to check you over, just to be safe. They'll be expecting your call."

"By chance," Chip asked, "would you happen to have any antacid medicine?"

"As an emergency measure, there are some packets of *sal de uvas* in the glove box. It's like Alka Seltzer in powdered form. It should neutralize the acid and minimize the gas, but you might be a little constipated tomorrow."

Chip found a packet, tore it open, emptied it into his coffee that had gotten cold, and drank it down before it fully dissolved.

"What you need," Mapache said, "is a tea brewed from *sosa,* a plant that grows wild all over Chiapas."

"Is it some kind of folk remedy?"

"My people have been using it for thousands of years."

"I'll have to write that down," Chip said, "and try it when I get to Chiapas." He brought his hand up to his left breast pocket. "Oh, no! That pen had sentimental value. That's something that can't be replaced."

"There are some cheap ballpoint pens and notepads in the glove box," Mapache said. "Take what you need."

As Chip tore out a page from the notepad, wrote the word *sosa* on it, and stuffed it into his pocket, he suddenly felt exhausted. With half-closed eyelids he turned to Mapache and mumbled, "Excuse me. I'm feeling sleepy again."

"Before you go under," Mapache said, "I've got a question. What was the name of the hotel you checked into in Nuevo Laredo?"

"*La Posada Del Camino*, The Highway Inn. Do you know where it is? It looked like it was a favorite stopping place for truckers."

"Sounds familiar," Mapache said. "And speaking of stopping places, we're coming up on a *gasolinera*. Do you need to drain a cup of coffee before you sleep?"

"Smart idea." Chip said. "I don't need my pants soiled more than they already are."

CHAPTER TWENTY-FOUR

After the truck's fuel tanks were filled and the splattered bugs were washed off the windshield, Mapache and Chip splashed water on their faces and drenched their hair. The moisture would keep their heads cool for a little while in the dry desert air. They climbed back into the truck cab and Mapache urged his vehicle on.

Stretching his leg muscles had given Chip a surge of energy. He was wide awake and ready to talk. "Tell me about the desert," he said. "How did you come to know it?"

Mapache didn't answer immediately. He handed the thermos bottle to Chip and said, "Pour us another cup. When I filled this up back there, the coffee looked pretty strong. I hope it doesn't activate your digestive acid producers too much."

While Chip poured coffee, trying not to spill it in the truck cab which rocked and bounced on a stretch of rough road, Mapache began his story.

"I was a student at the Monterrey Institute of Technology. You've probably heard of it—the M.I.T. of Mexico. My real interest was life science—biology and botany. I wanted to learn everything I could about plants, but I was forced to major in engineering.

"I lived in a boarding house with nine other Indians. *Indígenas* they called us. We ate, slept, and studied in that house. Except for going to classes and to church, we hardly ever went out. We were on a special, full scholarship, but we had almost no spending money. Most of the students in that university were from wealthy, powerful families. All ten of us Indians came from poor families.

"One day a classmate—one of the few friendly ones— invited me and two other Indian boys to go camping in the desert. It wasn't far from where we are now. He wanted to be a herpetologist, a specialist in reptiles. He wanted us to help him collect lizards and snakes in the desert. We called him *El Sapo*—The Toad.

"I will never forget that trip. I had never been to the desert before. At first, I was almost afraid. Everything was alien to me, like I was on another planet. It was so different from the thick, green vegetation where I grew up. It was only when the sun went down, when the sky turned dark blue, and a million stars began to twinkle, that I felt like I was home. And when the moon rose in the heavens, it was a big, yellow balloon, the biggest I had ever seen. I thought I could reach out and touch it."

"I saw a moon like that, once." Chip said. "I could almost feel the moonlight. Did you feel the moonlight that night?"

"It felt like golden rain. My friends felt it, too. We sat around a campfire and remembered the stories our grandfathers and grandmothers used to tell us about the spirit of the moon god that causes people to have strange dreams and do crazy things. We tried to tell ourselves we didn't believe in those old tales anymore, but before the night was over, we learned that no matter how hard we try to keep the god-spirits of our forefathers out of our minds, they find a way to haunt us and lurk in our hearts. And when they want to communicate with us, we cannot escape them.

"The desert that had been so hot under the sun, became cool under the moon. But as I felt the moon god warming my skin, I stripped off my clothes and bathed in the moonbeams. I ran, practically naked, out across the sand. I called out to my forefathers in the language of the ancients. And I wept."

Chip glance quickly at Mapache and saw no trace of shame or guilt.

"When morning came," Mapache continued, "I was physically exhausted, but spiritually refreshed. I felt cleansed. At the same time, my mind was confused. I wondered if I had been dreaming. I couldn't explain what had happened to me. But I didn't care.

"You can imagine how that experience affected me in the following days, weeks, and months. I was studying math, physics, and chemistry—the sciences of the modern world, in one of the best universities in Latin America. Why was I being visited by the spirit-gods of my ancestors?

"I was embarrassed and afraid to talk about my desert experience. I couldn't concentrate on my studies. It got so bad that my grades began to suffer. It became clear that I wouldn't be able to continue in the university, but if I dropped out, I would be too ashamed to go home."

Mapache paused to collect his thoughts. Both men drank a few sips of coffee in silence. The road had smoothed out.

"So what did you do?" Chip finally prompted.

"Somehow, I managed to finish the semester. Then, without telling anyone, I went to California. I was confused, desperate, and broke. I told you a little about that last night."

"I remember," Chip said. A picture was starting to form in his head, but there were still a lot of empty spaces in the puzzle.

"But you said you went to the university on a full scholarship, a special scholarship. What did you mean by that?"

"The ten of us Indians had been selected from various tribal communities because we had 'high academic potential.' It was a sociological experiment dreamed up by someone on the board of directors of Monterrey Tec. He had an obsession with solving Mexico's 'Indian problem.' He was convinced that the only workable solution was to integrate Indians into the mainstream of Latino-Mexican culture. Since there were no Indians enrolled in the university, he decided to rectify the situation. He spent a small fortune scouting for 'bright' Indian kids between the ages of seven and ten. His scouts identified twenty-four of us. They bribed our parents into letting them send us to a boarding school in Mexico City for an intensive, six-year, combined primary-secondary school. The eighteen of us who made it through were sent to the university prep school in Monterrey. As I said, ten of us made it into the university's *profesional* degree program.

"All this time we were not allowed to speak our tribal languages. We were forced to speak Spanish and study English. If they caught us speaking our Indian languages, we were beaten and locked in our rooms, usually without food. We were never allowed to wear our tribal clothes or eat our traditional foods, or practice any of our rituals or ceremonies. They wanted us to think in Spanish and pray like Catholics.

"They didn't have to tell us that we were being given the best education at the best schools in Latin America. And we knew we were good students. We were always at the top of our classes. But we were different. Since we had no money, we couldn't go out and have fun—no parties like the other students. We didn't have cars, either. So, we studied all the time and became the best students, the honor students.

"But that didn't make us popular. When the other students didn't study, we were the ones blamed for making them look bad. The professors liked us, though. They held us up as examples for the other students to follow, which just made it worse for us with the other students. Some actually hated us. They didn't want us in their school. The school administrators couldn't— or wouldn't— protect us from persecution.

"Consequently, the mixed messages we were getting had us totally confused. On one hand, the administration was telling us that we were expected to become more than *Ladinos*, meaning more than Spanish speaking Indians, we were supposed to be transformed into Latinos, truly Hispanic, and blend into mainstream society. On the other hand, from the lack of peer acceptance, we knew we would never be allowed into most of the normal social activities. No matter how well we performed in the academic world, we would be excluded from many professions. Often we were told that when we graduated, we would be expected to go back to our indigenous communities and teach other Indians how to become good Hispanic Mexicans. We were to lead our people out of their 'savage ignorance.'

"Only the churches, the pastors of the various religious denominations, appeared at first to have a genuine interest in us. But gradually we began to see that they, too, had a 'hidden agenda' for our lives. They wanted to groom us to be missionaries to go back to our tribal communities. They were smooth talkers with God on their side. 'Jaguars in goatskins' is what we called them."

Mapache took a sip of cold coffee and said, "I'll shut up if I'm boring you, or if you need to sleep."

But Chip wanted to hear more. "Who are your people? Where are you from?"

"I'm from Chiapas. I was born in a small town called Oxchuc, on the edge of the Lacondon Jungle. When I was four years old, my family moved to a town called Ococingo, where my father found work as a night janitor at a school.

"Some nights, my father took me to the school with him. I remember the first time I saw an indoor toilet. My father had to explain what all those big white *masetas* were for. He laughed when I called them flowerpots. He told me that many people in the town had a room called *el baño*, the bathroom, and in this room there was *una tasa*, a toilet bowl. When I asked him why we didn't have one in our house, he said, '*Hay mucha selva.*' And that was true; there was dense forest everywhere. Who would want a stinking *baño* in the house, when there was so much jungle around?

"While my father was working, I would run and play in the schoolyard, and explore through the classrooms. While he was sweeping the floors and picking up trash, he told me the names of many other things I had never seen before.

"Books were another new discovery. Often, when he finished his work early, my father would pick up a book and read to me. Then he taught me how to read. I was eager to learn, so it didn't take long. After that, I read while he was working, and if I came across a word or a concept I didn't understand, I would find him and get an explanation. Then he taught me how to use a dictionary. I've been reading ever since."

"So your father spoke Spanish," Chip said, "and knew how to read and write. Wasn't that unusual for an Indian in those days? How did he acquire an education?"

"When I was older, I learned that he had attended a church school taught by a priest from Spain. My father admired the priest so much that he decided that he wanted to become a priest, too. He studied and prayed and appointed himself as a personal servant to the priest. He was practically his slave. Then one day the priest told my father that he could never become a fully ordained priest because he was Indian. My father's heart was broken. He never spoke to the priest again. In fact, he never went inside a church after that. Even when he was dying, he made my mother promise that she would not have a church funeral for him. She kept her promise.

"After leaving the church, my father found a new life. He became active in tribal affairs and encouraged everyone to return to the gods of their forefathers. Eventually he became a respected tribal elder. And even though the Latino priests and community leaders considered him to be somewhat *loco*, they frequently came to him to interpret and translate for them.

"Was your language written?" Chip asked.

"No," said Mapache. "Not until my father developed a system to write it. He tried various ways, then finally found a way to transcribe most of the sounds using the Spanish alphabet. It didn't match up perfectly, but by using a few new characters he invented, he made it practical enough to work most of the time. And before he died, he made a small, bilingual dictionary."

"What motivated him to do that?" Chip asked.

"He suspected that one day the Spanish language and Hispanic culture would overwhelm the indigenous peoples. That time was coming like a river overflowing its banks. The floodwaters were already seeping under the doors of every home. It was only a matter of time before all our houses would be swept away, carrying our customs, our beliefs, our traditions, and our languages— our whole way of life—in an unstoppable torrent. What had started as a tiny stream would become a deluge. And it would carry our children away."

"There's a poet in you," Chip said.

"My father taught me to understand and feel the power of words. He loved the oral stories, but he told me many times how powerful the written word can be. He told me that when he learned to read and write, he felt as though he had escaped from a prison of darkness. His chains were broken and the walls crumbled to the ground. He possessed new powers. And he wanted to use this new power to save our people from the coming deluge. He saw himself as a kind of prophet. And he wanted to give the people something tangible. If they were going to survive, they would need something to cling to. They would need to remember the stories of our past. With that, we could always start over, begin again, continue the bloodline, and keep the spirits of our gods alive."

"Sort of like a modern day Noah," Chip mused.

"That wouldn't be stretching the analogy too far," Mapache said. "I think it fits."

"So what kind of ark did he build?" Chip asked.

"He made an ark of paper. He wrote an ark. A book not just for now, but for future generations."

"Did you know what he was doing? Did anyone know?"

"It was a project he kept secret from everyone. My mother found it several years after he died."

"What's it about?" Chip asked.

"It's really an epic poem," Mapache said. "It's the story of our people. It's practically an encyclopedia of our culture. He took the stories, myths, and legends that had been passed down from generation to generation, and wove them into a tapestry of heroic proportions. What the Old Testament is to the Jewish people, this saga will become to my people."

Chip sat spellbound. His mind raced. He could think of no such manuscript existing in any library. He couldn't even recall a reference to such a Mayan treasure.

"It's not just great literature," Mapache continued. "It tells the story of our gods and our beginnings. It explains how the gods gave us plants. Some plants they gave for food and others were given to heal our bodies. It must have taken my father years to make a list, a catalogue, of human ailments and how to cure them with specific plants. Some remedies require leaves, some use bark, and others call for roots and herbs. And there are specific preparation steps that must be followed."

"Where did he get this information?" Chip asked.

"I'm sure he got most of it from my mother." Mapache said. "I have no idea where or how she learned the magic of the *curanderas*, but she can cure anything."

"Where is the manuscript?" Chip blurted, unable to contain his excitement. His heart was pounding. He had a thousand questions, but didn't know what to ask first. "Do you have it with you? Where do you keep it?"

"A man does not carry his most prized possession around in his pocket," Mapache said. "It's in Chiapas. I left it with a librarian in San Cristóbal de Las Casas, in a secret hiding place. I wanted it protected. And I have been waiting for someone like you to come along to study it carefully, to make it known to the world, to share our ancient knowledge with the modern world. By doing that, you will awaken our people to their own heritage, to a history they can take pride in, preserve, and pass on to their children.

"I wasn't joking last night when I said that the angels sent you to me. I knew you would come. I just didn't know when."

"I've never had much belief in angels," Chip said, "but if guardian angels do exist, I've got a hunch that you're about as close as I'm going to get to one. You certainly came to my rescue."

Chip scribbled in his notepad, then asked, "What's the name of the library?"

"The librarian I mentioned works for the Martin Kirsch Library," Mapache answered. "It's a small library in the UNAM research center called Centro de Investigaciones de MesoAmerica. Everyone knows it as La CIMA. Although the librarian is technically employed by La CIMA, she actually works as an archivist at the Catholic cathedral. She is a specialist in the preservation of old documents. She's trying to help salvage the thousands of records that are deteriorating in cardboard boxes in the underground storage tunnels. She knows where my father's manuscripts are."

Chip stared at Mapache in disbelief. His jaw hung open. When he had recovered his composure, he said, "La CIMA. That's precisely where I'm going."

"I know," Mapache said.

"You know? How could you possibly know?"

"You told me in your dream talk."

"What a difference a night makes," Chip said. "Last night you and your friends made it clear that you didn't think it was safe for me to go to Chiapas. Why, all of a sudden, are you asking me to go there and see your father's manuscript?"

"Yesterday," Mapache said, " I didn't know the things about you that I know now. I didn't know that you were a scholar, a professor of linguistics. And I didn't know about your grandfather or the kidnapping of your mother and sister. Now I know that you must go there. That doesn't mean I think it's any safer. In fact, it's possible that what I'm asking of you could make it even more dangerous for you."

"What dangers are you talking about?" Chip asked. "Look, I know all about the Zapatistas and what's been happening since their uprising a few years ago, but, from what I hear, that's pretty much settled down. It's anybody's guess how long it will stay that way, but for now, I don't see much danger. In fact, I'm more afraid to go back to Laredo than I am to go to Chiapas."

"I'm not talking just about the Zapatistas," Mapache told him. "Uprisings like that break out once in a while, and when they do, they're violent and they attract a lot of attention. They're like volcanoes. They erupt when the pressure builds up under the surface. When forces crack the top open, all hell breaks loose. Then it settles down again.

"The Zapatista uprising was not new to Chiapas. My father's manuscript tells of many uprisings in our history.

Long before the Spaniards invaded, we resisted and rebelled against the Aztecs."

"I've got a pretty good handle on the history of Chiapas," Chip said, a trifle impatiently. "What does that have to do with me, here and now?"

"You gringos don't understand our way of thinking." Mapache said calmly.

Chip could tell by the tone of Mapache's voice that he was not insulting him. *It's his way of telling me to be patient and let him finish what he has to say*, Chip told himself.

"You *norteamericanos*," Mapache continued, "are instilled with the imperative to get directly to the point, to not 'beat around the bush.' You are taught to use 'economy of words.' We *Mexicanos*, especially us *Indios*, do not think in such a linear pattern. For us, there is a linguistic beauty in painting a word picture around an idea before we focus on it. Even the concept of 'main idea' is foreign to us. There is no word or phrase in our language that embodies that idea. So please be patient with me when I seem to be straying from the topic or 'talking in circles.' Just think of it as me adding a few more brush strokes to the whole picture."

"Are you aware," Chip said, "that what you just said was right to the point?"

"I didn't used to talk that way," Mapache said, giving a clue that he was going off on another tangent. "Don Wilbur would get so frustrated with me. He'd say, 'Cut the extraneous bullcrap. Don't tell me how to make a watch; just tell me what time it is.' Fortunately, Doña Mae was more understanding and tolerant of my verbal meanderings."

"Cut the extraneous bullcrap." Chip interjected. "Are you ever going to get around to telling me why Chiapas is a dangerous place for me?"

Mapache caught the sarcasm in Chip's voice and smiled. "The volcano may appear to be dormant again, but don't be fooled. There are deep rumblings still rocking the ground. Puffs of smoke are popping out in unexpected places. And people are taking notice. I don't want to press the analogy too far, but indigenous peoples are experimenting with new ways to confront the social injustices they feel and the exploitation they perceive. Some are working within the system, and others are still trying to fight the system. Either way, there's resistance and friction. And when the sparks fly, everybody is vulnerable. You'll be vulnerable in Chiapas. That's why I'm going to ask my friends to keep an eye on you while you're there."

"You still haven't told me why," Chip said, almost in exasperation. "Just what is this lurking danger you are so concerned about?"

"The conflicts in Chiapas are escalating." Mapache replied with gravity in his voice. "The gathering forces are bigger, more powerful, than anything we've seen before.
The players will be internal and external. International economic interests are coming into play. The stakes in the cultural war are being raised. You may have to choose sides in a collision where the outcome for the Indians could mean extinction."

Chip rolled his eyes and took out his notebook and pen again. "What's the name of that librarian who's got your father's manuscript?"

CHAPTER TWENTY-FIVE

*T*he sound of a jetliner flying low overhead jolted Chip awake. He had fallen asleep again somewhere on the desert highway. *How long was I out?* he asked himself. *What did I say this time under the hypnotic spell of a low-growling truck engine?* But as he looked around and became more conscious of his surroundings, he realized that the engine was quiet and the truck was not moving.

"*Buenas tardes, dormilon,*" Mapache said as he walked up to the truck door. "You really are a sleepyhead." Through the open window, he handed Chip a Styrofoam cup brimming with hot coffee.

Chip reached out and took the cup with his right hand while rubbing his eyes with his left fist. Without taking a sip, he opened the door and gingerly climbed out of the cab, being careful not to spill the coffee. Setting the cup on the running board, he stretched his legs muscles for a minute before attempting to walk. There was pain, but it was tolerable. The late afternoon air was beginning to cool, and steam was visible as it rose from the cup of dark, muddy liquid. Chip picked up the cup and blew slowly across the top surface several times to make sure he didn't scald his lips and tongue.

"Oh, I almost forgot. You'd better take one of these first," Mapache ordered as he handed Chip a small plastic bag of yellow capsules. "Your stomach was percolating this afternoon."

"What *curandero's* concoction have you prepared for me?' Chip asked.

"This is nothing more than a gringo acid suppressant with the generic name of 'omeprazole.' There's enough here to last you until you get to Chiapas. But remember, as soon as you get there, find some *sosa* plants, make a tea from the leaves, and then throw these pills away."

"That's one of the first things on my 'to do' list," Chip answered.

The smell of gasoline fumes was heavy in the air. Looking around, Chip saw that they were parked in the lot beside a large Pemex station. Dozens of trucks were in lines waiting to be refueled. Many more had already been filled and were parked in rows. The weary drivers were in the shower facilities, or were asleep, or were in the restaurant having a decent meal. Some were just stretching their legs and giving their trucks a well-earned rest.

Two young boys came running up to Mapache. Each carried his own bucket of soapy water, brushes, squeegee, and worn rags. After a brief, animated negotiation, Mapache dug some pesos from his pockets and tossed them to the boys. One climbed up on the cab and began to wash the insects and road grime from the windshield. The other boy snatched up his bucket and went to work on the tires.

"We're in Monterrey," Mapache said, "where I went to the university."

"I know a little bit about this place," Chip said. "There's a lot of industry here. When I passed through here several years ago, I was surprised at the number of smokestack factories I saw. Most of them are large, international companies. Another thing I remember about this city is that everywhere I went, most of the people spoke English, or at least they could understand it."

"That's because we're so close to the border," Mapache said. "The farther south you go, the less English you'll hear. When you get to Chiapas, English becomes rare."

Chip finished his coffee and set his empty cup on top of an overflowing trash barrel. "*Donde está el baño?*" he asked with a sense of urgency.

"That building over there," Mapache said, pointing with his coffee cup in his right hand. With his left, he handed Chip two large, bulging plastic shopping bags. "Go in there, take a hot shower, shave, and put these clean clothes on. And don't forget to brush your teeth and use the deodorant. You're getting ripe."

"You bought all this while I was sleeping?" Chip asked.

"I hope they fit. They should be your size." Mapache said. "Go on. I'll go ahead and get us a booth in the restaurant."

Twenty minutes later, Chip walked into the restaurant and found Mapache sitting at a booth, reading a newspaper. Chip slid into the plastic bench seat opposite Mapache.

"You look and smell better," Mapache said. "How do the clothes fit?"

"They're just the right size. How did you guess my sizes so perfectly?"

"I measured you while you were asleep."

"I didn't feel a thing."

"I know. You were dead to the world. It was like measuring a corpse. It's a good thing you're not very heavy."

Chip regarded him for a minute, trying to see any giveaway that Mapache was kidding. "Tell the undertaker to wait. I'm back among the living. And I'm rested, but what about you? You must be exhausted after driving and shopping all day without a break. Aren't you sleepy?"

"Don't worry about me. I've got a room for the night. After I get you on the plane, I'll get a good night's sleep."

"What are you talking about?"

"You're flying to Mexico City. Your departure time is 7:30 this evening. It's all arranged. I made the reservations for you."

Chip stared at the trucker in disbelief. He could only manage to say, "What time is it now?" as he again looked at his naked wrist.

"There's no rush," Mapache said as he pushed a menu across the table to Chip. "You must be hungry. Tell me what you want. I'll put in our orders while you go over there and make your telephone calls. I'm sure Xochitle is worried to death about you."

"Get me the whole left side of the menu," Chip said as he jumped up and took the handful of coins Mapache handed him.

Less than five minutes later, Chip was sliding back into the booth. "Every single number I called was busy. I'll try again later. What did you order for me?"

"A big, solid meal," Mapache said. "You may not get anything more than a little bag of salty *cacahuates* on the plane. A handful of peanuts is not very filling."

"I'm curious to know," Chip said, "how you're going to get me on a plane without any identification. And maybe you can tell me how to get through customs in Mexico City without a passport."

"It's not an international flight from here," Mapache answered.

"That's true," said Chip, "but they do have a habit of randomly stopping *extanjeros* to check their papers. Foreigners are dangerous, you know." Chip's concern was sincere. "Listen to me. Maybe you don't understand how serious my situation is. I need to call the American Embassy and get things straightened out." He felt a knot tighten in his stomach and was rapidly losing his appetite. *I'm going to need something stronger than omeprazole*, he thought. "Is there an American Consulate here in Monterrey? Maybe that's where I should start."

"*Tranquilo*," Mapache said soothingly. "Take it easy. I've got friends at the airport here and at Mexico City. I've already called them and they are going to take care of you. So, relax. *Todo está bajo control*. Everything is under control."

"Look at the bright side," he continued. "If things don't work out right, what are they going to do with you? They'll put you on a plane and send you back to Texas, right?" He stretched his lips into a wide gap-toothed smile.

Although Chip was not amused by the humor, there was something reassuring in Mapache's relaxed attitude. The knot in his gut began to loosen and hunger took its place. "Let me see that menu again," he said.

"I took the liberty to order a full *carne asada* dinner for both of us. It's the closest thing to a 'specialty of the house' they serve here. You won't be disappointed, and you won't go away hungry."

"Sounds perfect," Chip said, "but it had better get here soon or I'm going to start gnawing on the table leg." He was watching the *cocinero* slap wide, thin-sliced cuts of beef over the iron grate in the center of the dining room. The meat sizzled instantly on the red metal above the white-hot coals. Curls of dissipating smoke drifted through the room and widened Chip's nostrils on contact, almost choking him on his own saliva. No need for Pavlov's bell; he had been conditioned long ago.

When the *mesera* brought the orders to the table, both men attacked their plates without comment. Chip virtually inhaled the first few bites, then set his fork down and chewed slowly to extend the savory pleasure. He imitated Mapache in cutting a strip of meat and placing it in a warm flour tortilla spread with refried beans, guacamole, salsa, and *pico de gallo*, a mixture of chopped chili peppers, onions, tomatoes, and cilantro. When several such tacos had been devoured, he said to Mapache, "I'm in no position to make a suggestion, but *una cerveza bien fria* would really top this off."

"I agree," Mapache said. "A cold beer does sound good, but I think it would be best if we wait until everything is arranged at the airport. You'll have to get on the plane under your own power. Last night I had to practically carry you to the truck."

"I wondered how I got there," Chip said.

"I'm not completely sure how I got myself in the truck," Mapache said. "After you closed your eyes and went *mimi*, I helped Tom and Jerry empty another bottle of tequila. We made small talk and gossiped like a bunch of old women in a mercado. It's true. We really are *chismosos*, but there's a reason for that. We get lonely on the road and sometimes we start talking to ourselves. Getting together once in a while at truckers' watering holes is our only real social life. What am I going to do when you get on that plane? I won't have anyone to talk to."

"I'm sorry if I haven't been a good conversationalist," Chip said. "I think I was asleep most of the time."

"Maybe you weren't awake," Mapache said, "but even in your sleep, you were an excellent listener, and sometimes you were a pretty good talker. I like a good listener. Most people aren't very good at listening; they love to hear themselves talk."

"I think you've mastered the art of listening," Chip said. "And you do more than that. You observe what people do, and try to figure out why they say what they say, and do what they do. You're a people watcher."

"I've been a people watcher as long as I can remember." Mapache said. "I'm not sure when I began, but one day I realized I was distinguishing the differences between the way Indian families lived and the way Hispanic families lived. In those days, Hispanics were called Latinos. I'm not sure if either of those words is politically correct today."

"Get to the point," Chip kidded him.

"I'm getting there. The point is I watch and I noticed many differences. Beyond the obvious difference in language, I was curious why our clothes, our food, our houses, our music, our religion—our everything—was different. In those days I didn't know that all these things combined were called culture.

"I was fascinated by the things Latinos invented to make their work easier and faster. They were always making new tools, not just for work, but also for their houses. The word 'appliance' didn't even exist in my vocabulary. Years later, when I learned the word 'technology' I knew I had found the precise term to describe this phenomenon. I watched as my family—and many other families—adapted technology from other cultures and it spread through a community and then through a whole society. Sometimes it was a gradual process, and at other times it seemed to happen overnight. You wake up one morning and discover that a part of your culture is changing. It's evolving into something new, almost unrecognizable. It's not something static, but unstoppably dynamic.

"And I saw that the emerging Indian culture was not like the evolving Latino culture. They, too, were borrowing, adapting, and creating new technology and incorporating it into their culture. I was shocked when I first realized that Latinos were borrowing certain aspects of Indian culture. But it was clear to me that the two cultures would never blend into one. The two cultures had different starting points and they were traveling at different velocities. More importantly, they were not headed in the same direction. These differences create friction, or sometimes an explosive collision.

"Long ago I came to the conclusion that Latinos and Indians would never fuse into a single, unified culture. I saw that Latinos possessed the tools, the wealth, and the weapons—the power—to impose their culture upon us. They would be dominant, but they would never completely assimilate the Indian culture.

"You're an educated man, so what I'm saying may sound simplistic to you. I'm well aware that I have oversimplified my argument here. I know that in addition to technology, there are many other factors that influence culture. So many psychological, sociological, and environmental factors relate directly—or indirectly—to culture. And I don't want to get into the 'nature vs. nurture' debate. What concerns me now is how people, as individuals, and as communities and societies, adapt or don't adapt, accept or don't accept, new technology into their lives, their social worlds, and into their cultures.

"I know I'm beating around the bush, but I'll try to tie this all together. Let me tell you a story. After my father died, I came home from California and stayed with my mother for a while. With the money I had saved, I wanted to help my mother. I tried to convince her that she needed a refrigerator. If she had one, she wouldn't have to get up early every day and go to the *mercado*, the big community market, and fight the crowds to buy fresh food for the day's meals. She would be able to buy enough food for several days—maybe even a week—and it wouldn't spoil if she put it in the refrigerator.

"I didn't understand why, but she always resisted. She came up with excuses like 'It costs too much,' or 'It'll use too much electricity.' Then, one day I overheard her chatting with a neighbor and I learned the real reason she didn't want a refrigerator. She actually wanted to go to the mercado every morning. She liked going there to see and visit with her neighbors, her friends, and her relatives. She enjoyed those encounters where she could gossip with the women and exchange juicy bits of information with the butcher and the bean seller. This was how she learned what was going on in the community. This was her way of finding out who was getting married, who was having a baby, who was sick, who died, and who was cheating on who.

"How could I have been so blind? You see, a refrigerator—that piece of technology—was a real threat to her way of life. It would destroy her opportunity to have daily, face-to-face contact and conversation with her friends. It would destroy her social life and confine her to her house. Since she couldn't read a newspaper, it would cut her off from her primary source of community news. It would be like sending her to prison, or at least placing her under house arrest. I don't think it would be an exaggeration to say it might have killed her.

"If you stretch the analogy, carry it out to its logical conclusion, you can see that technology has the potential to affect, to modify so many areas of social life, and that if the cumulative affect reaches a critical point, an entire lifestyle—a culture—can be threatened with extinction."

Chip's mind was once again spinning. The discussion of ideas had always transported him to another world, and this impromptu lecture was exciting his mind. Only vaguely was he aware that he was sitting in a truck stop restaurant in Monterrey, Mexico, and not in a graduate seminar. At this moment he felt more the student than the professor. "Are you suggesting that entire cultures may be compared to biological organism?" he asked. "Are you a social Darwinist? Do you believe that cultures must adapt to the changes in their technological environment, or die?"

"Not entirely," Mapache said. "I do think that some degree of social evolution is inevitable and necessary. To what degree is not so clear. This all goes back to what I have said before—that some cultures have the ability to do more than adapt. They have the ability to resist, and even modify a hostile environment. There's something in their cultural genes that makes them practically immune to extinction. That's the cultural ark I was talking about. It's something they cling to that helps them rise above the flood."

"I'm impressed," Chip said. "How would you like to teach a seminar for me?"

"In a classroom?" Mapache replied. "Not a chance, but if you've got a few good students who would like to ride with me for a while, they might learn some things about life they'd never learn in school. Besides, I could use the company.

"Just one quick footnote," Mapache said. "There will always be inequality in the level of technology among cultures. Some cultures will have more, and some will have less. The ones with more will always look down on those with less. Those with more will describe those with less as 'third world,' 'underdeveloped,' or 'primitive,' but those terms can be totally irrelevant and meaningless. It all depends on one's perspective. If survival is the name of the game, then cultural values will trump technology every time. No culture, whether high-tech or low-tech, will escape extinction if it doesn't have an ark in which to float the values system which it has developed."

With that, Mapache stood up, left a generous tip on the table, and headed to the cashier to pay for the meal. Chip went to the door and waited. As they went out into the evening air, they were joined by two men coming out of the shadows.

"Don Mapache!" one of the men shouted.

"Don Chipotle!" the other greeted loudly.

"Tom and Jerry," Chip gasped in instant recognition. "What are you doing here?"

"Professor Windbag didn't tell you?" Tom asked in mock surprise. "He sent us on a mission to find your belongings. Well, here they are. Here's your truck, your suitcases, your passport, your cheap watch, and your expensive fountain pen."

"What about his *dinero*?" Mapache asked.

"Most of that was gone," said Jerry, "but I think all the credit cards are still in the wallet."

"Did they give you any trouble?" Mapache asked.

"Once we found those *maldito banditos*, it didn't take long to interrogate them. Jerry's machete can be most persuasive. Those boys said they were real sorry," Tom said with a sinister laugh.

"Excuse me," Mapache said. "I'll join you at the cantina in a few minutes. I've got to go cancel an airline flight."

CHAPTER TWENTY-SIX

Stopping only when necessary for gas and bodily relief, Chip pushed his pickup to its limits. Impatiently, he slowed in the cities and towns, then sped through the open spaces between populated area. His mind reeling with the possibility of an uncirculated Mayan manuscript—a codex—he drove past wide expanses of farmland, barely realizing he had crossed through them.

With a sigh of relief he plunged into the beehive of swarming traffic that never seems to slacken in the metropolitan spread of the Mexico's national capital, *el Distrito Federal*, known to everyone as *D.F.* Somewhat dazed, he found a reasonable motel in the area called University City where UNAM, *Universidad Nacional Autonomous de Mexico*, houses its mother campus. It was late afternoon, but Chip telephoned the Linguistics Section of the Anthropology Department and was assured that the departmental director would be working late and would try to squeeze Chip into his schedule. After a quick shave, shower, and change of clothes, he hurried over to the administrative offices, only to wait interminably for the departmental head.

Though his body ached from the long drive and the residual bruises from his mugging, and the wooden bench was most uncomfortable, his mind ignored these physical irritations. He worried anxiously about his grandfather, his mother, sister, and especially his daughter. Then his focus gravitated deep into things Mayan. *How is it possible that Mapache's father had accumulated so much information about Mayan culture? Did he really obtain some authentic, ancient manuscripts, perhaps even a 'codex' without any of these UNAM scholars being aware of it? Could this treasure really exist?* He knew he would have to go to Chiapas to find out. He had no intention of telling anyone here. *Maybe they already know and are keeping it a secret. Some scholars are like that,* he thought.

Chip began to squirm on the hard bench, then stood and paced for a while. He walked across the office and asked the secretary if he might get a cup of coffee somewhere.

"I'm sorry," the woman said. "I should have offered you a cup sooner." Her English was quite good. She stood and poured him a cup of strong, dark coffee from the coffee maker behind her desk. Handing the cup to Chip, she explained apologetically, "This coffee has been cooking all day. I hope it is still drinkable. Would you like sugar and cream in it?"

"*No, gracias, señora,*" Chip replied in Spanish.

"By the way," the secretary said, "my name is Dolores. Please call me Lola." She held out her hand, the gesture of a professional, liberated woman in Mexico. "I already know who you are, Professor Oatley. I'm pleased to meet you."

"The pleasure is mine. I'm Chip. You can call me Chipotle."

She caught the humor immediately and laughed.

"I'm sorry you have had to wait so long, don Chipotle," she said sincerely. "It's getting late and I know that you must have driven a long distance. The director knows that you are here, but he is very busy."

"I'm sure he is," Chip said. "But don't worry. I'm on my way to Chiapas and I just wanted to pay my respects. I had hoped to discuss the situation in Chiapas with him and look through your library stacks, but circumstances have made it urgent for me to get there as quickly as possible."

"If he's not aware of that," Lola said, "I'll bring it to his attention. Right now all of his attention is focused on union negotiations. It's not that he thinks you are unimportant; it's that there seems to be no end to their demands. I hope you will understand if he's not able to see you."

"I understand completely," Chip assured her. "I'll wait a little longer to see if he can break free, but if not, then I'll be on my way."

Chip returned to the bench and observed the secretary as she moved around the office answering the phone, taking messages, opening mail, and filing correspondence. He was impressed by her efficiency. Mentally he compared and contrasted her to "Princess" Gretchen in Dean Lambert's office. Lola was slightly taller and thinner than average and her near-sixty years had stooped her shoulders. And though her lips were thin, a pleasant smile was pasted on her gaunt face. Most noticeable, Chip thought, was an air that bordered on sophistication. Smooth and polished, she could probably trace her lineage to the Spanish aristocracy. Wide streaks of silver added dignity to the hair she had pulled back into a large bun. The image was shattered by her flowery—but plain—cotton dress and worn shoes. *Her only jewels are the sparkles in her eyes,* Chip said to himself.

It suddenly occurred to Chip that he was the one who was keeping Lola late at the office. From a scattering of photo frames on her desk, he guessed that she was married and had children and grandchildren, "You must be anxious to get home to your family," he said. "I hope I haven't kept you overtime."

"I wish that were true," she said, "but I have no family to go home to. My husband died several years ago and my children are grown and gone. I live alone now."

Chip heard the loneliness in her voice. "Would you like to have dinner with me this evening? Don't get me wrong. I'm harmless. I just need someone to talk to tonight, and you sound like you could use a little diversion. Besides, it looks like I won't get in to see the director and I suspect you know as much or more about the operation of this department than he does." The look and the nod she gave confirmed his suspicions.

"I'll finish up here at 7:30. I'll meet you at the front entrance of this building," she said. "While you're here, you might as well go ahead and sign all these papers that say you understand the authority this department has over you, and that you agree to obey the rules and regulations that apply to all the employees of this university. Of course, you are in a special category. Your pay comes from your home university, so we don't really have the same control over you that we have over other professors. All this is nothing more than a bureaucratic formality."

Chip spent the next half hour initialing and signing papers and reading over packets of orientation information, most of which was out of date. When he was certain that he had reached the last of the documents, he ceremoniously took out his Montblanc fountain pen and wrote a grandiose *Pancho Villa,* knowing that no one would ever check the signature.

****

When Chip drove up to the front entrance at 7:25, Lola was exiting the building. *She's right on time,* he noted, *in a culture where punctuality is a rare commodity.*

Lola didn't wait for Chip to open the pickup door for her. She walked up to the pickup, pulled the door open, and climbed in. She had changed out of her flowery office dress and high heels into a sporty blouse, loose-fitting jeans, and white tennis shoes. Her bun was gone; her hair fell loose half-way down her back. On her left arm hung a light windbreaker and she clutched a small purse. The change didn't make her look any younger, but it did give her an air of youthful vigor that had been missing in the office.

Before Chip could ask, Lola gave directions. "Turn left at the next traffic light. About two kilometers down the road there is large Bimbo bread distribution warehouse. Across the street from that is a colonial house that has been turned into a low-budget *cantina.* In addition to bad music and cheap beer, they have the best *tacos de lingua.* It's a typical college hangout."

"Sounds good to me," Chip said. "It's been a long time since I've since I've had cow tongue. I'm hungry enough to eat the whole cow."

"This is my treat," Lola made clear.

"Looks like we beat the crowd," Chip said when he saw that the parking lot was not crowded.

"This is the best time to come here," Lola said, "while we can hear each other. Later on, the music gets loud."

"Then we had better take advantage of this opportunity," Chip said as they went in and found an empty table. "What can you tell me about the situation in Chiapas? Do you get reliable reports from field researchers there?"

"We get lots of reports from the field, but I'm not sure how reliable they are. I keep my eyes and ears open for any news from there, but lately I find that I'm being left out of the loop. There's been a big shake up in the administration of the department. We have a new director who will probably clean house and bring in a whole new staff."

"What brought that about?" Chip asked.

"The old director was opposed to the priorities forced on us by big money grants from giant corporations. There were 'philosophical differences' about academic independence and objectivity. But, like always, he who has the gold makes the rules."

"Who is the big gorilla with all the gold?" Chip asked.

"There's a big new bully on the block called Rainwater Pharms," Lola answered. "It's a transnational pharmaceutical that came in flexing its muscles and rocking the boat. If I'm not mistaken, they're the ones who are funding your trip down here," she said cautiously.

"That's correct," Chip said. "And I, too, have already had some philosophical differences with their representative who is my point of contact. The more I learn about Rainwater Pharms, the more apprehensive I am. What's the former director going to do?"

"He's being forced into retirement, and that has created a ruthless game of musical chairs. Many personnel moves are in the works."

"How does all this affect you?" Chip asked.

"I'm being kicked out the back door. The new director is bringing in his own administrative assistant."

"I'm sorry to hear that," Chip said. He could see that Lola's smile was evaporating. "It's none of my business, but I'm curious about what you're going to do now. Are you planning to retire, or would you like to find another job?"

"It has all happened so fast," Lola said, "I haven't had time to make plans. I'm still in a state of shock and denial. I've been thinking about retirement, but I wanted to work for a few more years. I never expected to be dumped out into the street without any warning."

"You said that you have some grown children. Do they live around here?"

"My son is studying electrical engineering here at UNAM. He thinks he's too old to stay at home. My daughter is married and lives in Chiapas. Her husband has a degree in computer programming, but his family marimba business takes up his time. He has a marimba-making shop in their house in Chiapa de Corzo."

"Do you get to see them often?" Chip asked.

"Not often enough. I have a year-old granddaughter that I haven't seen since she was born. They send pictures and I talk to them on the phone, but I'm dying to spend some time with them and spoil my granddaughter. Maybe I'll have time to do that now. But that's enough about me, Chip. What is it you want to know that will help you with your research?"

"I have a thousand questions, but I think they can wait. Some other questions have crowded into my mind. I'm sure you know a lot about La CIMA, the research center where I'll be working. What do you know about Ollie Krahn, the head of the center? He has a reputation worldwide as the preeminent Mayan linguist in Mexico. I hope he isn't going to lose his position. He has been a friend of my family for many years. He has been most helpful in this trying time for me. I'm assuming you know about my grandfather and the kidnapping of my mother and sister. I will always be grateful to Ollie for taking care of things at the Mission Station until I can get there. I need to call him tonight and find out if the police or the military have uncovered any new information."

Lola's expression became totally serious. Her eyes took on a far-away look and she had difficulty controlling her emotions. Her voice quivered when she spoke.

"I heard about the attack on the Mission Station," she said, "and about the situation with your family. I'm really sorry and I hope your mother and sister have not been harmed. I heard that the staff nurse was taken, too. This must be a terrible time for you. If anyone is in a position to help you, there's no better person than Ollie."

"You know him personally," Chip asked, surprised.

"I've known him more than thirty years," Lola admitted. "I met him right here at UNAM. In fact, we were classmates."

"Were you good friends?"

Lola's eyes were misty. There was a knot in her throat. She looked down and whispered quietly, "We were more than friends."

Chip was quiet for a moment, then spoke suddenly, "Lola, how would you like to go to Chiapas with me and be my research assistant? Sort of like my personal secretary? Help keep me organized and help me put a doctoral dissertation together. As you know, the position has already been authorized and budgeted. I can't think of anyone more qualified for the job. In fact, you're over-qualified."

When Lola looked up, there were tears in her eyes. "When would we leave?" She asked.

"Can you be ready by dawn tomorrow?"

CHAPTER TWENTY-SEVEN

Early the next morning, Chip and Lola were caught in the congested morning traffic that crawls in and around *El Distrito Federal*, the governmental center of Mexico. The camper shell of Chip's pickup was now packed with Lola's suitcases and an assortment of plastic bags and cardboard boxes. No longer was there any space for Chip's luggage to shift, slide or rattle.

Looking like mother and son, Chip and Lola chatted like old friends. Lola's eyes were red and her face was puffy, but she was energetic and cheerful. In the middle of the bench seat, Lola had placed a wicker basket of soft tacos; freshly made, they still steamed. One whiff and Chip's stomach growled in anticipation.

On the floor in front of her, a large birdcage rocked with the motion of the vehicle, but Lola held it securely between her calves and feet. Her jeans were wrinkled.

"Sorry if I look like a mess this morning," she said. "I've been packing and making phone calls most of the night. The first call was to the new department director. I was hesitant to mention I was quitting to take the position you offered me, but when I told him, he seemed pleased that he could now put his favorite secretary into my slot in the organizational chart.

"Then I called my daughter in Chiapa de Corzo, and told her what was happening. She was so excited! She said one of the extra bedrooms will be ready for me when I get there and it will stay ready for me to come visit anytime. They have a large colonial house with lots of rooms built around a central patio."

"What about your son? What was his reaction to this sudden, drastic move?"

"I could tell he had his doubts at first, but after I told him I wanted him to live in my house and take care of it, he saw the advantages, so he encouraged me to go. As long as I send him money each month to take care of the utility bills, I know he'll keep everything in good condition. He's a good boy and a serious student, but he's still immature in some ways. I don't trust him to take care of Scorpy." She patted the top of the cage. "Thanks for letting me bring him. I'm sure he won't be a problem."

"As long as he doesn't criticize my driving," Chip said. He had been a little apprehensive about the bird, but had agreed since the cage was covered by a cotton slip cover that would keep the bird asleep most of the time. But even with the covering, the unmistakable smell of bird droppings lingered in the air. Chip cracked his window open, sending a draft of cool air circulating through the cab.

"How long have you had the toucan?" Chip asked.

"You're one of the few people who know the difference between a parrot and a toucan," Lola said. "I've had him for more than thirty years. These birds have long lives."

"Where did you get him?"

"It's a long story."

"This is going to be a long day," Chip reminded her. "If I recall correctly, it's about a sixteen-hour drive from here to Tuxtla Gutierrez, the capital of Chiapas."

"Then we should get there late this evening," Lola said. "Then it's another half hour to cross the river to Chiapa de Corzo. They'll have dinner waiting for us when we get there.

"It'll sure be nice when they finish building the new *carretera*. It's supposed to cut the driving time in half. But that will probably take another two or three years."

"I doubt if I'll be here when that happens," Chip said.

"Do you know why many people keep pet parrots and toucans?" Lola asked as she lifted the cover off the cage just far enough to see if Scorpy was awake and in a talkative mood.

"I have no idea," Chip admitted.

"For two main reasons," Lola told him. "Because they imitate human speech, and because they eat insects, spiders, and scorpions. That's important, especially when you have small children around."

"What do you mean?" Chip asked. "Do people catch scorpions and feed them to the toucans?"

"No," Lola laughed. "The wings of the birds are clipped so they can't fly. When the birds are let out for exercise, they hop around, flap their wings, and eat insects." She leaned forward and spoke to the bird, "*Qué quieres?*"

"*Quiero alacrán*," the toucan screeched. Lola smiled with delight.

"What's so wonderful about him saying he wants a scorpion? I don't suppose you brought any scorpions to feed to him, did you?"

"He said much more than that," Lola said mysteriously. "If you listen closely, you'll hear that he said '*Quiero*...Ollie...Krahn'—I love Ollie Krahn."

"What are you telling me, *doña* Lola? You told me you and Ollie had a special relationship back when you were both university students. It's really none of my business, but are you telling me now that you have been secretly harboring some special feelings for Ollie all these years?"

"I warned you; it's a long story."

"I'm a sucker for a good story."

"It started in 1967. Ollie and I were both graduate students in the UNAM linguistics department. I was working on my master's degree and he was about to finish his doctorate. He was teaching one of my classes when we fell in love. That summer he went on a research trip to Chiapas and brought back Scorpy for me as a birthday present.

"It was the most exciting year of my life. I was young, in love, and saw nothing but roses in my future. But all over the world there was revolution in the air. It was a time when students protested and took over their universities. Mexico was no exception. Here at UNAM, the student revolutionary movement was controlled by radical Marxist leaders who had dreams of eventually overthrowing the Mexican government. And in their eyes, the end justified every means.

"The student movement grew powerful and they pressured all of us to join in, but Ollie tried to avoid them and remain neutral. He had no interest in political activism. Besides me, his only interest was finishing his dissertation and becoming a full professor so we could get married. Well, it didn't work out that way. In 1968, the students occupied most of the administration buildings."

"I've heard lots of stories," said Chip, "about how the government was so worried about the students disrupting the Olympic Games, they called the Army out to crush the demonstrators in the main plaza. They shot live rounds and killed hundreds of students."

"That's really true," Lola responded. And that only made the revolutionaries more determined to bring the government down. At the university, in addition to destroying many buildings and most of the furniture, the students hunted through the cabinets for files on students like Ollie who refused to participate in their revolution. They made bonfires of their class records and transcripts. When it was over, there was not a single document to prove that Ollie had ever been enrolled in the graduate program.

"In order to end the student occupation, the administration caved in to many of the students' demands. They stood by helplessly while the destructive storm played itself out. Ollie and the other student who had not actively supported the radical revolutionaries were ostracized, threatened, and barred from entering the facilities. Ollie was told never to set foot on campus again. And he was never awarded his PhD."

"Ollie must have taken that pretty hard," Chip commented.

"He was devastated. He felt as though the world had been totally destroyed. He didn't eat for days. He just stayed in his room. Several times I went to see him and tried to talk to him, but gradually he even stopped talking to me. I was afraid he would might even try to commit suicide. So one day I told him he had to face reality. 'Go to Chiapas and do what you do best. Go find a Mayan dialect and show the world you are the world's best anthropological linguist. You know the researchers down there; go show them how it's done. Don't worry about the degrees and the diplomas.' He held me and we cried in each other's arms. Finally, he agreed to go. One day he went away without telling anyone where he was going. But I knew.

"I didn't hear anything for months, the finally I learned he was living in the jungles of Chiapas, documenting and analyzing indigenous languages. Except for his contact with the Indians, he was living like a hermit. Some of his former professors were secretly supporting him. They knew what a loss it would be to the study of Indian languages if Ollie were not allowed to continue his research. It turned out that they were right. As you know, he has become one of the most respected linguistic scholars in the world."

"So how did you deal with all that?" Chip asked, mesmerized by this tragic love story. "Obviously you didn't become a nun."

"I cried a lot. My world had been destroyed, too. When I finally resigned myself to the fact that he wasn't coming back, I tried to forget him. Eventually I married another man, a high school math teacher. He was a good man and we had a good life together, but I never loved him in the same way I had loved Ollie. And all through the years there was never a rumor that he had found another woman to take my place.

"I've always thought it was poetic justice that those barbarians who tried to destroy Ollie are now dead or forgotten, but Ollie vindicated himself. Over the years, as the more rational elements have regained control of the university, Ollie has finally—but quietly—been given the recognition he deserves for his research and was appointed director of La CIMA in San Cristobal. But he was never awarded the PhD..." Her voice trailed off.

Chip glanced at Lola's profile and saw a question in her expression. He waited and was rewarded when she spoke. Abruptly—but softly--changing the subject, she asked, "Did you say anything at all to Ollie about me?"

"Not a word," Chip said. "And now I'm thinking it's good that I didn't. That's for you to handle yourself—in person."

"*Gracias, don Chipotle.*"

CHAPTER TWENTY-EIGHT

The telling of Ollie's story—and her own—left Lola emotionally drained. Evoking thirty years of repressed feelings came with a price. Raw and exhausted, she lapsed into a trance-like stupor. Memories paraded through her semi-consciousness. Slumping back and down into the pickup seat, she drifted into a troubled sleep.

While Lola fought for sleep, Chip dealt with a rising tide of troubling thoughts of his own. *I've known Ollie for more than twenty years and I've never heard about UNAM denying him his doctorate. How could he have kept that a secret? Did Grandpa know? What would I do if that happened to me? Did Grandpa have any secrets hidden away? Does Mom have secrets I don't know about? Even me—how much am I hiding from the world? Is it necessary for the world to know everything about us? There's a lot I'd like to learn about my family. I can keep a secret.*

The trip to Chiapas was taking longer than he expected, but Chip refused to drive fast, especially with Lola in the truck. A healthy respect for the fast-moving flow of cars, trucks, and busses barreling in both directions kept the conscious part of his mind on the act of driving. Below the surface, however, his mind alternated from "rewind" to "fast forward," from Xochitle to Grandpa, from Dean Lambert to Mom, from Ollie to Sis. And into the stream of images, he injected subconscious sound-overs. *Xochi, I miss you...Grandpa, can you hear me?...Mom, Sis, I hope you are all right...Hold on...I'll do everything I can to find you...God, please help me...God, please protect them...What?... How did I bring God into this?... I haven't allowed God into my life for years... How did I stray so far from the God I used to have so much faith in?... Grandfather, I really don't know who I am anymore.*

Chip thought about pulling over to the shoulder of the road for a short siesta, but decided to push on. An hour later when Chip was again about to surrender to fatigue, Lola roused from her coma feeling surprisingly refreshed. Chip mumbled a line from one of his favorite poems, "...and miles to go before I sleep."

As if reading Chip's mind, Lola nudged his arm and suggested, "Why don't you let me drive for a while?"

"If you're sure you can drive this old buggy, I could use a breather. When we get to the next town, we'll make a pit stop and you'd better call your daughter and tell her we won't get there until morning."

After the rest stop, Chip and Lola switched off every hour in the driver's seat. Scorpy didn't seem to mind when Chip held the cage between his knees.

The trip south was one of contrasts. From state to state, sprawling modern cities gradually transformed into rural towns and villages, then populated areas became increasingly sparse and isolated in wide expanses of abundant vegetation.

The city of Puebla was like a wealthy suburb of Mexico City. The oil-rich state of Veracruz flaunted its recently acquired wealth with newly-paved highways.

The extreme poverty of Oaxaca was reflected in its crater-pocked roads. Although competing with Oaxaca for lowest rankings in economic indicators, Chiapas was making an attempt to keep its major highways patched and passable. Road crews were finding it impossible, however, to repair the highways as quickly as overloaded trucks and Army convoys tore them up.

Dropping sharply from a high plateau into the valley of the Grijalva River, both the temperature and the humidity rose steadily. In the morning twilight Chip and Lola saw the glow of city lights rising from Tuxtla Gutierrez. Lola felt the thrill of anticipation of new beginnings—a new life—stir within her. Although Chip was relieved at coming to the end of a long drive, he could not shake the uneasiness of entering a dark and foreboding world where evil, treachery, and danger lurked in ambush. But this was where he had grown up. *I'm ready for whatever comes*, he told himself. *I'm on my turf. I've got home field advantage.* Even Scorpy the toucan roused and squawked his delight at being back in the atmosphere of his natural habitat.

Entering Tuxtla, the modern-day capital of Chiapas, Chip avoided the traffic of *el centro*, the downtown business district, taking instead the *periférico*, the bypass road that skirted the city. Then, after crossing the mile-long bridge over the Grijalva River which flows into the Sumidero Canyon, with its sheer, vertical, thousand meter rock walls, Chip took the turn-off to Chiapa de Corzo. Squinting into her compact mirror, Lola competed with Scorpy in a preening process. Lola was now completely awake with the adrenaline of anticipation coursing through her system.

Passing the *parque* central, circling around the huge, brick kiosk in the shape of a crown, and squeezing between the closing mercado and an old convent church,

Chip followed Lola's directions down a narrow cobblestone street with colonial houses along the banks of the wide, muddy river. When they reached a large adobe house at the end of a rutted street, Leticia came running out to meet her mother with a chubby little girl tucked under one arm. Lola was out of the pickup before Chip could even set the emergency brake.

"*Hola* Leti! *Hola* Gordita!" Lola sang out, her arms flung wide. Hugs, kisses, and joyful chatter kept Lola busy while Chip unloaded her bags from the pickup. A crowd of neighborhood children gathered around Scorpy's cage on the sidewalk as he screeched and hopped up and down on his swinging perch. He enjoyed the attention and mimicked their squeals of laughter.

Chip was tired and hoped the obligatory round of introductions would not take long. Not wanting to interfere with Lola's family reunion, he wanted to slip away and find a hotel room in Tuxtla. Desperate for news, he wanted to be alone to make some phone calls. And he wanted to hear the sound of Xochi's voice. But, first things first.

Chip found himself being introduced to everyone around a cast-iron table in the center of the large, interior patio yard, most of which was covered by the outspread limbs of Flamboyant trees. Their branches, blanketed in a kaleidoscope of emerald green and splotches of neon scarlet, canopied the entire patio, providing needed shade from the burning afternoon suns. Lola and Leti herded everyone to pull up a cast-iron chair and crowd around the outdoor table to partake of a fruity *jamaica* drink. The sweet, reddish *bebida* closely matched the flame-colored flowers overhead.

Leti bubbled with joy, repeating her gratitude to Chip for bringing her mother to Chiapas and giving her a job. "Just last week," she said, "Nando and I were talking about how we could convince her to come live down here. Nando will be out in a minute. He's dying to meet you. He's been on the phone and the Internet all day making arrangements to ship a marimba to the music department at the University of Illinois."

As she was speaking, Nando came up beside her, grabbed her and gave her a peck on the cheek. "*Buenas noticias, mi amor*," he said, his face beaming. Then to Chip he said in English, "It's a pleasure to meet you, Professor Oatley. I'm Nando, Leticia's husband. I'm sure she has already expressed our thanks to you. I was just telling her I have more good news. Three more universities want to buy marimbas from us for their music departments. If there is any good side to the publicity Chiapas is getting, it's that people all over the world are learning about our folkloric Mayan culture, including its music. Today there is nothing more representative of *Chiapanecan* music than the marimba. I have a feeling that we're going be getting lots of orders from music departments and metropolitan symphony orchestras all over the world. We're changing the way the world does music," he grinned, paraphrasing a popular TV commercial.

"While Leti and her mother are catching up, let me give you a quick tour of our little marimba factory."

Chip followed Nando into a neatly kept workshop that smelled like a lumber yard for exotic woods. Nando noticed chip sniffing and enjoying the musky odor. Picking up a dark plank of wood, he said, "Marimba keys are made from a special hardwood tree that grows only in the Lacondon jungle. With the Zapatistas and the Army fighting for control of the transportation routes, we are finding it harder and harder to get the wood we need. Another problem is that a lot of illegal logging goes on in the jungle. We hope that the 'midnight tree suppliers' don't reach into our territory. "

As they walked among the marimbas in various degrees of completion, Nando volunteered his observations concerning the uprising in the highland forests. "On January 2, the day after the uprising began, I went to the Teran airport with a boxed-up marimba to ship to the University of Kansas. When I got there, the place was swarming with military troops. Fresh units were arriving and casualties were being flown out. Bundles of body bags were being unpacked, filled with dead soldiers, and laid out along the edges of the tarmac. I tried to make a quick count of the dead, but I soon lost count. I'm positive there were more than seven hundred. A few days later, I couldn't believe my ears when a government spokesman said that there were about one hundred casualties. Why would they lie to us?" he asked, not expecting Chip to answer.

When Chip and Nando walked back out onto the patio, Lola and Leti were setting the table with cool fresh fruits, bowls of hot pozole, a spicy soup made from pork and hominy, and a basketful of warm quesadillas, melted cheese in tortillas. Chip resigned himself to the fact that he was not going to be able to slip away soon, so he asked Nando to let him use the phone before eating. He let Ollie know he had arrived in Chiapas, but did not tell him that Lola was with him.

"Stay in Tuxtla tonight," Ollie told him. "I'll come down there tomorrow morning. I have to buy some supplies for La CIMA and I want to go see the governor in the afternoon. He's called a meeting of his senior officials and advisors to discuss the mission attack and kidnappings. I want you to go with me. I want you to hear it first-hand."

"Okay," Chip agreed, "I'll go to the immigration office in the morning and get the paperwork started to make me legal here. I'll meet you at the San Marcos cathedral at noon."

Chip's next call was to Xochi. She seemed happy to hear her dad's voice and prattled on about how she was doing fine at school and she was taking care of herself at home. The façade cracked a bit, though, when she asked how much longer she would have to wait before she could go to Chiapas. When Chip tried to assure her it wouldn't be long, Xochi wanted to believe him.

Back out at the breakfast table, Chip found himself answering a barrage of questions.

"Yes, my grandfather and my mother brought me to Chiapa de Corzo several times when I was a boy. I'm surprised at how it's grown into a big town."

"Yes," Leti said, "there are several museums here now, and many arts and crafts shops. Lacquer ware— especially lacquer masks—is a big thing these days. We've become a well-known tourist attraction. And, of course, it doesn't hurt that dozens of tour boats still go up and down the river through the Cañon de Sumidero every day."

"My grandfather told me the legend of the Indians who resisted the Spanish conquest here," Chip said. "After years of bloody fighting, they realized that they could not hold out much longer, but still refused to surrender. So, rather than live as a defeated people subject to torture and slavery, they all decided to fling themselves from the top of the canyon's rock walls and die in the river waters below."

"We still tell that story to our children," Nando said seriously. "Indian resistance is not a modern phenomenon."

"When you came here as a boy, did you take a boat trip down the river through the canyon?" Lola asked Chip.

Before attempting to answer the question, Chip looked around to make sure that there were no children near enough to hear his story. He wasn't sure that he really wanted to tell his story, even to adults, especially to some near-strangers. Reluctantly, he opened up and bared an emotional scar from the past.

"I was hoping you wouldn't ask that," Chip said, "but I'll tell you about my trip down the river. I don't remember why, but my sister and I came here with my grandfather and my mother when I was about nine years old. I think my grandfather was here for a conference with some other missionaries. One morning I went exploring along the river banks where I met a boy about my same age. His name was Chel and he was an Indian. I could speak enough of his language that we could understand each other. He had made a small raft from tree limbs and used it mostly for fishing in the deeper waters. Sometimes he would paddle out to the little islands in the middle of the river. The next day he invited me to take a trip with him down the river on his raft. I got permission from my mother, packed a lunch, and we set out. When we had been drifting with the current for about an hour, a motor boat full of drunken young men came speeding down the river and nearly hit us. The wake of their boat rocked our raft so much that Chel fell into the water. He was a good swimmer and was swimming back to the raft when the boat turned around and came back toward us. 'It's only an Indian kid,' someone yelled from the boat. 'Run him over,' someone else said. And they did. They ran the boat right over Chel, cutting him up badly with the propeller of the outboard motor. Then they sped away. I tried to save Chel, but I wasn't strong enough to get him back on the raft. I was holding onto the raft with one hand, and holding on to Chel with the other. I will never forget the look in his eyes when he asked me, 'Why?' and then he died. I finally had to let him go and let him drift down the river. I maneuvered over to the shore, let the raft go, and watched it follow Chel until it was out of sight, then walked back to town. My grandfather and I did everything possible to find Chel's family to let them know, but we never found anyone who knew him. To this day, I try not to think about that river. I try to forget those beseeching eyes, and I try to answer that haunting question, 'Why?' And I still haven't found a satisfactory answer."

Lola came to Chip's side, placed a motherly arm around him and said, "Chip, I used to ask myself that same question when Ollie was ripped out of my life. I'm going to give you a bit of advice. Let it go. If you don't, you'll go crazy."

CHAPTER TWENTY-NINE

Lola, Nando, and Leti did their best to persuade Chip to stay the night in one of their spare bedrooms, but he insisted on going to Tuxtla. When it was clear that Chip was going to find a hotel, Nando told him that the Hotel Vagabundo, right in the middle of downtown, had a good reputation, and gave him the address.

As they walked out to the street where Chip had parked the pickup, Nando asked discretely if he had any news of his grandfather or his mother and sister.

"At first," Chip said, "we heard that my grandfather had been killed, but later there were reports that a curandera had attended to his wounds and then somehow managed to sneak him off somewhere. At this point, we don't know where he is, and we don't know if he is still alive. Ollie believes my grandfather is recuperating in some jungle cave. If he had died, word would have gotten out. And if he dies tomorrow, the news will spread through every Indian village within hours. Ollie knows the Indian ways."

"Well, I hope he is alive and well," said Nando, "but if he should die and there is a memorial service for him, I will personally put together the biggest and best marimba band this state has ever seen."

Chip was moved and gave Nando an abrazo. *"Gracias, amigo. Muy amable,* that's very kind of you," he whispered, then turned to open his pickup truck. He drove off without another word.

Back in Tuxtla, Chip missed a turn and found himself at a stoplight, tired and lost. In the lane beside him was an empty taxi. Honking his horn, Chip got the taxi driver's attention.

"Donde está el hotel Vagabundo?" Chip shouted out his window.

*"Sigame,*follow me," the driver yelled back and sped away.

Chip followed the taxi several miles and was thankful when it finally drove straight into the underground garage of the Vagabundo Hotel. He took a ticket from the attendant and parked in the space pointed out for him. The *taxista* pulled into an empty spot, jumped out and began helping Chip with his bags.

Once in the lobby, the taxi driver went behind the check-in counter and woke up the clerk. *"Primo!* Give this man a good room!" he ordered. Then, turning to Chip, he explained, "This is my cousin. He'll take care of you."

After the driver had helped carry the bags to the room, Chip pulled out his wallet to give him a tip, but the *taxista* refused. "I'm through driving for the night, but I'd appreciate it if you'd buy me a drink or two at the bar. Besides, I want to practice my English."

"You got it," Chip said. "I'll meet you out on the patio bar in fifteen minutes. Have a shot of tequila waiting for me." He grinned slightly. "And not any of that cheap, rot-gut stuff like they usually serve to unsuspecting gringos."

"You got it!" the driver replied.

As soon as Chip found his way to the Nucú Cantina, the patio bar, the taxi driver escorted him to a table near the bar. A barmaid had two shots of tequila on the table before they sat down.

The taxi driver, a young, robust man in his mid-twenties, introduced himself. "I am called Valdo," he said. "And I would like you to meet my friends. The bartender's name is Ignacio, but we call him Nacho. I'm sorry I don't know the waitress's name, but we all call her Chis because she is *chismosa*. She knows all the gossip about every guest in the hotel. Soon she will know everything about you, so be careful what you say to her."

Apparently it was a slow night at the bar; it was almost empty. It didn't require any persuasion to get Macho and Chis to accept Chip's invitation to get a drink and join him and Valdo at the table. Chip introduced himself ordered another round of drinks for his three new acquaintances. Soon Chip had them chatting like old friends. He was especially interested in pumping Chis for gossip from the jungle highlands. The liquor loosened her up and she liked to talk. Valdo hadn't exaggerated when he said she knew it all. Her gossip was not always coherent and cohesive, but Chip took her bits and pieces and strung them together.

"My uncle who is a mechanic says that every day there are more military convoys arriving...big troop buildups...non-military trucks are being hired to haul in supplies, especially food for the troops... My cousin who is a priest says that the Indian villages are not getting food...they are being starved out...there's a silent war being waged against the Indians...a handful of Indians are being killed every day...almost none of the killings are being reported by the media...it's a real guerrilla war...the army officers who come in here are saying that the Indians are fighting back...some say at least a dozen soldiers are found dead every day...the Zapatistas are getting help from international sympathizers ... sophisticated communications equipment is coming in from Italian sources by way of Guatemala ... reports from everywhere that the Catholic church is involved, maybe even the major player in the game...some are saying that Bishop Samuel Ruiz is acting as the intermediary for arms dealers...the business people are saying that even the banks are involved..."

It was the first time Chip had heard most of these rumors. Some he thought were believable, others seemed incredible. *Could there be any truth to those allegations?*

"Do you really think the banks are involved?" Chip asked.

"All I can say," Valdo interjected," is that while a lot of other businesses were being robbed, looted, and burned, banks kept their doors open for business as usual. Normally, when there is any trouble, the banks are the first to close and lock their doors."

When Chip realized that there was no gossip about missionaries or kidnappings, he excused himself, thanked the trio for their company, and started for his room.

"I'll help you tomorrow morning," Valdo said.

"How's that?" Chip asked.

"You're going to need me to get you through immigration's red tape."

"This could be the beginning of a great relationship," Chip grinned. "*Nos vemos. Hasta mañana.* See you in the morning."

CHAPTER THIRTY

Both Chip and Valdo were red-eyed when they met in the lobby of the Vagabundo at 7:30 the next morning.

"Why so early?" Chip asked. "No government office is open at this hour."

"We need to have some *menudo al diablo* before we do battle with government bureaucracy. I'll take you to a place where their *al diablo* is hotter than the devil."

"Just what I need," Chip said, "but I don't care if it builds my confidence. If it'll rid the cobwebs from my brain and clear my vision, I'll eat a bucket of cow stomach."

"The place is just down the street. It's a hole in the wall and doesn't have any fancy furnishings, but every *taxista* in town eats there, so it's gotta be good. And it's only a few block from *la migra*, the immigration office. So let's walk."

Chip was not disappointed in the menudo *al diablo*. "Believe it or not," he said to Valdo, "I do feel somewhat fortified of spirit."

"If that means what I think it means," Valdo relpied, "you're going to need all the 'spirit' you can get when you deal with Rita this morning."

"Who is Rita?" Chip asked.

"Rita is an old maid school teacher who is somehow related to the governor. He used his political influence to get her appointed as chief of the immigration office for this state. The salary is low, but she has learned how to gouge foreigners who come to her office for work permits. I watched her in action as she scalped two university professors from Canada. I should have known she had mastered the art of using bureaucracy to her advantage."

"Then you knew her before she became *la jefa de la migra?*"

"Oh, yes," Valdo said. "She was my *maldita* high school math teacher."

"I'm ready to do battle, now," Chip said. "Let's go meet the enemy."

When Chip and Valdo entered the immigration office, the air was heavy with stale cigarette smoke. Señora Rita Perra stood beside her desk behind the counter. She held a black coffee mug in her left hand and with her right hand was lighting an unfiltered cigarette which dangled from her smeared red lips.

"*Muy Buenos dias, Señorita,*" Valdo began, but was cut off before he could continue.

"I am not *señorita*, young man. I am *señora*! I'm sure you are old enough to know the difference."

"*Por supuesto,* of course," Valdo answered sweetly and unruffled. "*Señora,* I'm here to assist Professor Oatley obtain the necessary *permisos* to work here. He is a *norteamericano* and will be working under contract with UNAM's research center called La CIMA in San Cristóbal. If you will be so kind as to provide the forms needed for the *trámite,* I will assist Mr. Oatley in initiating the application process."

Rita sneered and said, "Do I look like an illiterate idiot? I know what La CIMA is. And I am not impressed by pompous professors.

"Señor Oatley, if you will please provide me three copies of your passport and your employment contract, we can get started. But I want to make it very clear that your application will be processed in the same manner as any other applicant. You will not receive any special treatment or consideration. Do you understand?"

"*Sí, señora*," Chip answered respectfully.

"Give me your passport and contract," Valdo said. "I'll run and make the copies."

"Relax, Valdo," Chip said, putting his hand on his arm. "I anticipated this. I've got six copies of everything right here in my briefcase." He took the copies out and placed them on the counter.

Rita took the copies and handed Chip a stack of forms to fill out. Chip and Valdo spent the next hour completing the paperwork. When they had finished, Chip went back to the counter and politely asked Rita if she would check to see that he had given all the required information.

Rita glanced at the forms, pulled several aside and said, "These forms must be signed by your employer, Mr. Oatley. And here are three more forms that must be completed. And I will need copies of your driver's license and the rental agreement for the place where you will be living."

Chip recognized the bureaucratic run around, but couldn't be sure if he was if the "supporting documentation" was really necessary, or if a discrete fifty-peso *mordida* would expedite the process.

Rita picked up her purse and was headed toward the door for her mid-morning snack when Valdo whispered in Chip's ear.

"Señora Rita," Chip called out just before her back disappeared into the back hallway, "before you go, I'd like to see some of the *recuerdos* you have in that basket. Are they for sale?"

Rita stopped in her tracks, turned, and actually smiled. She walked back behind the counter, picked up the basket and brought it to where Chip was standing. "They're very economical and they make wonderful gifts."

Bingo, Chip said to himself. "You're absolutely right. And they are so colorful. I'll take the whole basket full. In fact, if you'll sell it to me, I want to buy the basket, too."

As she passed in front of Valdo, she said politely, "His work papers will be ready this afternoon."

"*Momento, por favor*," Valdo said respectfully, and whispered in her ear.

Rita smiled and went back to her desk. Setting her purse down, she said, "I will be glad to give your *trámite* special attention. Your papers will be ready in about an hour."

Valdo grabbed Chip by the elbow and pushed him out the door.

"What did you say to her?" Chip demanded, grinning at Valdo.

"I told her you are here on a special assignment for the governor. You are helping to find the governor's missing niece."

"Is that all?"

"I also promised we would bring her an assortment of *pan dulce*, the Mexican sweet breads and a liter of *café de olla*, the coffee we make in a large pot with lots of sugar and flavored with shavings of cinnamon bark."

"We all have our price," Chip said, then asked, "Why didn't you give her that line about the governor when we first got here?"

"I would have— if I had thought of it earlier."

CHAPTER THIRTY-ONE

While waiting for the wheels of the immigration office to grind out its paperwork, Valdo guided Chip to the landmark Café Avenida where the majority of customers are grizzled old men who sit around metal game tables and reminisce over freshly ground and brewed coffee.

This place is famous," Valdo told Chip, "for the aroma of roasting coffee beans reaching out onto the sidewalk, grabbing those who pass by, and drawing them into the open-bay storefront."

"With good reason," Chip answered. "Chiapas has some of the world's best coffee. I remember coming to Tuxtla when I was just a boy. Even then, the smell of roasting coffee beans was so rich I wanted to eat them."

Once inside, Valdo ordered the house espresso for both of them. Chip asked the old waiter with a long, white apron to prepare four, one-kilo bags of the best coffee to be ready when they finished their *exprés*. The old waiter smiled and discreetly tucked his ten-peso *propina* under his apron. It occurred to Chip that the man probably depended on such tips for his livelihood.

After Valdo had sipped his coffee, he told Chip he needed to get back to his taxi. He assured Chip that he and his friends at the Nucú Cantina would keep their ears open for any news of the kidnappings. Chip thanked him and gave him a generous *propina*.

"Thanks," Valdo said, "I go get a wagon load of *pan dulce* and a gallon of coffee for the old bag."

"Here's another fifty pesos," Chip mumbled and laughed.

Just before noon, Chip returned to the immigration office and picked up the packet of documents granting him permission to work and pay taxes in Chiapas. Then following Valdo's directions to the Zocaló, the main plaza, he walked to the rear of the cathedral and found Ollie seated on a park bench, basking in the warm sunshine. Ollie's hair was whiter than he remembered, and he had gained a few pounds.

Ollie stood and greeted Chip warmly and consolingly. He sincerely shared Chip's concern for the missionary's disappearance and the taking of the women from the Mission Station. As he led Chip to the governor's conference room, he told Chip that there had been more unofficial reports that his grandfather was being kept alive in a cave, but was in serious condition.

"Where are these reports coming from?" Chip asked. "Are the sources credible?"

"My driver at La CIMA has relatives all through the jungle," Ollie said. "His sources are seldom wrong."

The governor's conference room was actually a small auditorium with a slightly raised platform at one end. A dozen chairs were arranged in a semicircle behind a slim wooden podium. When Chip and Ollie arrived, less than a quarter of the one-hundred audience seats were filled and two administrative aides were on the stage waiting for the governor. When he saw Chip and Ollie enter the room, one of aides motioned them to come and sit on the front row. Immediately after they took their seats, a young military officer opened a side door and the governor strode in. Before he reached the podium, a hush fell over the room. With a curt *"Buenas tardes,"* the meeting was called to order. There were no ceremonial preliminaries or wordy introductions. The governor was clearly not in the mood for humor or trivia.

"Caballeros, gentlemen," he began, "I am not pleased with the turn of events in this state. The attack on the Baptist Mission Station, the violence done to the missionary, and the taking of women hostages are all actions of cowardice that will not be tolerated. As you are aware, I am deeply angry and distressed by this situation, not only because it is my official duty to ensure safety and security for the citizens of this state, but also for personal reasons. Not just because I have known the missionary and his family for many years and consider them my friends, but as you know, my niece was working as a nurse at the Mission Station, and she is one of the kidnapped women. I assure you, I will not rest until this situation is resolved. May God have mercy on anyone who harms those women."

The governor stepped down from the stage and stood beside Chip. After placing a patronizing hand on Chip's shoulder, he turned and stepped back up onto the stage and took his seat of honor. In quick order, various members of the governor's inner council came to the podium to brief the gathering on any new developments in the case. When they all had reported they had no new information, the governor stood up again. His fists were clinched and displeasure radiated from his reddened face.

"I have placed a good sum of my personal fortune," the governor fumed, "at your disposal to investigate this matter. If you cannot get results, I will be forced to turn this over to the federal police and the military. I had hoped that wouldn't be necessary. I will give you three days more. If you have not uncovered the culprits by that time, most of you will be looking for new employment. Now, get out of here and do your jobs."

Except for Chip, Ollie, and the governor, the room emptied in less than a minute.

When they were alone, the governor spoke emotionally to Chip and Ollie. "Yesterday I received a call from the President of Mexico. He had just spoken with the American ambassador, who was relaying the concerns of the President of the United States. The President of The United States, it seems, is concerned about Baptist missionaries. And Baptists constitute a block of at least twenty million voters in the United States. No president can afford to lose that support group. If I cannot control this situation, and if I allow it to escalate into a negative 'international incident,' I will lose the favor of my President. Of course I assured the President that I will do what's best for this state and whatever is in the nation's best interest. But, I am telling you personally, it is not pressure from the president of my country or your country that motivates me most in this matter; it is my heart that I am listening to. Even if I destroy my political career, I will stop at nothing to save my family and friends. I will not rest until we avenge this crime."

Chip took the governor's hand and said, "Yes, the bastard's will pay, but don't do anything rash. I want my mother and my sister back alive."

CHAPTER THIRTY-TWO

C hip and Ollie left the governor's office planning to retrieve Chip's pickup truck from the Vagabundo Hotel and go directly to San Cristóbal. Ollie's driver had already left with a van full of supplies. But before they could get out of the governor's conference room, a young aide came to them with a message. "The governor wanted you two to be his guests for lunch at the Las Delfilapa seafood restaurant, but some pressing matters have come up. He asks that you go ahead and enjoy yourselves, on him. His secretary will call and arrange for the tab to be paid." The aide handed them a *croquis*, a crude, hand-drawn map showing how to get to Delfilapa. Chip and Ollie looked at each other, shrugged, and accepted the map.

When Chip and Ollie arrived at the Las Delfilapa, the owner Luis Mariscal was on the front step waiting.

"The governor's secretary didn't waste any time making that call," Ollie remarked.

"Yeah," Chip responded, "Looks like we're going to get the VIP treatment."

"Well, I'm not going to object. I'll just submit to their fawning and allow them to pamper me. I don't see any harm in that, do you?"

"Of course not," Chip answered, grinning, "especially when the governor is paying the bill."

Luis personally escorted them in a booth away from the noise of the kitchen and near enough to watch and hear the three-marimba band, but not close enough to be overwhelmed by the music.

"You are my guests," Luis said as he seated them. "Please excuse me. I'll be right back." Before he left the table, two *meseros* materialized, spreading a fresh blue-and-white linen tablecloth, placing an array of silverware and crystal, appetizer dishes, and the obligatory basket of warm *totopos*, triangle wedges of crispy fried corn tortillas, and a bowl of homemade salsa—traditional Mexican chip-and-dip.

"Maybe you were wrong about the governor paying for this," Chip said. "I'm guessing that Luis is astute enough to know that he might need a favor from the governor someday, so he probably told the governor to forget about paying the tab."

"He's also smart enough to know that the governor will conveniently forget to pay anyway," Ollie said with a chuckle. "So he's just turning a small financial loss into a substantial political gain."

One waiter filled the water glasses. Another brought a pitcher of the house *sangria*, a grape-flavored wine punch with freshly chopped apples and thin slices of orange and lime floating on the top. He filled two glasses, then left the pitcher on the table. Yet another waiter brought them each a shrimp cocktail. Then Luis returned with a large silver tray loaded with raw oysters on the half shell.

Without being invited, or asking for permission, Luis slid into the booth beside Chip, picked up an oyster, squeezed lime juice over it, splashed it with chipotle cocktail sauce, then slurped the shucked oyster from its barnacled shell into his mouth. A gesture of his hand conveyed the invitation for Chip and Ollie to join him in this tasty treat. As they each extracted a shell from the shaved ice, Luis introduced himself and began to chat like an old friend. "I'm sorry to hear about the attack on the mission and the kidnapping of your mother and sister," he said to Chip. "I hope your grandfather will recover from his wounds, and that your family members will be rescued soon."

"You seem to know a lot about my situation," Chip said. "Has the governor given you most of the details?"

"I'm sure the governor didn't tell you," Luis replied, "but the truth is that in this case, he has gotten most of his information from me."

"How is that?" Ollie interjected, not certain whether to believe Luis.

"To give you a bit of my history, my father started this business with one small fishing boat on the coast not far from Tapachula. In fact, he opened our first *mariscos*, seafood, restaurant in Tapachula about sixteen years ago. We have grown into a chain of twelve locations throughout Chiapas, and we are now wholesaling seafood to twenty-eight states throughout the Republic of Mexico. Seventy-two of our trucks are on the highways of Mexico every day. Our truckers talk to truckers who talk to truckers. This truckers' grapevine hauls in much information about many places and many people.

Luis stopped for a moment letting his words sink in, then looked directly at Chip and continued, "We heard about the attack on the Mission Station the day it happened. We also heard about a professor of linguistics who was mugged in Nuevo Laredo, and about how he came to be known as '*don* Chipotle.' Surely you recall two talkative truckers known as Tom and Gerry?' They're making you famous."

With a quick gesture indicating they should enjoy their meal, Luis slipped out of the booth and began to circulate through the crowd, working the now-full dining room. Ollie and Chip watched as he shook hands, hugged friends, slapped backs, and brushed ladies' cheeks with welcoming kisses, all with the skill of an experienced politician campaigning for office.

Within moments an enormous platter bearing a large red fish stuffed with shrimp, crab, scallops, and baked clams arrived at the table. As if on cue, at the precise moment when they could eat no more, Luis reappeared to ask if they would like dessert. When they declined, Luis slid back into the booth and ordered strong black coffee for the three of them.

"How is it that you speak English so well?" Chip asked Luis.

"I started taking English lesson after school when I was six years old," Luis replied. "And then I went to Baton Rouge, Louisiana, as an exchange student for my junior year in high school. For ten months I lived with a family of three boys and two girls. One of the boys was my age, so we were in the same classes at school. And we were both on the junior varsity basketball team. So I learned a lot about the English language and American life that they don't teach you in the classroom."

"What did the parents do for a living?" Chip asked.

"The father was retired from the military. He had been a Master Sergeant in the Army, and had been stationed all over the world. In fact, his wife was Korean. They met when he was assigned there after he had spent a tour in Vietnam."

Chip did not want to talk about Vietnam so he quickly changed the subject. "Did you learn to like Cajun food?"

"I fell in love with it at first bite," Luis said. "My favorite is their gumbo made with okra. I have an idea that my customers would like a special Mexican gumbo made with shrimp and okra. What do you think? Of course, I would have to find an okra supplier. As far as I know, nobody grows okra here in Chiapas."

"Have you ever had okra dipped in cornmeal batter and fried in a skillet?" Chip asked. "It's a common dish in Oklahoma. Maybe I can hook you up an okra farmer there. Luis handed Chip one of his business cards and said, "I'd appreciate any lead you could give me. I've been trying to get one of the chili growers out in Villaflores to experiment with a small crop of okra. It might work out to be a valuable cash crop, but so far, no one is willing to try it."

"There's a trucker they call *El Mapache*, the raccoon," Chip suggested. "Maybe you're aware that I hitched a ride with him outside Nuevo Laredo. He grows and hauls jalapeños out of Villaflores. He's a pretty enterprising guy—he might be interested in growing a few *hectareas* of okra for you."

"How can I contact him?" Luis asked with great interest.

"You said you have truckers who talk to truckers. He won't be hard to find."

"Please excuse us, Luis," Ollie broke in. "We must return to San Cristóbal. I need to see if there is any news from my field workers."

"I understand," Luis said. "Please let me know if you hear anything." His voice cracked slightly and his eyes misted over.

Surprised at Luis' sudden display of emotion he mistook as anger, Chip asked, "Have any of your trucks been hijacked in the conflict area? Have any of your drivers been hurt?"

"I could deal with something like that," Luis said.
"But they have taken something much more precious
from me. They have taken my Teri."

"Are you talking about Teresa—the Mission Station
nurse?" Ollie asked. "Are you related to her?"

"Not yet." Luis whispered. "I love her very much. She
is my fiancée. We were making plans to be married this
summer. Please, help me find her." He abruptly stood up
and walked toward the kitchen.

CHAPTER THIRTY-THREE

It was late afternoon when Chip drove Ollie from Tuxtla to San Cristóbal. Passing by Chiapa de Corzo, Chip wondered when, where, and how Lola was going to make her grand entrance back into Ollie's life. It would be a "must see" show. Even so, he restrained himself from letting the cat out of the bag, so he shut the image from his mind and began talking to Ollie on another subject .

"Ollie, when I was a boy here in Chiapas, groups of *perigrinos*, pilgrims, would gather in Chiapa de Corzo on New Year's Eve. After a short mass in the Catholic Church in the early evening, the people—men, women, and children—would walk up the mountainside all the way to the cathedral in San Cristóbal. They walked all night and into the next day. Do people still follow that tradition today?"

"Only a few people still keep that tradition alive, Chip. Young people are too busy, or have invitations to *fiestas del año Nuevo*. Some just don't see any point in hiking up a mountain. And the older folks don't know how to articulate the mystical experience they find in pushing their bodies to the limit through a long night, then witnessing the dawn of a new day on the mountain top."

"The articulation sounds pretty easy when you say it," Chip said, laughing out loud. "And you're right. My grandfather took me on one of those pilgrimages when I was twelve years old. I still remember the elation I felt when we reached the top of the mountain. It was a religious experience.

"I've been thinking, when Xochi—that's my daughter—comes down here this summer, I'm going to take her on a trek up that mountain. I know it won't be New Year's Eve, but it'll be a special holiday she'll never forget.

"I need to call her as soon as we get to your house."

****

As soon as Chip and Ollie had unloaded the pickup into Ollie's living room, Chip tried to call Xochi. When there was no answer, Chip called Dean Lambert's office. Gretchen took the call.

"Where've you been?" she demanded. "I've been trying to reach you all day at La CIMA. Nobody knew where you were." There was urgency in her voice.

"I've been in Tuxtla with Ollie Krahn, the director of La CIMA, Chip said, trying to keep the defensive note out of his voice. "We met with the state governor. We just now arrived in San Cristóbal. Why? What's going on? Is something wrong?"

"Anything wrong?" she mimicked. "You bet there is. Honey Bee—Xochi—or whatever her name is now, called me this morning. I could tell she had been crying. She said her mother didn't come home last night, and still wasn't home this morning. I told her to wait where she was and I would be right over.

"Well, when I got there, Marlene's mother and father were there and they were packing up all of Honey Bee's things. When I asked what was going on, they said it was none of my business, but they were her grandparents and they were taking her back to El Paso with them. They said Marlene had called them and told them that you had gone to Chiapas and that she couldn't take care of a child anymore."

"Tell me it isn't so. Please say they didn't take her," Chip moaned.

"I did everything I could to stop them. I think old preacher man Moffett was scared when I threw him up against the wall and threatened to knock his teeth out. That's when his wife said she was going to call the police. Well, I backed off and asked them to at least wait until I could contact you. But they didn't want to talk to you or anybody else. Honey Bee was crying her eyes out, but they dragged her into their car and took off.

"I told Dean Lambert what happened. He called the police, but they're not going to get involved in what they called 'a family affair,' especially with a prominent Baptist minister. As you know, the Chief of Police is a Baptist deacon."

It took a moment for Chip to catch his breath. His immediate reaction was to see how quickly he could catch a plane and fly back to Oklahoma. To Gretchen, he said, "See if there is any way I can call Xochi. If you can get through to her, tell her to try to get along with her grandparents and I'll do my best to get her down here to Chiapas as soon as I can. But be sure not to mention that to her grandparents. By the way, where is the dean now?"

"He's on the other line with Rainwater Pharms. They're concerned that you haven't made contact with Ted Cravens since you were resurrected from the dead. What are you waiting for?"

CHAPTER THIRTY-FOUR

The next morning, after he finished piling his bags and boxes in Ollie's guest room, Chip washed up quickly and walked back down the hall to the kitchen where he found Ollie on the phone with his driver, Chete, instructing him to wash and service Chip's pickup. "If it needs a tune-up, do it. If it needs new tires, put them on. And then fill it up with gas. Do whatever you would do for my vehicle." Hanging up, Ollie grunted a "good morning" and headed to change clothes.

Obliged to follow Ollie's morning routine, Chip soon realized he had returned to Chiapas time—and Chiapas ways. There was no alarm clock, no early morning scramble to eat a quick breakfast and beat the rush hour traffic. There was no smell of frying eggs and bacon; no biscuits baking in the oven. The only thing Chip recognized as a "breakfast smell" was the rich aroma of coffee from a neighbor's kitchen. Without waiting for Ollie, he rummaged through several cupboards until he remembered to look in the oven, where he found a one-quart sauce pan. Like most other people in Chiapas, Ollie didn't use his oven for baking; that would only add heat to an already warm house. Instead, the oven was just another storage cabinet for pots and pans.

Filling the pan with water, he set it on the gas stove to boil. Into a *calcetín*, a "sock" on a circular wire mount, he measured out a half-cup of coffee grounds. When the water came to a boil, he lowered the coffee sock down into it until the water turned dark brown and the aroma filled the house. It brought Ollie out from his bedroom with an empty coffee mug in his hand. It also lured in Ollie's driver Chete who had come to get Chip's truck. The chore of servicing the truck could wait.

After introducing Chete and Chip to each other, Ollie took delight in explaining the origins of their names—Chete and Chipotle. "Chete's real name is Chext, but when he was a young man, he acquired a taste for *mescal*, the Mexican version of 'white lightning,' and frequently went on a *borrachera*, a binge of drunkenness, picking machete fights, and acquired the nickname 'Chete.' He has a few nasty scars to remind him. I'd say he's lucky he lived through that suicidal phase of his life. He doesn't drink much anymore, but he hasn't forgotten how to use a machete. You should see him peel and slice a pineapple."

After all three had enjoyed their first cup of morning coffee, Chete drove them to the La CIMA compound. On the way he stopped at Ollie's favorite taco stand and purchased a dozen *tacos de canasta*, soft, steaming hot *machaca* tacos, wrapped in cloth and usually carried in a basket. These shredded beef tacos would serve as breakfast at the 10 o'clock break.

Upon their arrival at La CIMA, Ollie escorted Chip on a tour of each office and introduced him to the research "investigators" as well as the administrative staff. In the library, he introduced Lydia Molina, the Chief Librarian, and then Ramona Ramos, an archivist who spent most of her time on loan to the governmental agency charged with salvaging the state and church records now stored in the basement tunnels under the cathedral. Ollie informed Ramona that she was to make time in her schedule to show Chip around. She was also to act as his "sponsor," help him find a place to live, get his utilities turned on, set up a bank account, and anything else that would make his transition smooth and problem-free.

Chip found both of these young women outwardly attractive, but their personalities, even on brief first impression, vastly different. Ollie himself seemed warmer when speaking to Ramona, even though she was clearly not pleased with her added responsibilities for assisting Chip. Although her words indicated she would do as she was told, her expression made it obvious that she was being imposed upon. Lydia, In contrast, Lydia's reaction could only be called flirtatious. Even as Ramona and Ollie were concluding their arrangements, she beckoned Chip to follow her for a tour of the library moving her hips seductively as she led him deep into the stacks. But when they returned to the front desk where Ollie and Ramona were waiting, Lydia's smile was gone. Her attempts to engage Chip in something more than dusty tomes had been turned down. Ollie was unable to keep a small satisfied smile off his face, as he had a good idea what had happened, even if he didn't know the particulars.

The charged atmosphere in the library was heightened further when Chip informed Ramona he wanted to get started immediately on the search for an house. Then, to Lydia's further dismay, he asked Ramona if he could take her to lunch. If Lydia had known what Chip had on his mind, she wouldn't have bothered pouting. Chip had recognized immediately that Ramona was Mapache's daughter, and he figured a nice lunch might ease her into telling him what she knew about where the Mayan manuscripts were hidden.

Chip was distracted for an instant, remembering that he still hadn't spoken to Ollie about this mysterious collection of Mayan writings—and the possible existence of another ancient "codex" that went with it. He was jerked back to his immediate surroundings when Lydia tossed a small stack of library loan request forms to him and said coolly, "Make sure you fill these out in triplicate if you need anything from this library."

And if you ever need some company on a Friday night, you handsome young stud, you'll find that Ramona's not any fun, Lydia muttered to herself as Olli, Chip and Ramona walked out the door. *You just don't know what you're missing.*

CHAPTER THIRTY-FIVE

Upon leaving the library, Ramona said she needed to go to the cathedral and let her supervisor know that she would be busy for a few days. Coolly she took her leave and politely declined Chip's invitation to lunch, so Ollie and Chip returned to the La CIMA compound office.

"What seems to be Mona's problem?" Chip asked. "Did I say something wrong?"

"No," said Ollie. "Her husband left her a few years ago. She almost went crazy, but finally pulled herself together and found this job. She's been a man-hater ever since. I guess you can't blame her."

Back in the office, Ollie found his secretary Corina sitting at her desk with her face in her hands. She was sobbing into a handkerchief. When she saw Ollie, she blurted out, "I'm sorry, Ollie. I'm so sorry!"

"What are you talking about, Corina?" Ollie demanded.

"I couldn't stop them. They just went right in to your office." She sobbed again.

Ollie went into his office and saw that it had been ransacked. The desk drawers and file cabinets were open and papers were scattered everywhere. Ollie froze in his tracks. His face paled as his mind flashed back to 1968. His lips trembled as he sank to his knees. "Not again," he said as he fell to the floor. The stress was too much for his system.

When the word reached Chete, he came running in with his sharpened machete at the ready. Chip calmed him down and recruited him to help get Ollie back to his house.

As they tucked Ollie into his own bed, he was talking incoherently. Chete disappeared, but was back in a few minutes with Ramona and a small bag of brown powder. She mixed it with water and carefully spooned it into Ollie's mouth. Within moments Ollie was sleeping soundly.

Chip asked Ramona what the medicine was, but she was vague and elusive. When Chip pressured her for an answer, she would only say that it was an herbal *receta*, a recipe or prescription, from a tribal curandera.

"Do you know this medicine woman?" Chip asked.

"I should," Ramona snarled as he glared at him. "She's my grandmother.

****

Chip went to Ollie's study and closed the door. He sighed in relief when he got through to Lola on the first try. When he explained what happened and that Ollie may have had a mild stroke, she cut him off.

"Say no more, Chip. Nando is right here. He'll drive me up there. I'll stay by Ollie's side and nurse him back to health. What's the address? Tell me how to get there."

CHAPTER THIRTY-SIX

Ted Cravens wasted no time going to Chiapas when he learned that Chip was alive. Using the Rainwater Pharms corporate jet, it didn't take long to get to San Cristóbal. Having visited this colonial city before, he knew his way around. His fluency in Spanish and a pocket full of pesos helped him learn much about La CIMA in a short time. Realizing that Chip would be relying heavily on the library's research services, he took a taxi to the La CIMA compound. He walked into the library and posed as a visiting scholar and found exactly what he needed in the person of Lydia Molina, who wrongly assumed her flirtations were having the effects she desired; she had no idea she was the one being seduced for a specific mission. Ted's invitation to an evening of fine dining—and whatever that might lead to was quickly accepted.

****

When Ted picked up Lydia, it was just before 8 p.m., still a little early for a Chiapas dinner. Glad the traffic was heavy and slow, Ted used the drive to ask Lydia several pertinent questions about her gastronomical tastes. His suspicions were confirmed that she was not a connoisseur of fine dining: a pizza and a bottle of cheap wine would probably suffice, but he directed the driver to El Restaurante Paris-Mexico, where he could order a passable French dish and Lydia could have a well-done steak. She seemed pleased at his choice.

Two margaritas with appetizers, a bottle of wine with the meal, and a snifter of cognac afterward had their desired effect on Lydia. Ted's flash of *dinero*, a roll of currency too big for a money clip, wasn't lost on her either. She melted in his hands.

"Lydia," he said smoothly over dessert, "I'm a sociologist. But I'm more than that. I'm also a businessman—a very successful businessman."

"What kind of business are you—" She cut herself off in mid-sentence, clearly regretting her indiscretion.

"It's okay," he said quickly, patting her hand. "I also do some research for a large pharmaceutical company that wants to contribute to the world of medicine by developing new drugs from traditional herbal cures. But there are some people who think we're robbing the *curanderos* of their intellectual property. I'm sure you can see how crazy that is, can't you?"

"Why would anyone want to keep that knowledge from the world?" she asked.

"Maybe it's a business tactic," he answered. "Maybe it's just one company trying to keep the other companies from profiting the herbal knowledge."

Ted leaned closer and spoke in hushed, conspiratorial tones. "I'm sure you've met the new linguist who just arrived at La CIMA. His name's Oatley. Charles Oatley. His nickname is Chip, but some people are calling him Chipotle now."

"I met him yesterday," Lydia said, pulling back and frowning.

"I don't know if you are aware, but his salary is being paid by a big drug company to keep my company from getting what we want," Ted lied. "So, I'd like to stop him from ruining our business." He looked her straight in the eye and asked, "Can you help me?" He could almost see the dollar signs in her eyes.

"How can I help you?" She asked "What do you want me to do?"

"I'd like to know everything he does, everywhere he goes, everybody he talks to, and especially everything he requests from the library—every book, magazine, newspaper, manuscript, and every inter-library loan he wants."

Then changing the tone of the conversation, Ted said, "You know, Lydia, I saw your face when I mentioned Chipotle's name." And looking down at his half-full glass as if it required his attention, he remarked, "I take it you two didn't hit it off so well."

"I'll poison him if you want me to." she snarled and Ted wondered how many others had suffered from her spite.

CHAPTER THIRTY-SEVEN

C hip waited impatiently at Ollie's house for Lola to arrive from Chiapa de Corzo. He used the time to call Gretchen to see if she had any news of Xochi.

"I talked to Marlene's mother this morning. They have Xochi in El Paso now. I guess they're finding it more difficult to control her than they thought it would be. Like you, Xochi can be stubborn when she wants to be. And they are not happy about some of the honky-tonk language Xochi uses—expressions you don't hear in church. I'm guessing that it won't be long before they'll be begging you to take her off their hands."

Chip smiled as he imagined the consternation in the pastor's parsonage. "I'll wait a few days and then I'll call them. First, I need to find a place to live and get settled in. Thanks for all your help, Gretchen. You're a real princess." Chip dismissed her protest and asked to talk to Dean Lambert. Without another word, she transferred his call.

"What are you doing down there?" Bert demanded. "In less than a week you've managed to create an international border incident, steal the secretary from the UNAM anthropology department, and disrupt La CIMA enough to give Ollie a stroke. You leave the proverbial trail of destruction in your wake. Don't bother to explain; just tell me how you are going to straighten all this out and do what you are getting paid to do for Rainwater Pharms."

Chip didn't know how to answer. All he could say was, "Ollie's going to get better and I'm going to do my job." He hung up the phone and asked himself: *How does he know about Lola coming with me, and how does he know about Ollie's condition? Where is he getting his information?*

When Lola arrived, she took charge of seeing that Ollie was resting comfortably, and then began to clean and arrange his room. Ollie had not regained consciousness, but she planned to be there when he did. Chip wished he could be there to see the expression on Ollie's face when he recognized Lola next to his bed, but he decided that would have to be private, intimate reunion. He asked Chete to take him back to La CIMA.

When Chip reached Ollie's office, Corina was waiting to show him the office she had arranged for him. She apologized that it was some distance away from Ollie's office, but Chip assured her that it was perfect. He preferred to be as far away as possible from the foot traffic of the central office.

Corina handed him a set of keys for the door, the closet, the file cabinets, and the desk. "You can move your things in whenever you want," she said.

"Just one more thing," Chip said. "Would it be possible to put a sofa in here? There may be times when I work late and I may even want to spend the night right here."

"You must have learned that from Ollie," she laughed. "But he uses his sofa for his afternoon siestas." Then her laughter stopped as she suddenly remembered Ollie was home unconscious.

"He's going to be all right." Chip assured her.

When Chip and Corina walked back to her office, Ramona was waiting inside. After greeting her, Corina excused herself to go clean up the mess the intruders had made in Ollie's office. Ramona approached Chip and said, "I need to talk to you, *señor* Oatley."

"Sure," Chip replied. "I need to talk to you, too. Let's go to my office."

As they walked down the long hallway, Ramona spoke quickly. "I told my supervisor about having to help you find a place to live. He was actually very understanding and told me not to worry about taking time off. But I would like to do this as quickly as possible. I don't like to leave all the work for Che to do by himself."

"Che?" Chip asked.

"Father Gabriel Guevara, a Catholic priest. Everybody calls him Che, like the revolutionary Che Guevara associated with Fidel Castro."

"Well, I hate to interrupt your work, Ramona," Chip said as he ushered her into his new office and shut the door. "Please sit down. I have something very important to talk to you about."

"I'd rather stand," she said stiffly, letting him know she was not sold on him or his business in Chiapas.

Chip stopped to collect his thoughts, then spoke in hushed tones. "I know your father Mapache, the trucker. Actually, I was mugged and left beside the road for dead. I would have died if your father hadn't found me and taken care of me. As I recuperated, I rode with him across the northern Mexican desert, and he trusted me enough to share the secret of his father's manuscripts. Ramona, he asked me to study those papers and publish them in a form that would not only bring widespread attention to the conditions of your people, but also become a source of indigenous pride—something they can use to keep the language and culture from extinction. He told me you know where the papers are hidden. He said you would help me." Then he added, "Your father is very proud of you, Ramona. He loves you."

Ramona stared at him, and he watched the play of emotions cross her usually controlled face as she processed what he had told her.

"Please call me Mona," she said finally, as her eyes and her voice softened. "My father told me that he would find the right person for the task. He didn't tell me that you were his choice. Of course, I will help you. I'm sorry I have been rude to you. I suppose it shows that I am an angry woman. She didn't explain further, but Chip hadn't forgotten that her husband had left her. This moment was not the time to reveal everything he knew—it might put her back on the defensive.

"Don't worry about it. I've been an angry man myself," Chip assured her. He felt an immediate attraction to Mona and had a sudden impulse to reach out and touch her cheek. But he restrained himself. Besides thinking that romance was the last thing he had planned on, he suspected that if he made any such move, he would probably destroy any chance of gaining her full confidence.

Mona steered them both back on track when she stated in a business-like manner. "I rent a room in a boardinghouse not far from here. My meals are included in the monthly rent. When I went there for lunch today, I told *la duena*, my landlady, about you and asked her if she knew of any apartments for rent. She said that the little cottage in the back that was built as a maid's quarters is available. It's fully furnished. If you're interested, let's go look at it.

CHAPTER THIRTY-EIGHT

At the *casa de huespedes*, the boardinghouse, Mona introduced Chip to the landlady *doña* Sabel. They had found her in her small sitting room sipping a small, crystal shot glass of anise, a licorice-flavored liqueur. "A small nip in the evening helps me sleep better," she explained without being asked.

Chip felt concerned. Even without having met her before, it was obvious that *doña* Sabel did not feel well. Her face distorted with pain when she stood and with every step she took. Chip suggested that he could come back the next day, but she insisted they stay. In spite of her discomfort, she was clearly eager to show Chip the small cottage behind the main building. Chip guessed that the old woman had financial needs.

Chip was pleasantly surprised that the rooms in the cottage were spacious, with high ceilings. Even though he didn't plan to be here for long, it would be nice to have a base where he felt comfortable. "I like this place," Chip said, "but it looks like someone still lives here. How soon will it be available?"

"All these things you see here," *doña* Sabel explained, "belong to the last person who rented this place. He was an anthropologist named Bjorn Sorenson, who came here to study the religious beliefs and practices of the ancient Mayans. He was especially curious about their use of hallucinatory mushrooms and began to experiment with them. They say he began to have mystic visions and heard spirit voices from the past."

"Where is he now?" Chip asked. "What happened to him?

"One day," *doña* Sabel said, "he just got up and walked into the woods and never came back. Some people say they have seen him wandering along the trails in the forest and in the jungles. And they say he hasn't trimmed his snow-white hair or beard; both flow down to his waist. He wears only a loincloth and is known as 'The Crazy Viking.' The Indians fear him and worship him as though he were a spirit ghost.

"If you want to rent this place, I'll pack up all his belongings. Or, if you prefer to do the packing, you can keep anything you want for yourself. The rest I'll give away or throw away. I think that if he had wanted me to keep any of his things, he should have told me before he left."

The cottage was exactly the kind of place Chip had in mind, and the rent was well within his budget. "Don't worry. I'll go through these things, starting tomorrow." He had spotted a number of books on the shelves he wanted to take a closer look at. And from the looks of things, the old Norseman might have even left behind scholarly notes—probably handwritten—on a variety of Mayan topics.

"I'll need three months' rent in advance," *doña* Sabel said quickly.

Although Chip had not yet opened a bank account, he had withdrawn enough cash from an ATM to cover the expense. After he had paid and received a receipt from *doña* Sabel, he found Mona sitting in the dining room waiting for him.

"Would you like to see my father's papers now?" she asked, "or do you need time to make any other arrangements?"

"Let's wait until I have enough time to study them," he said. "Right now I need to get something to eat. I didn't have lunch."

"There's a taco stand right around the corner, if that sounds good to you."

"Sounds fine," Chip answered. "I know you told me you had lunch already, but if you'd care to join me, I'll buy you something to drink, and you can tell me more about your father's papers."

"I can talk for a little while," Mona agreed, "then I need to go to the mercado and buy a few things. Wait just a moment while I ask *doña* Sabel if she wants me to get anything for her while I'm there. I'll meet you out front."

When Mona came out, she was smiling. Chip hoped it was another indication that she was warming to him, but he may have misinterpreted her cheeriness when she said, "*Doña* Sabel said to tell you that the utilities are included in the rent. And since they are already in her name, and she's never had them turned off, you don't need to do anything to start using them. I think you got a good deal."

"Yeah, it's better than anything I had expected to find. Thanks for your help."

Chip noticed that the air had turned cool and Mona was wearing a sweater and was wrapped in a heavy wool shawl. "I'd better see what I can find in the Crazy Viking's closet to keep me warm," he said. "I'm going to need more than this thin cotton shirt. I'll be back in a minute."

It took Chip less than a minute to find a fleece-lined leather jacket in a small closet. It fit well enough to have been tailor-made for him.

Chip and Ramona walked quickly along the sidewalk toward the taco stand at the end of the block. The sidewalk was narrow, so Chip walked in the cobblestone street while Mona led the way on the high-curbed, concrete sidewalk. Looking up at her, Chip felt like a child tagging along with his mother. He half-expected her to frown and tell him not to step in the water that trickled beside the curb. The words formed in his mind, *I miss you, Mom. Please, God, don't let anything happen to her.*

CHAPTER THIRTY-NINE

T he aroma of *carne asada* sizzling over a charcoal grill under a small canvas awning brought Chip back to his immediate surroundings, his stomach suddenly responding with a growl. As he gazed at the meat on the grill, he became aware of the two children tugging at his wrists, begging him to buy them each a taco. The taco vendor, a vigorous, middle-aged man with an old sheet wrapped around his waist and tucked into his pants as an apron, waved his hands out and attempted to run off the ragged street kids. They looked pleadingly up at Chip, paying no attention to the man's ranting threats.

At first, Chip pretended not to understand the young pair, a boy and his older sister. Neither had yet reached puberty. But as he submitted tolerantly to their solicitations and listened to their speech, he heard frequent lapses into Tzotzil, the language of the nearby Chamula Indian community. In his turn, Chip shocked them when he used their language to ask them how many tacos they wanted. Even Mona was surprised. Then Chip shocked everybody when he ordered tacos, speaking clearly in the Tzeltal dialect of the indigenous Mayans who populate the region of Oxchuc, in the rainforest northeast of San Cristóbal. The vendor nearly dropped his spatula and Mona was incredulous. "You speak my mother tongue better than I do!" she exclaimed.

The children stood speechless until Chip invited them to sit with him on the high curb and share his tacos. He also bought each of them a tall glass of *agua de limon*, the local lemonade, and began chatting with them. They weren't shy—they were orphans and were being raised by an older sister. Their life was tough and they often went to bed hungry. They thanked Chip many times for his generosity.

When the children had finished eating and began to play in the street, Mona stood up from the wooden stool where she had been sitting several feet away. She and the taco vendor had been chatting together, but neither had been unaware of Chip's ability to connect with the children. She walked over to him and sat down beside him. "Do you have any children?" she asked bluntly.

"I have a daughter," Chip said, "who is just about the same age as these kids. And I can't stop thinking about her. I wonder how she's doing, and what she's doing right now, and what she had for dinner this evening. I miss her."

"I don't understand," Mona said. "Where is she? Where is her mother?"

"Her mother and I divorced not long ago. She got custody and I got visitation rights. But I just found out that her mother has disappeared and my daughter's grandparents have taken her to El Paso, Texas. I haven't been able to call her since then." Then he turned to Mona, deliberately shifting focus from himself to ask, "What about you? Do you have any children?"

"Not long after we were married, my husband Eloy decided to go to the United States to find work. He left and followed the crops in the San Joaquin Valley of

California. The first six months he sent money to me. Then one day I got a letter saying that he had found another woman. It hurt me so much I wanted to die. I don't ever want to hurt like that again. Well, I divorced him. Now I don't know if he's alive or dead. The truth is I don't care anymore." She paused a moment, then said, "We didn't have any children."

Both Chip and Mona were silent for moment. Chip wanted to know more about Mona, but decided to change the subject. "Maybe we should go to the mercado now. We both have some shopping to do. I need to buy some cleaning supplies."

"I'll show you where to get a broom and a mop," Mona grinned, "but I will *not* help you clean your house."

The two children, who had been listening while they played nearby, came running to his side. "Our sister will work for you," the little girl offered eagerly. "She works very hard and she knows how to cook, too."

"Bring her here tomorrow morning," Chip told them. I'll put her to work for a few days, but I don't need anyone to cook for me."

"Okay, okay!" they both screamed.

"Well, then, we must introduce ourselves," Chip stated solemnly, extending his hand. "I am called Chipotle," he said with a wink.

"Chili Chipotle," they giggled. "*Señor* Chili Chipotle."

"Have some respect for your elders, *niños*," Mona broke in. "Please call him *don* Chipotle! Now act like you have been raised properly," she scolded, "and introduce yourselves."

"*Si, señora,*" they said in unison. The girl took the lead and said respectfully, "I am called '*Chispa*' because when I get angry, you can see sparks flying from my eyes. And this is my little brother '*Chango.*' They call him a monkey because he can climb up and over anything. He can climb up the side of a building!" They reached out and shook Chip's hand. "And our sister's name is *Luna*—because her face is round like the moon."

Chip laughed, but suddenly his face wrinkled and he pressed both hands to his lower chest.

"What's wrong?" Mona demanded. "Are you all right?"

"My stomach is on fire," he said. "I ate too much of that hot sauce on my tacos. You know the old saying: *picoso, pero sabroso*, hot and spicy, but delicious."

"Are you taking any medicine to control the heartburn?" Mona asked.

"I've been taking omeprazole, but your father told me to find a plant called *sosa* and make a tea from its leaves. Do you know where I can find that plant?"

"Certainly. All you have to do is walk out to the wooded areas around here and you will see that it grows everywhere like a weed. But if you want, we can go to an herbal shop in the mercado and buy a handful. It's very plentiful and cheap. Come on. I'll show you where to get it."

"Be careful if you go there," Chispa said. "This morning someone robbed all the herbs and destroyed most of the shop."

"Who would do such a thing?" Mona asked in surprise. "What are the people in the mercado saying?"

"They say it was done by a *Chilango*, someone from Mexico City. And they say he was paid by a company called Rain Farm, or something like that. He has lots of money and everybody is afraid of him. Even the police don't do anything to stop him."

The burning in Chip's midsection flared to new heights.

CHAPTER FORTY

After shopping at the mercado and depositing their purchases in their respective rooms, Chip and Mona met in the dining room. Mona described to him how she would brew the *sosa* tea, then Chip went into *doña* Sabel's private study to make his calls. His first call was to Ollie's house.

Lola answered with excitement in her voice. "Oh, Chip, we've been waiting for you to call. Ollie is feeling so much better. He'll have to stay home and rest for a while, but he's going to be fine. I'll make sure of that.

"But there's more news—wonderful news—from the Lacandon jungle. From the field investigators' grapevine, the word is that your grandfather is alive and has been taken to the Mission Station. Isn't that wonderful?"

"Then I must go there immediately," Chip replied. "And what about my mother and sister? Any news or jungle rumors about them?"

"The only thing Ollie has heard is that the Zapatistas are making it clear that they had nothing to do with the raid on the Mission Station. In fact, the Zapatistas have sent out several search parties looking for them. That's all we know now. But listen, Chip, "I've already spoken with Ollie and made arrangements for Chete to take you there in the La CIMA vehicle."

"How soon can Chete be ready to leave?"

"He's ready. Where are you?"

"I've just rented a place," Chip said, "at the boardinghouse where Mona stays.

"I assume you'll want to leave tonight so you can arrive there in the morning. Shall I send Chete over to pick you up now."

"As soon as I drink a cup of sosa tea, I'll be ready to go. But just one more question. Is there any news from Oklahoma—or El Paso—about my daughter?"

"I'm sorry, Chip," Lola said sincerely, "but there's been no word. Ollie himself called Dean Lambert's office twice this evening and his secretary said she hasn't been able to make contact. From what Ollie says, Gretchen— the secretary—is furious."

"Thanks, Lola," Chip said. "I'll have Chete bring me by to see you and Ollie before we leave. I hope it won't disturb him too much if I talk to him a few minutes before I go. I wish he was well enough to go with us."

"Ollie's expecting you. Sometimes I think he worries more about you than he does about himself."

"I'll bet he thinks a lot less about me, now that you're back in his life, Lola."

CHAPTER FORTY-ONE

Chip went to his newly rented cottage behind the main boardinghouse building. There he found a small suitcase in the extra bedroom, placed it on the bed and opened it. From the closet, he grabbed a pair of jeans, a long-sleeve, wool shirt, and a sweater from the Crazy Viking's wardrobe. He tossed them into the suitcase. In the bathroom he found a travel-ready shaving kit and shoved it into the suitcase beside the clothes. From a chest of drawers, he took a change of underwear and socks he hoped would fit. In less than ten minutes he was back in the boardinghouse reception room pacing the floor, waiting for Chete.

Chip was startled when he heard the honking outside the main entrance. Looking out the window, he saw Chete behind the wheel of the La CIMA van. He snatched up his small suitcase and headed out the door.

"Why the big, old van? Wouldn't it have been better to use one of those new sedans on the mountain roads?" he asked Chete as he climbed in and slid his suitcase between two of the rear seats. "Or is someone else coming with us?"

"I have more confidence in this old goat than I do in those pretty, new lambs. It hasn't failed me yet." Then he turned and looked Chip straight in the eyes and said, "And perhaps you may not have considered it, but it may be necessary for us to bring your grandfather back here or to Tuxtla for medical care. Maybe you will want to bring some of your grandfather's possessions back to San Cristóbal. I'm sure you know that Ollie already brought some things here that he thought were important, and there must be many personal items you will want to bring here if it becomes necessary. This old van can hold a lot of baggage."

"You're right. I hadn't thought about that," Chip said. "I'm sorry I questioned your judgment. I'm not thinking very clearly right now.

"You think he might be dying, don't you?" Chete said. "And if that is so, you want to get there and see him before he dies. Am I right?"

Chip tightened his jaw and said nothing, but his head moved slowly up and down.

"Then you better buckle your seat belt and hang on, because I'm going to make this old goat run through these mountains like a young kid billy goat. And since I plan to fly through all those silly military check points, you'd better be ready to duck when the bullets start zinging through the windows. But don't worry, those *soldados* don't have anything that can catch me." To prove his point, he stepped on the gas pedal, making the tires squeal on the pavement.

Chip was flung back against his seat, but turned to grin at Chete. "Is that the best you can do?" he asked.

As Chete careened the old van through through the streets of San Cristóbal, Chip looked out his window, clenched his fists and muttered, "Hang on, Grandpa! Please don't die before I see you one more time. Let me have one more talk with you, Grandpa. I just want to know what you meant when you told me to know myself. Don't leave me hanging."

A montage of memories crowded into his mind--some from childhood and others from summer visits through the years.   One after another, as the images of his grandfather flashed across his mental screen, he realized every one was now precious beyond words.. And suddenly he felt compelled to write down these memories. Pulling his Montblanc pen from his pocket and digging some scraps of paper out of the glove box, he scribbled away even as Chete drove into the night. One day he could hope to share these memories with Xochitle. And he hoped that there was still time for Xochitle and him to create their own special memories. Silently, he promised her, *Xochi, when I get out of this mess, I'm gonna straighten things out for us.*

****

Dark clouds hung heavily over the compound clearing when Chete and Chip arrived at the Lacandon Baptist Mission Station the next morning. No one came to greet them as they parked in front of the chapel. No smoke came from the kitchen chimney. Although there was no breeze, Chip felt a chill in the air. The compound was like a ghost town. For a moment, Chip feared the jungle rumors had not been accurate. As he stood anxiously surveying the buildings, a solitary figure appeared in the dining room window motioning for the men to come in.

Cautiously, Chip walked to the open side door. Machete waved him on, indicating that he would stay with the vehicle. Seeing the machete that Chete gripped in his hand, Chip nodded his agreement and stepped into the dim room. The only light came from the small windows. A tiny Mayan woman came from the darkness and stood in front of him and he recognized her as one of the cleaning staff who had been employed by the Mission Station for many years. Even in the dimness, Chip could see that her eyes were puffy. She wept as she spoke.

In her Ch'ol dialect she whispered, "Señor Chip, your grandfather was brought here yesterday morning. He is in very bad condition and may not live much longer. I believe he is preparing himself for the next life. He is praying and he is talking to his wife who has already gone on to heaven. And he is talking to his son—your father—who died in Vietnam."

"Where is he?" Chip demanded. "Please take me to him."

"I begged him to stay in his bed, but he would not listen to me. He is in the garden behind the chapel, kneeling beside your grandmother's grave. He wants to die and go be with her. Please, go to him now before it's too late."

"Thank you, respected ancient one. You have been most helpful. Now, wait here, please; I wish to be alone with him."

"Of course. I understand completely," said the old woman, moving back toward the kitchen.

****

In the cool, damp garden surrounded by a low adobe wall behind the chapel, the old missionary's eyes shone brightly with fever, yet they flickered with recognition and pleasure as Chip approached. Chip's eyes filled with tears as he wrapped his arms around his beloved grandfather. "Oh, Grandpa, I thought you had gone to heaven before I had a chance to tell you how much I love and honor you—before I could tell you goodbye." The words caught in his throat.

The old man's grip on Chip's arm slackened slightly and his breath became labored, but he fought to speak. "Chip, my time has come to leave this world and go to a better place. And I'm ready. I've been ready for a long time. I'm going to be with my Sarah. She's waiting for me, you know. She's calling me now. I must go to her side." He gasped for breath.

"I don't want you to go yet," Chip sobbed, "but if it's time, then I cannot keep you here

"Chip, I can see you still have many questions, just as when you were a boy," the old man said. "You have always had that questioning look. I saw it long ago when I told you to know yourself. You wondered what I meant by that, didn't you?"

"Yes, Grandpa, I've always wondered why you said that to me."

"Well, there are some things I need to tell you, Chip—things that will help you understand who you really are," the old man whispered. He put one hand around Chip's head and pulled his ear close to his trembling lips. When he had spoken his last words, his hands dropped and his eyelids fluttered for the last time.

Chip was still rocking his grandfather in his arms an hour later when Chete lifted him to his feet and led him back to the dining room.

Lightning lighted the sky and thunder shook the buildings of the mission compound as Chip dug a grave that afternoon for the old missionary next to his beloved wife in the garden behind the chapel. Chete offered to help dig, but Chip refused to let him. "I cannot explain why, but this is something I want to do by myself." And a line from an old hymn stuck in his mind: *I come to the garden alone....* He was hardly aware of the driving rain pelting his face. His grandfather's last words rang in his ears.

CHAPTER FORTY-TWO

After his all-night vigil at his grandfather's grave, Chip was physically and emotionally exhausted. He was thankful when Chete brought him a cup of hot *atole de avena*, a thin brew of sweet, spicy oatmeal. The old woman had disappeared sometime in the night, so Chete had prepared the drink himself.

As he drank his *atole*, Chip went into his grandfather's bedroom and collected everything he could of sentimental value to take back to San Cristóbal. He was especially interested in an old leather briefcase under his grandfather's bed. Although he would be coming back to the Mission Station, it was entirely possible that looters might break in and take or destroy anything they could get their hands on.

As if he were reading Chip's mind, Chete said, "I'll get some of my people to come here and guard the place."

"Thank you, Chete. I'll rest easier knowing this place will be protected," Chip said and decided to stop his collecting efforts for the moment. "Let's get back to San Cristóbal."

****

Chete seemed less nervous this time about driving through the jungle, but he still kept a cautious eye out and drove as fast as the muddy road allowed. The intensity of his focus told Chip that this was not a good time to distract him with small talk.

To distract himself, Chip retrieved his grandfather's old leather briefcase. Inside he found packets of yellowed letters and several cloth bound books that turned out to be diaries. The cover of one thin volume was cut from a rough, faded seed bag pasted on cardboard. Pulling it out, he carefully untied the old leather thong from around it and opened the brittle cover. On the first page, in the simple, delicate cursive handwriting he recognized as his mother's, were the words "My Summer in Chiapas." Turning a few pages, he realized that he pages in his hands were his mother's diary of that first hot summer she had spent as a college student in the company of Dad and Bert Lambert.

Reading through the pages, Chip found himself reliving her youthful, carefree days almost as if he had experience it all himself. Forgetting the bumpy road and, for the moment, his dead grandfather, he began to see the world through his mother's eyes. The diary related a love story and as he read through to the end, it became clear: this story was his story. Lost in thought, he realized that what he now knew would forever change his life.

CHAPTER FORTY-THREE

When at last they left the rut-filled, jungle track and pulled onto the asphalt road, Chip and Chete were both relieved and conversation came naturally and easily, almost a necessity for releasing pent-up emotions.

At one point, without bothering to frame his question in any context or lead-in, Chip asked directly and unexpectedly, "What's it like to be an Indian?

"There was a time when I was offended when people called me '*Indio*,' but now I like to be called '*Indio Maya*.' Why do you ask? Is that what you have been thinking about since your grandfather died? Or have you been reading about *Indios* in that little old book that's had your undivided attention for most of our ride so far?"

"I know this sounds strange," Chip replied, "but my question actually relates directly to something my grandfather told me before he died, as well as to what I've been reading."

"Oh. Well, it is truly strange that you should ask me how I feel about being *Indio* because I have been asking myself that very same question for the last few years."

"Why?" Chip asked.

"When I was a boy," Chete began to explain, "it didn't take long for me to realize that I was part of a special social group. At the time, I wouldn't have described it as special, more likely as 'weird' compared to the others around us because my family and the community where we lived were different from the people who had control over us. Those other people—the ones who had authority over us—spoke another language, dressed in different clothes, went to different schools, ate different foods, sang different songs, worshiped in different churches, and prayed to different gods." He spoke without emotion, as if he had learned not to care.

"How did you deal with those differences?" Chip asked.

"First I gradually I came to hate, even detest the fact that I was an *Indio*. I was ashamed and I rejected my people. I left my community and tried to pass as a *Ladino*—maybe you know that's a term we use to describe *Indios* who speak Spanish and adopt the culture of the people who came from Europe. But I was never successful. No matter how hard I try, I cannot get out of my jaguar skin."

"What happened to change your feelings about being *Indio Maya*?" Chip asked.

"Ever since the Zapatistas organized and started their revolution against the government, I have had to ask myself where I stand. I think 'Who am I?' is the real question. I don't want to fight and kill people, but I do want to identify with the revolutionary movement because I want equality for my people. I want better treatment and better conditions for my people. And I want to be proud of my heritage. I want to be proud of who I am." Chete paused for a moment, then asked, "Do you understand what I'm saying? Do you have any idea how it feels to be pulled by two cultures, one of which is the real you but you are ashamed of, the other which will never accept you no matter how hard you want it to and anyway you resent it because it's not really you? Did that make any sense?"

"Do you know what this is?" Chip asked as he held up the burlap-covered book. "It's a diary my mother wrote right here in Chiapas when she was eighteen years old. It's a very personal journal of her daily life, her thoughts and her feelings. She describes her first thrill of romance, love and lust. She bares her desires and her doubts. And in her writing she remembers what it was like growing up in a small, country town in Oklahoma. I've just been reading in her words the anguish she suffered, like you, because she was Indian. And I discovered something that no one ever told me. My mother is half Potawatomi Indian. Why didn't she ever tell me? Why didn't my grandparents ever talked about it? I should have been told something so very important. I learned that Why? Why didn't she tell me? Was she that ashamed of her Indian blood, her Native American heritage?"

"I have never heard of the Potawatomis," Chete said. "Where is their community?"

"For as long as they could remember, the Potawatomis made their home in the forests below the big lakes in the north-central part of the United States," Chip explained, certain that Chete would not be familiar with the Great Lakes. "But when the European settlers formed a new nation and spread across the North-American continent, these Native Americans were pushed off their lands or rounded up and placed on reservations. Even massacres were not unknown. The Potawatomis were forced to leave their territorial lands and walk to a place called 'Indian Territory' in Oklahoma. That 'death march' became known as the 'Trail of Death.' I know this part of their history because I live and work

in Oklahoma where they are known as the Citizen
Potawatomi Nation, the People of the Fire. I've even
visited the tribal headquarters and cultural center and
seen some of the original 'treaties' they were forced to
sign with the United States government. And every single
one of those treaties has been broken or totally
disregarded. One was even signed by Thomas Jefferson
when he was President of the United States and I'm sure
he fully expected that treaty to be honored, but many
settlers moving westward did not share his values."

"Did your mother write about how she was treated,
and how she felt?" Chete asked. He had no interest in
worthless treaties.

"She wrote that most of her classmates insulted her,
shunned her, and made fun of her. She was a tomboy who
could run faster and ride a horse better than the boys, yet
she felt inferior and ashamed to be an Indian. Eventually
she stopped telling anyone she had Potawatomi blood in
her veins. She says she cried when they called her 'half-
breed' at school, and for a while, she wanted to quit school
and run away, but she had nowhere to go. So, she decided
to prove that she could do everything better than the
other kids. She was an honor student and she became the
best barrel-racing rodeo cowgirl in Oklahoma. That's how
she got a scholarship to go to college."

"I bet she was prettier than all the other girls, too,"
Chete said with a grin. Then he became serious again and
asked, "And now, what about you? How do you feel, now
that you know that you are *un Indio*?"

"I haven't had time to absorb it yet," Chip said. "But
I'll tell you this: I want to learn more about my Indian
heritage. I want to learn the language and culture of the
Potawatomi. I, too, feel the urge to identify with my
people, now that I know they are my people. I just haven't

been Indian long enough to know what it feels like. Give me a few more hours," he joked.

"That's not entirely true, my Indian brother."

"What do you mean?" Chip asked.

"You have been learning the Indian ways since you were a little boy. You are a student of our languages, our customs and our traditions. You are already half jaguar."

"And how do I become a full jaguar?"

"You must commune with our God and feel the spirit of the universe. And you must experience the sacrifice of your own blood. Only then can you know what it is like to be *un Indio de las Mayas*."

A chill ran up Chip's spine as he recalled what Ollie had told him long ago about the bloodletting rituals in the sacred caves.

"And you already have an *Indio* name," Chete added.

"What? My name's not Indian." Chip said in confusion.

"*Chipotle* is not a Latino name, my friend. Nor is it a gringo name."

"You're right, Chete," Chip admitted. "And, now that you mention it, there's someone else in my family who has an *Indio* name. It's my daughter Xochitle and I've got to find a way to communicate with her—she's back in Texas."

"We will stop and refuel at the next Pemex gas station," Chete told him. "You can call Ollie and let him know about your grandfather's death—although he probably knows already. That kind of news travels quickly through the jungle. There might even be more news concerning your mother and sister."

"I'll do that," Chip said. "And then I'll try to call Xochi. I'm worried about her."

As they rode down the road, again in silence, Chip vaguely recalled hearing about a Potawatomi ceremony which conferred tribal names on those individual wishing to embrace a part of their heritage. *I'll have to check into that,* he thought. *And Xochi would probably like that, too. Although a Potawatomi name would be chosen for her by the Chairman of the tribe, it would give her another option. Hopefully it wouldn't be a name that included the word 'dog.' "*

****

When Chete stopped for gas, Chip made his phone call to Ollie's house. Lola was waiting and Chete had guessed right about Ollie already knowing about the missionary's death. Convoys of fish-hauling trucks and gotten the word and had relayed it by CB radio to everybody in the known world. Ollie had called the governor, who had already been informed by Luis, whose fish haulers were still getting the word first. Plans for a memorial service were already in the works, but the actual date would have to wait until there was some sort of resolution to the kidnapping situation. The service would have all the dignity and pomp of a State funeral at the *palacio* in San Cristóbal and it was believed that the President of Mexico would attend. And, although the Reverend Matthew Oatley was not Catholic, Archbishop Samuel Ruiz would hold a special mass in honor of the venerated missionary. When Chip made it clear that Nando's marimba band was to be the featured musical group for the service, Lola was pleased and proud.

Lola also told Chip that there were unsubstantiated rumors that his mother, his sister, and the nurse were being held captive in a cave. Chip's heart beat a little faster.

When Lola told Chip that Ollie refused to stay home any longer because he wanted to get back to his office,

Chip laughed out loud and told her, "Then you had better meet me at my office in the morning and be prepared to start earning your pay."

"Aren't you going to let me finish?" she asked. "I saved the best news for last."

"I'm afraid to guess what that might be," Chip said, holding his breath and gripping the phone more tightly.

"Ollie called Dean Lambert's office this morning and spoke to Gretchen. Your daughter Xochi ran away from her grandparents in El Paso. Apparently, she pinned her hair up, put a boy's cap over it, and dressed up like a boy. Then she took a Greyhound Bus to Oklahoma. We found out about all of this because she went straight to Gretchen's office and demanded to be taken to Chiapas. Well, Gretchen thought that was a great idea and told Dean Lambert that if he wasn't going to take her to Chiapas, then she would do it herself. So, using the power-of-attorney you signed, Gretchen applied for Xochi's passport. They're flying down as soon as the passport is ready. That could take as about six weeks. Gretchen threatened to knock off the head of anybody who got in her way!"

"I should be shocked," Chip said, "but for some reason, I'm not surprised. What did Gretchen say she was going to do when she gets here?"

"She said she's going to take charge of the rescue operation. She's coming down to show us how to organize a posse—just like in the western movies."

Chip laughed and said, "I'm not sure that Chiapas is ready for Princess Gretchen!" By the way, did she say what number I should call to talk to her and Xochi?"

"She gave me a number and said not to tell anyone but you."

****

Immediately, Chip called Gretchen. Before passing the phone to Xochi, Chip stressed to Gretchen that now was not the time to bring Xochi to Chiapas. He said he was going to be extremely busy for a while. He didn't tell her that he thought it was too dangerous and that he didn't know for sure where the danger was coming from. He told her that his grandfather had died, but said nothing about the rumors concerning his mother and sister. Gretchen told Chip that Dean Lambert had gone to Chicago to work out the details of the grant from Rainwater Pharms.

When Xochi took the phone, she was animated. "I just couldn't stay with those people. They wanted to keep me locked in the house like a prisoner. They treated me like a little kid. I couldn't choose my own clothes, my own books, or my own TV programs. Everything I wanted to do or watch was sinful. And the worst part was that they were always talking bad about you. They said it was all your fault that Mom went away. You drove her out of the house. When I told them that was a lie, they tried to lock me in my room. I had to get out of there." She sniffled quietly and begged, "Daddy, please let me come down there and be with you."

With all his heart, Chip wanted to yes, but he had to say no.

CHAPTER FORTY-FOUR

Although it was already late afternoon when Chip and Chete returned to San Cristóbal, neither had any time to rest. Ollie had a list of errands for Chete take care of and as soon as he walked out, Chip found himself in a conference with Ollie, a military general, several politicians and government bureaucrats, and one of La CIMA's senior field investigators. Lola and Corina were there to take notes.

Even though the conference was informal, expressions were somber. Everyone had condolences for Chip on the death of his grandfather. Briefly the memorial service plans were discussed, then the talk turned to hopes that the women would be rescued in time to attend the service. No one dared to hint in words or on faces the possibility that the women might not be found alive—a situation which would create a need for more memorial services.

At last, Chip was asked to give an account of his visit to the Mission Station. Before he had finished, the military commander spoke up, demanding that Ollie release Chete from his normal duties to contact all his relatives and friend to help find the *curandera* who had treated the missionary, and bring her in for questioning.

The commander's "suggestion' left Ollie with little choice, but in fact, he was in total agreement.

After the serious business had been covered, a prominent politician, El Leon, an energetic man who appeared to be in his early forty's, smoothly changed the topic and invited all the men in the room to the birthday celebration for El Tigre, the *cacique*, the regional political boss, at his expansive colonial *hacienda* located in the middle of a 500-acre *rancho* originally granted to his ancestors more than 400 years ago. For some unknown reasons, the *cacique* had specifically requested that Chip attend the *fiesta*. Giving the request little thought, as his mind was solely occupied with concerns about his family, Chip readily agreed to attend, even though he had no idea whether he would even be in the area at the time of the celebration. Still, he had no desire to offend the most powerful politician in the area.

When the outside guests had left, Raymundo Vasquez, the field investigator, quietly mentioned that the Zapatista committee of elders was planning an inter-tribal council meeting as soon as they could gather themselves together at a secret hideout near San Andreas, about 100 kilometers north of San Cristóbal. Mundo, as the investigator was called, suggested that he and Chip should try to attend that meeting. This time, Ollie readily agreed on Chip's behalf. If the elders would let him attend, Chip would be invaluable as a translator, since some of the attendees spoke dialects incomprehensible to attendees who spoke other dialects. And there was a possibility that they might pick up some word about the kidnapped women. Ollie asked Chip and Mundo to stay in close contact with each other for the next few days and was given the assurance they would.

When they were alone, Chip turned to Ollie. He quickly related the things his grandfather told him before his death, as well as what Chip had read in his mother's diary. Ollie's eyes grew large as the pieces of the revelation fell into place. "Some things are beginning to make sense to me now," he said in awe. Then he cautioned, "You be very careful now, Chip. This roadshow could easily get out of control."

Chip left Ollie's office with his head down, thinking this long day was nearly over. Chete hadn't had time to service the pickup, but Chip took it anyway. He drove to Ollie's house and collected his suitcases, boxes and bags, then drove to his new cottage behind the boardinghouse. Just as he was about to take off his shoes and relax, Mona knocked at his door. Chip invited her in, but she had other plans.

"*Doña* Sabel is out of town," Mona said. "She went to see a friend who lives near Palenque and won't be back until tomorrow. I know where she keeps the key to the library, so let's sneak in and look at my father's papers."

Chip hesitated, but only out of pure weariness. His curiosity overpowered him and he stood. "Let's do it," he said, grabbing his own keys.

Once inside the library, Chip realized that it would soon be dark and he had no desire to turn on the lights. Instead, He suggested that they retrieve the papers and take them back to Chip's house. No one noticed as they relocked the library.

In the darkened hallway, Mona pressed the papers into Chip's hands. "You take them and look through them tonight," she said. "You look tired and anyway it's best if I'm not seen alone with you in your house. The *chismosos*, the gossips, will talk. This way, you can read through as much as you can tonight and give the papers back to me in the morning so I can put them back in the library before *doña* Sabel returns." She gave him a last look then turned and hurried away before Chip could respond. He stood there immobilized by physical exhaustion, yet a wave of excitement was slowly rising in his chest. It wasn't just the expectancy of what he might find in the papers that aroused him; something else had stirred within him when Mona came close and touched his hands. His face flushed as he hurried out the back door.

Once inside his cottage, Chip quickly moved to lock the doors and pull the curtains closed. Opening the packet of papers on the kitchen table, he began to read through the pages. Within moment, what he saw took his breath away. *Mapache was right,* he said to himself, *this is a veritable encyclopedia of Mayan history and culture!* In less than an hour he found dozens of references to an existing collection of writings that scholars would call a "codex" hidden in a cave. And that cave had a name and a location. If Chip understood the ancient glyphs correctly, the cave was part of an abandoned amber mine complex. Along with the written record, there were hand drawn sketches of the ancient painting on the cave walls. And there they were—depictions of the bloodletting ritual that Ollie described to him when he was twelve years old. In addition to the piercing of the old woman's tongue, there were unspeakable mutilations performed on the male genitals, drawing forth spurts of blood which, when set afire, became a burnt offering to the gods. Included were descriptions and drawings of many other rites and ceremonies. As he read, Chip determined to do whatever was necessary to preserve these papers. And he desperately wanted to find the cave and get his hands on the codex.

Late that night, Chip carefully tied the packet of papers back into its protective wrapping and locked it in a closet. His mind reeled—as it had done when Mapache first told him about these papers—with the implications, the possible consequences of this treasure. Already he knew that these papers, the codex, and the cave drawings held the potential to help an endangered culture survive, but more than that, on a very personal level, the codex possessed the power to change his own life. With these papers he could salvage his professional career and redeem his reputation, but beyond that and even more important to Chip, he would have a legacy to leave his daughter, something that would make her proud of him in spite of his tarnished reputation in other areas.

After much consideration, Chip decided not to share his find with Ted Cravens or anyone else from Rainwater Pharms, even though the papers included pages of herbal remedies and brewing preparations. When it came down to it, Chip realized Ollie was the only one he thought he could trust. Even the enticements of fame and fortune couldn't remove his distrust of Ted Cravens and the pharmaceutical industry. All the red flags were signaling that Rainwater Pharms couldn't care less if tradition medicines were intellectual property or not, or whether a people's customs and tradition were preserved. Their only concern, it seemed, was bottom line profit.

CHAPTER FORTY-FIVE

Chip slipped into the boardinghouse dining room well before the other guests would come in for *desayuno*, a light breakfast. The kitchen workers were noisily setting out plastic plates and tableware for the sleepy-eyed students who would soon straggle in. From the kitchen prep room came the sounds of chopping, scraping, and mixing as the crew readied dishes for the day's meals. When a large aluminum pot of hot *atole de avena*, was brought out and placed at one end of the table, Chip didn't wait for the workers to bring out a tray of tall glasses. Taking the foot-long ladle which dangled from the side of the pot, he filled the empty mug he had brought.

Chip had not slept well and had awakened early. He had gone to bed knowing that the excitement caused by what he had read in the papers would probably prevent him from sleeping. But what he had not expected was the image of Mona crowding out all other thoughts. He had been trying to deny it, but there had been the twinge of attraction he felt every time he got near her. *What is it about her?* He asked himself. *I'm not looking for an affair. What's with me? I've only known her for a few days, and suddenly I can't get her out of my mind.*

Chip nearly dropped his cup when he felt a soft poke under his left shoulder blade. Looking around cautiously, he saw Mona backing out into the hallway motioning him to follow her. She held up a finger to her lips to stifle his sputtering.

"Where are the papers?" Mona quietly asked. There was urgency in her voice.

"I have them locked up," Chip told her. "Why? Do you need to put them back in the library right now? I thought you said *doña* Sabel would be away most of the day."

Mona took Chip's arm and pulled him into a vacant sitting room and closed the door. "A man named Ted Craven has been here asking about you. He's from a company called Rainwater Pharms. Do you remember? They're the ones that people at the mercado said were responsible for the destruction of the herbal market. Chip, I'm afraid of this man—and his company. What do you think we should do?"

Before he could stop himself, Chip slowly pulled Mona close and wrapped his arms around her. Forgetting about the problems and the danger he seemed to be attracting, as well as the bombshell potential of a codex discovery, he thought only of the woman he now held in his arms. *I think I'm falling in love with this beautiful creature*, he said to himself. *As if I don't have enough complication in my life already!* It took all the self-control he could muster to stop himself from lifting her chin and pressing his lips to hers.

But then Mona gently pushed him away.

"Chip, what do you want to do about Ted Cravens? What do you know about him?" Her own face was confused, as if she was trying to ignore what had just happened, while trying to keep her voice normal.

Chip's own voice shook slightly when he finally answered, "I'll get your father's papers. I think you should take them and hide them in the archives under the cathedral."

"Yes, I agree, because whoever's after your research will probably suspect that if you have any old manuscripts, you might bring them here. Get the packet now and give it to me. I'll get a taxi—alone—and take it to the archives. You go to La CIMA and see Ollie. Find out if there is any news of your mother and sister. Then meet me at the Tulúc Restaurant—the one that has a carving of a wild turkey on its wooden sign that hangs out over the door. It's a favorite breakfast spot for European tourists and Mexican who like to think they're cosmopolitan. If I get there first, I'll get a booth."

Chip barely heard her over the pounding in his heart. Mona turned him around, opened the door, and pushed him out. "Go get me the papers," she snapped.

"Oh, yeah," he said. "I almost forgot."

****

After regaining some semblance of control over his senses, Chip cautiously removed the packet from his cottage. Then, making sure no one was watching, he slipped inside the boardinghouse and passed it to Mona, then got into his pickup and drove to La CIMA. As he made his way along the streets he found himself increasingly concerned about Mona's safety, especially now that she was the holder of the manuscripts. And he felt responsible for passing on the danger that those papers attracted.

Chip wished he had more time to sort out the chaos that surrounded his life, more time to consider his choices, more time to spend with Mona, getting to know her. *But wherever this is going*, he told himself, *it'll have to wait until I get my mother, my sister, and my daughter back.* But he wasn't totally sure it could or would wait.

Inside the La CIMA compound, Chete stopped Chip and said "Give me your keys and let me give this dirty thing a bath, if you've got time."

"Make it quick," Chip said. "I won't be here long. I need to go to the Tulúc Restaurant."

"You can walk there," Chete replied. "It's only three blocks from here."

"Great," Chip said, "Then you'll have time to wax and polish it, too."

"Don't forget who works on your engine," Chete shot back and they both laughed.

Once inside the main office, Chip found Ollie surrounded by three women trying to slow him down. Chip was amazed, but not actually surprised to see him scurrying around like a man possessed. His secretary, Corina, tugged at one of Ollie's sleeves while Lola held his other arm, and an old woman in Mayan garb chanted in his face and tried to make him swallow a spoonful of purple liquid. Moving forward, Chip came to the aid of the women, pushing Ollie down firmly in a chair. "Would you slow down a minute before you have another attack? And would someone care to tell me what's going on here?" he demanded.

Lola spoke up first and explained that Ollie had been working on a linguistics project for many years, researching the "remains" of a Mayan dialect everyone thought was extinct. Only yesterday, one of the field investigators came across an old woman who spoke that dialect. It was actually her native tongue, which she spoke until she was given as a bride to a man from another community."

"She could very well be the last person alive who speaks that language!" Ollie interrupted. "I'll be able to record the vocabulary, the sound system, and the grammar of that dialect. And then we'll know whether my theories about the language are correct."

"Wow, that's fantastic!" Chip said. Being a linguist, Chip shared Ollie's elation.

"Is this the woman?" he asked, pointing to the old lady in colorful clothing.

"Oh, no," Corina corrected him. "She's in Mundo's office recording her speech. We're not wasting any time. This good woman here is Mona's grandmother, the *curandera* who's working her herbal magic on Ollie. Whatever she's giving him seems to be working wonders. As you can see he's suddenly got more vim and vigor than he's had in years. I'm ready to try some of the stuff myself."

Turning to the old woman, Chip introduced himself in her own Mayan dialect. She recoiled in disbelief. "Where did you learn my tongue? And how did you know that was my tongue?" she quizzed him sharply. This old woman showed no sign that her age had impaired her mental processes, much less her determination to pursue her ancient practices.

"I heard the incantation you were chanting when I came in," Chip explained. "I first heard those words when I was a boy at the Lacandon Mission Station, which is also where I learned your tongue. Please accept my sincere appreciation for what you have done to remove the unwanted spirits from my friend. We all will be forever thankful." He held out his hands, palms up and bowed slightly.

The old woman visibly relaxed as she reached out her weathered hands and picked up the invisible offering from his palms. "Your gift is worthy, my son. I accept it and give back blessings and honor upon you." Leaning forward, she pulled his head down and kissed him on the forehead. Then she added, "I am Servidora. Please call me Dora."

While the others in the room stood watching this interchange in surprised silence, Dora said to Chip, "Young man, I can see that you are well educated in the manners and courtesies of my people. But from the untamed defiance I see in your eyes, you have not yet learned how to conduct yourself in the accepted ways of your own people. Like a wild horse, you must learn to contain your wild spirit."

Dora's words embarrassed and stung Chip. *How right she is*, he thought. Then speaking quickly to cover the awkward moment, he asked Ollie, "Has there been any news about my mother and sister?" When no one could offer an affirmative answer, he asked to be excused so he could go meet Mona for breakfast.

As Chip walked to the door, he failed to see Dora watching him with even more interest. The sharp old woman hadn't missed the intimate way Chip pronounced her granddaughter's name. *He'd best behave himself*, she thought. *But he does have potential.*

Before Chip could slip away, Lydia the librarian sashayed her shapely body into the office. Sliding her spike heels, gyrating her hips, and tossing her hair, she came up beside Chip and slipped her arm through his and nudged him toward the door. "Come with me again to the library stacks, handsome, we have some unfinished business to attend to." Somehow Chip managed to escape her seductive clutch and quick-step out the gate, heading for the Tuluc Restaurant. More than ever, he wanted to be with Mona.

As Lydia waltzed out of the office with a grin on her face, Corina and Lola just stood shaking their heads in disgust. Dora, however, vocalized her reaction. "That woman is an evil snake," she said. In her mind she began to plan how she would work her black magic on the shameless wench. She hadn't yet decided if she wanted to play matchmaker or matchbreaker for Chip and Mona, but she was not about to let Lydia work her wiles on Chip. Dora determined to take Lydia out of the picture. *This will be fun*, she thought.

When Dora was left alone to administer another of her curative concoctions to Ollie, he whispered in her ear. "Do you know, Dora, that this young man we call Chip was robbed and beaten in Nuevo Laredo, and left for dead in the burning desert? He has suffered a lot."

"Why are you telling me this?" she asked.

"He was rescued by a passing trucker," Ollie continued, watching Dora's expression for understanding. He wasn't surprised when her eyebrows lifted a notch. "That trucker was your son. After nursing Chip back to health, Mapache sent him on his way, down here to Chiapas, but with a new mission. It just might have something to do with a bundle of your husband's papers. That might be why Chip is overly friendly with Mona."

"You caught that, too, did you?" Dora asked. "But I think it goes deeper than that." Then she demanded, "Why didn't you tell me about him and Mapache before?"

"I haven't had an opportunity, have I? There's always somebody else around who doesn't need to know these things."

"Well, I think you were wise not to tell anyone else. And if Mapache thinks that Chip is the one to take care of my husband's papers, I'll make sure no one else gets their hands on them."

CHAPTER FORTY-SIX

E ven though the wooden sign with a turkey image carved on it was smaller than he had imagined, Chip had no trouble spotting the Tulúc Restaurant. Looking up the street before he pulled the door open, he saw that the plaza was just two blocks away with the cathedral looming on the far side.

Inside Tulúc, he suddenly felt as if he were in the Jewel Family Diner back in Tecumseh, Oklahoma. He took a quick glance at the plates on the tables around him. There were platters of eggs and bacon—with a side of hash brown potatoes, saucers of toast and jelly, glasses of orange juice and milk, and practically everyone with a heavy, white mug of coffee waiting to be refilled by a passing waiter. The waving of Mona's hand from a side booth caught his eye.

Chip looked in both directions before sitting down on the red leather bench across from Mona. It wasn't until he looked up that he saw there was a man in a dark suit sitting next to her. Chip was startled to see his white collar until he remembered that Mona worked with a priest. He greeted them both, trying to hide his frustration at not getting to be alone with Mona. *It's too soon to feel jealousy*, he told himself sternly. *I have no right to feel this way. After all, they do work together, and why shouldn't they be close friends?* But Chip's mind wouldn't let go. *Is it just my imagination, or are they sitting closer than just co-workers?* There was something about the way they looked at each other and smiled that Chip interrupted as a degree of intimacy inappropriate for a priest. Chip tried to act as though he saw nothing unusual between the two, but it was difficult to ignore the slow burn in his stomach.

Introducing the two men, Mona was somewhat casual, telling Chip, "This is Gabby Chavez, who works with me in the archives." It seemed odd that she failed to use the priest's title; she did not say 'Father' or '*Padre.*' But her presentation of Chip was almost formal. "And this is Professor Charles Oatley, a linguist from Sooner Institute in Oklahoma, who is doing research for his doctoral dissertation concerning modern Mayan dialects. He's here with an arrangement with La CIMA."

While the two men simultaneously reached out and shook hands, the priest modified his introduction. "I prefer that you just call me 'Che.'

"As in Che Guevara, the idolized revolutionary companion of Fidel Castro?" Chip asked, warming slightly to the priest.

"You're exactly right, Professor Oatley," the priest said. "When I was a rebellious young man, he was my hero. Maybe that's why later I was so attracted to a movement called 'Liberation Theology,' especially its revolutionary manifestation in the Zapatistas here in Chiapas. Of course, I try to keep my enthusiasm and my activities within the restraints of the Church."

"Before we go any further, Che, just call me Chip, or as some folks do now, call me Chipotle."

"That sounds so disrespectful for a man of your stature," Mona interjected.

Chip wanted to take her comment as a compliment, but instead he almost blushed at her insinuation that 'Chipotle' sounded childish. He responded, "If you insist on formalities, I'll consent to being called 'Professor Oatley' only if Che is comfortable with 'the Right Reverend Father Chavez.' " He was relieved when Mona laughed.

"Please go on, Che," Chip suggested. "I'm afraid I'm not as informed as I should be about Liberation Theology. I'm familiar with the term, but could you refresh my memory as to what it's all about?"

"Sure," Che said, "and I'll try to keep it brief. Back in the 1950s and '60s, most of Latin America was ripe for revolution. The vast majority of the people suffered under poverty, illiteracy, and every other kind of social injustice. It's easy to see why revolutionary leaders sprang up everywhere—it wasn't just in Cuba. And it was so widespread, the Roman Catholic Church couldn't ignore it. At first, the old bishops saw it as a threat and threw their considerable weight in with the military dictators to crush the movement. But a strange phenomenon happened. Some eccentric old priests began to protest and voiced the 'heresy' that Christian love was much more than a philosophical ideal. They were convinced that Jesus wanted us to go beyond charity for the poor and concern for their souls; they began to preach that the Church was morally obligated to help the poor and weak fight for social reforms."

"That idea is not restricted to Catholicism," Chip remarked. "The concept of 'social gospel' has caused divisions in almost every Protestant denomination."

"Well, it definitely caused an uproar in Catholic circles. The new social crusaders said that the Church had a mission to literally 'liberate' the oppressed from their suffering. This new approach found fertile ground in the hearts and minds of many young priests. It ignited a whole movement. Conferences were held and books were written."

When Che paused a second, Chip broke in, "Excuse me, could I interrupt you for a minute so I can order a cup of coffee and a short stack of hot cakes?" He motioned a waiter to the booth.

When Chip glanced at Mona, she rolled her eyes and said, "I should have warned you. Once Che gets started on this topic, it's hard to stop him. I know because he goes on about it when we're working." Then, directly to Che, she said, "Don't lecture him. If you guys want to go have a beer some evening and talk about this, that's fine with me, but for now, let's stick to stick to current events, okay?" To Chip, she sounded almost like a wife who had no interest in her husband talking football with his buddies.

"Please forgive me, Chip," Che immediately apologized, "but this topic is so exciting to me that I get caught up in my enthusiasm and forget where I am and actually lose any sense of time. Yes, please make your order."

After Chip's coffee arrived and he had taken a few sips, he prompted Che to continue. "I assume this liberation movement was not popular with many Church leaders."

"Indeed not!" Che emphasized, eager to tell more. "It was highly controversial. But because it became so popular with the poor, hungry masses, the old conservatives were caught in a dilemma. They could not condemn the movement publically, and they had to be careful how they worded their scolding of the inflamed priests. It didn't dampen the debate when some priests took their ideology to extremes and openly identified themselves as Marxist Communists; that brought the wrath of the Vatican down upon their heads. That heat pushed the movement underground most of the time, but it never died. Right here in Chiapas, it's common knowledge that the Archbishop surrounds himself with 'liberation' priests. When they go out into the *indigenas* communities to hold mass, marry and bury, and give catechism classes, they take the opportunity to actively organize political action groups. They teach the men and women to read and write. They explain how the economic system works and how it is stacked against them. They even give real-life tips on how to run a business and how to be competitive. It's called 'praxis' because it's meant to be practical in the real world."

"Is that why some people accuse the Church of instigating the Zapatista revolution?" Chip asked with false innocence.

The priest smiled, but did not answer the question.

While Che pushed on through his monologue, Chip noted that Mona kept silent and at times fidgeted with her napkin. For her sake, Chip at last changed the subject. Addressing Mona, he said, "Tell me about what you do in the archives." He wanted to reach out and place his hands over hers.

Mona's eyes told Chip that she was thankful to be included in the conversation. She spent the next several minutes explaining how she and Che were trying to salvage the mountain of documents, papers, letters, newspapers, and official records of every sort that had accumulated in the cathedral basement over the centuries. "They're all in danger," she said, "of destruction and deterioration caused by the damp climate and insects. And, of course, the ravage of time."

At that point, Che broke in to describe the process of classifying and cataloging the documents with library codes and numbers, before scanning and applying chemicals to preserve them. But Chip soon cut him off to ask if they had ever come across any references to old Mayan manuscripts or possibly a codex.

"Once in a while we do find such references," Che told him. "And just the other day a man dropped in to see me and asked if we ever came across references to Mayan medicines, especially traditional herbal cures. He said he would pay us well for copies of those documents. I told him we couldn't accept personal payments, but if he wanted to make a donation to the church, that would be fine."

"Do you remember his name?" Mona asked, alarmed. And when she heard the answer, both she and chip knew she had been right to be concerned.

"Wait, he gave me his business card. I've got it right here. Oh, yes, his name was Ted Cravens, from Rainwater Pharms."

Chip was relieved that Che failed to notice their expression and instead of pursuing the topic of Ted Cravens, he leaned over the table and lowered his voice to ask, "What have you heard about the Zapatista confab tomorrow? It's some kind of inter-tribal council of elders."

"I heard something," Chip confided, "but I thought it was supposed to be a big secret. Guess I was wrong. Does the whole world know about it?"

"Many people know about it," Che informed him, "but very few non-participants will be allowed to observe the proceedings. Mona and I have been invited to attend as spectators. Would you be interested in going with us? We're leaving as soon as this meal is over and we can get you in."

Chip couldn't hide his surprise. "How can you—?"

"Mona has told me all about you," Che interrupted with a wave of his hand, "and I have heard from my 'Liberation' sources about what happened to you family at the Baptist Mission Station. You have my deepest sympathies, and I can assure you that the Zapatistas had nothing to do with that raid, and are doing everything they can to find your mother and sister."

"Say no more," Chip said. "I'll go with you. Is it possible for a friend of mine from La CIMA to go along?"

"Not this time," Che said firmly.

"Can I make a few phone calls?" Chip asked.

"Sorry, Chip," the priest said. "We really do have to leave now. There's a vehicle waiting in the cathedral garage to take us out by way of a secret tunnel that goes to a nearby residence. Once we get into the mountains, Mona will be our guide."

"I grew up in that region," Mona said. "I used to ride with my father when he drove his truck. I know all those roads and trails." She looked at Chip and said, "You go with Che while I let Ollie know that you'll be tied up tomorrow and won't be coming in to the office. Then I'll buy a few supplies and meet you at the cathedral in an hour."

Chip could have sworn that he heard the priest whisper, "*Sí, mi comandante.*"

CHAPTER FORTY-SEVEN

Deep in the dense rainforest, under a large brush arbor, the senior elders from thirteen Mayan communities sat in council session. Chip, sitting with Che and Mona two rows back from the main participants, estimated that there were eighty people under the shade provided by the leafy covering, and about two hundred more—most of them armed—were milling about in the chilly mountain air. Except for Chip and a handful of other spectators, all attendees wore black woolen *pasamontañas*, pullover ski masks. No cameras or recorders of any kind were allowed.

In their various dialects, often through interpreters, they discussed the latest proposals from the Federal Government of Mexico to end the hostilities and mollify the Mayan people. For the most part, the discussion was calm, even friendly, but there came a point when a disagreement arose among translators were having difficulty with some of the vocabulary for modern technology, such as "microwave relay" and schools with "satellite television" for distance learning. Without clearance from Che or Mona, Chip abruptly stood and volunteered his services. To the hushed elders he explained the questioned terms in simple everyday vocabulary, offering translations in several of the languages being used. Some of the elders were horrified at Chip's breach of protocol and signaled the guards to come apprehend him, but as several guards rushed toward Chip, one of the elders quickly stood and spoke up in his defense.

"My brothers, wait! This young man is the grandson of the old gringo missionary who was killed at the Lacandon Mission Station. This is the boy who became a legend in our communities because the gods blessed him with the gift of tongues."

At that, the rest of the elders stood and gathered around Chip as though he were a god in their midst. The guards backed off and the conference was totally disrupted as most of the participants gathered around Chip wanting to touch his lips and his tongue. Almost desperately, Chip stood on a chair and told the crush of admirers, "I will permit you to touch my lips only if you will tell me where my mother and my sister are being held."

The senior elder spoke up for the whole assembly, "My son, we swear to you that we had nothing to do with the attack on the Mission Station, nor do we know where your mother and sister have been taken, but we give you our solemn promise to help you find them and bring justice to the ones who are responsible for this crime."

When the elder had finished speaking, Chip felt the familiar poking in his back just under this shoulder blade, the same poking he had felt in the boardinghouse. Turning around, he knew Mona would be standing there.

"Come on, Chip. We've got to get you out of here. The old men may adore you, but there are some young hotheads in the assembly who would like to feed you to the jaguars."

CHAPTER FORTY-EIGHT

Darkness was falling on San Cristóbal as Che, Mona, and Chip returned from the inter-tribal council. Mona drove the entire time, speaking very little. Che kept Chip awake with a steady stream of questions about language extinction. Although this was Chip's area of specialty, he made an effort to not get carried away in a lecture like Che had done on the subject of Liberation Theology.

"My main thesis," Chip said, "is that cultures rise and fall with their ability to harness technology and use it for their economic advantage."

"Aren't there are other factors that may be just as important?" Che asked.

"Of course there are," Chip agreed. "Some cultures rise, some cultures fall, some culture die off, and some just seem to ride along with a few ups and downs, but never die. For some reason, they manage to survive all the social forces that doom other cultures into extinction."

"Why do you think they survive?" Che asked with genuine interest. "Is there any way to predict which cultures will survive and which will die out?"

"I have come to my own conclusion," Chip said, "that only those cultures which possess a fanatical belief that they have been chosen by God for a special purpose in history have any hope for survival. Such a people will fight and sacrifice their lives to ensure that their way of life—their beliefs, their customs, their traditions, and their values—survives.

"You draw your thesis from the Bible, right?" Che asked.

"Well, yes, Jewish culture is a prime example," Chip answered, "and Christian culture continues its basic value system. But there are other religions that instill their followers with an equal zeal."

"The obvious question then for us here in Chiapas now is the survival of the Mayan who are being swallowed up by a Latino culture with much greater technology and economic resources at their disposal. Realistically, do these *indigenas* have any chance of survival?"

"Only if various factors come into play," Chip told him. " First, they must learn and remember their history and be convinced that they have reason to be proud of their cultural achievements. Second, they must have a written record to constantly remind them of their heroic deeds and how they have overcome hardships. Third, they must learn to use technology. Fourth, they must never forget the language which expresses their cultural beliefs and values."

"That's a big order to fill," Che commented.

"Oh, but there's more," Chip said. "There's a requirement for religious shepherds like you to persuade them that God has chosen them for a special mission in His plan. And they must become so passionate about that belief that they will die for it."

Mona smiled and said, "That's one of the best sermons I've heard in a long time."

Chip grinned broadly at her, but Che turned and looked out the window as his cheeks turned red. *That's wasn't a very subtle way of saying that there is something lacking in my sermons.*

****

After the vehicle had been returned to the cathedral and Mona's *hasta luego*, 'until tomorrow,' sent Che to his priestly quarters, Chip suggested to Mona that they walk the quarter mile to the boarding house. He knew that even in a taxi, he wouldn't feel free to talk. Once they were out on the street he opened up. "I was going to tell you earlier, but I didn't feel it was safe to talk about this around Che. I've found some things in your father's papers that I'm not ready to announce to the world yet. There are numerous references to a sacred cave and descriptions of its location. As a librarian, do you know where I can get some maps with the locations of caves marked?"

"Those should be pretty easy to get," Mona said. "If Lydia doesn't already have them, she can use the inter-library loan system to get them for you in a few days."

"That might be a problem," Chip said with a forced chuckle. "I haven't been receptive to her amorous advances. I'm not so sure she'll be willing to help me."

"Oh, I see. When we get back to the house, I'll call one of my old friends. She married a gringo who likes to climb mountains, rappel down cliffs, and explore caves. If he's in town and he thinks you know about a treasure in a cave, he'll be over tonight."

CHAPTER FORTY-NINE

E arly the next morning after a quick shave, a hurried shower, and a clean set of clothes, Chip rummaged through what the Crazy Viking had left in his kitchen. Under a dish towel, he discovered a vintage dial telephone. To Chip's amazement, when he picked up the receiver, he heard a dial tone. Just to confirm that this antique piece of equipment was functional and someone was still paying the monthly bill, he called Ollie to see if there had been any news and give him a rundown on the unplanned trip to the Intertribal Council meeting. But Ollie stopped him before he could articulate a question. "Why on earth are you calling me at this ungodly hour on a Sunday morning? I don't have any news. If I did, you can be sure I would have sent Chete to find you. Now let me go back to sleep. I was out late last night with Lola and we had a nice bottle of wine. Where were you all day?"

When Chip quickly explained where he had gone and what had happened, Ollie calmed down, but still sounded grumpy. "Unless you learn anything about your mother and sister, don't bother me today. I'm supposed to be recuperating, don't you remember?" Chip heard the familiar 'click' sound of the old telephones when they disconnect.

Chip continued his exploration of the kitchen and was disappointed when he found an assortment of South Asian tea leaves in tin canisters, but failed to find any coffee. He had no option but to go to the boardinghouse kitchen. Since he was already dressed, he grabbed the biggest mug he could find and headed out the door. He was already making a mental list of people to call this morning. Gretchen and Honey Bee were at the top of the list. Somewhere at the bottom of his list was Ted Cravens. Chip had been delaying that particular call, but now he felt it wasn't in his best interest to wait any longer.

In the dining room Chip was pleased to find Mona waiting for him. She wore a sleeveless blouse, faded jeans, and dirty white tennis shoes. Chip thought she looked absolutely beautiful.

"I like your hair in a *trenza*, braided down your back," he complimented her with a rather foolish grin.

"I like it that way now," she said, "but I haven't always. When I was a teenager, I didn't want my hair in a *trenza* because I thought it made me look like a peasant, a farm girl. Isn't it strange how our attitudes change as we grow older? Now I'm proud to be identified with the *campesinos*, the peasants, the laborers." She stopped and looked him up and down. "You're dressed as if you're getting ready to go to the office today. What's happening? Did Ollie call you in?"

"I didn't realize today was Sunday," Chip admitted sheepishly. "With everything that's happened this week— especially yesterday—I completely lost track of time."

"Sunday is supposed to be a day of rest, so why don't you go change into something more comfortable and go with me to the Museum of Mayan Medicine. It's right on the outskirts of town and it has an herbal garden that's very relaxing to walk through."

"Sure, I'll change clothes and go with you, but first I need to make a few phone calls," Chip said. "Also, I need a cup of coffee. I'll meet you back here in half an hour."

Just the thought of spending some time with Mona raised his spirits. But he was anxious to get back to the packet of manuscripts.

****

Chip's calls went unanswered. When he returned for Mona, his spirits had taken a downturn. Frustration showed in his face as he drove Mona in his pickup to the walled compound that housed the Museum of Mayan Medicine. At the entrance gate he paid the modest entry fee, drove down a dirt road, and and parked in the shade of a large *almendro* tree in the grassy area which served as a parking lot. Ever since he was a boy, Chip had wondered if these *almendros* were the same as the almonds that supplied the tasty, edible nuts to the world. *I'll have to check into that*, he told himself.

Before going into the museum building complex, Mona suggested they take one of the paths and stroll through the herbal gardens that radiated out in all directions. Every row was headed by a small square sign which identified the plant and its medicinal uses.

"There's even an herbal pharmacy inside," Mona said. "They've got a remedy for every ailment under the sun."

"Is this where your mother buys ingredients for her herbal concoctions?" Chip joked.

"The truth is that they buy their herbs from her."

"I'm curious," said Chip, "as to why Rainwater Pharms and other international pharmaceutical giants don't just come here and buy their traditional herbal curatives right over the counter. What do they need me for?"

"They need more, detailed information about how these herbs are prepared and combined," Mona explained. "And the curanderos won't tell their secrets, especially now that they know the bio-pirates are in a war to get the secret cures first. They need you to get the secrets from people like my mother, and from the ancient manuscripts."

"That's exactly why we can't tell a soul about your father's papers," Chip said.

"That's right, because the information in those papers could be worth hundreds of millions of dollars to the drug companies. And that's what makes it worth robbing and killing for. That's what makes you a target, Chip. You have to watch your step."

Chip was about to make a foolish comment about how much he'd rather be watching her, when his attention was suddenly distracted by a familiar voice. Just a few yards in front of him stood Valdo, the taxi driver he met in Tuxtla. Valdo was herding two dozen old German women in what was obviously an organized tour group. Moving closer, Chip listened in on Valdo's speech.

"As you ladies have probably heard," he said in broken German, "there are some herbal remedies here in Mexico that are available for experimental treatment of cancer. These treatments are not approved for use in the United States or the European Union and they are becoming very expensive." Valdo's eyes misted over, his voice cracked, and his lips trembled. "I'm praying that the treatment works because I have a six-year-old son who is dying of cancer. I hope these *curanderos* here will agree to treat him. I hope they have something to ease his pain and cure his body." By this time, he had most of the old women in tears. They patted his arms and pressed 500-

peso notes into his hands. He thanked them and struggled to regain his composure.

As the women returned to inspecting the fragrant plants, Chip walked up beside Valdo and whispered, "That was a low-down trick, but I'll have to admit it was a pretty good show."

Valdo turned and grinned, gaving Chip a quick wink and said, "Works every time."

Still whispering, Chip asked, "Have you or Chisa heard any gossip at the hotel in Tuxtla?"

"The only thing of any interest is that the governor has hired practically every mountain climber and cave explorer in Mexico to do some special project. It doesn't take a genius to figure out what he wants them for."

Before Chip could ask any more questions, Mona strode up beside him and spoke quietly through her teeth. "Four men following us. I'm sure they're all armed. Let's walk back down the path like we're going into the museum, then run to your truck."

Chip's eyes widened and his pulse quickened as Mona pulled a small pistol out of her tote bag and pressed it into his hand, blocking the transaction with her body. "Here. Put this in your belt. I hope you know how to use it."

CHAPTER FIFTY

Chip and Mona jumped into the pickup and sped away from the Museum of Mayan Medicine. After six blocks Chip slowed to see if they were being followed. Mona checked over both shoulders, but seeing nothing, she relaxed and faced him. "I didn't want to say it earlier, but it is possible that those men were actually assigned to protect you," she told him. "I wasn't going to take that chance because we couldn't be sure they weren't *los tipos malos*, the bad guys."

Amazed again at this woman's audacity, Chip gaped at her momentarily but said nothing until they arrived back at the boardinghouse compound and parked in front of his cottage. He turned off the engine, but when Mona started to open her door, he placed his hand lightly on her arm.

"Mona, when I promised your father that I would take care of his papers I had no idea I would be so attracted to his daughter. I don't have any idea where all this is going, but I think I need to tell you my feelings. I don't know much about you, but it's clear that you are more than just a librarian, more than an archivist. And I don't want to interfere with whatever extracurricular activities you're involved in. I just want to know if there's any chance I might fit into your life because I can't help myself from wanting to be near you. Is there a chance for us?"

Looking down, Mona took a breath. "I think you're a wonderful person, Chip, and because my father chose you to take charge of his papers, I will do everything I can to help you. And I will be your friend. But that's as far as I can go in a relationship with you. There are too many other things going on in my life, and I'm sorry I can't tell you about them. I hope you can understand." She leaned over and gave him a friendly peck on the cheek, then opened the door and jumped out.

Before closing the door, she turned back to Chip and made a suggestion. "*Doña* Sabel is probably back and she loves to have guests over. It reminds her of the old days. It would make her day if you would invite Ollie and Lola to come and visit with us this afternoon. And I'll have my mother join us."

"I'll make a few calls and see who might like to come over," Chip said.

"And I'll invite Che. He should be finished with his Sunday mass duties by then," Mona added before she walked away.

I knew it! Chip said to himself. *She and that priest have got the hots for each other. Talk about an unholy alliance.* A slow burn spread through his stomach.

****

After the regular boardinghouse guests had eaten their two o'clock Sunday lunch and drifted off to their respective rooms, Dora gathered the invited guests into her comfortable sitting room. Everyone that Mona had suggested to had accepted their invitations. Chete had chauffeured Ollie, Lola, and Dora the *curandera*, who was still nursing Ollie back to health over his protest.

Doña Sabel was in her element. She loved to entertain and stimulate conversation. After sending Mona to round up some *botanas*, some snacks, from the kitchen, she hobbled to an antique china cabinet and lifted out an old bottle of mango wine. When Mona returned with a tray of *carnitas*, little chunks of fried spicy pork, *doña* Sabel instantly sent her back with an order for fried *cotija*, small cubes of pungent cheese, deep fried to golden brown on the outside, but soft and gooey inside.

Ollie had been raised as a Lutheran and always enjoyed a good theological debate. It didn't take much for him to engage Che in a discussion about denominational differences. Chip tried to stay out of it, but was drawn into the armchair confab when Ollie asked about his Baptist viewpoint on church organization and structure.

"Most churches," Ollie commented, "have a formal hierarchy of authority. Che, here, takes orders that come down from the Pope, through Cardinals and other layers of authority before they get to his level. We Lutherans don't have a pope, but we do have bishops that keep a close eye on their subordinate ministers."

"Baptists are very different," Chip said. They've always prided themselves on the fact that each congregation is considered to be independent but they have used various methods to create some form of unity. For example, groups of Baptist church form associations, usually in a single county. These alliances are headed by a senior minister, a sort of 'pastor to the pastors' called an 'Associational Missionary' or 'Director of Missions,' but they have no real authority over any of the allied churches or their pastors. And there are state and national Baptist 'Conventions' that administer the mission offerings and commission missionaries, but these organizations are directed by elected officials who, again, have no actual authority to tell a local church pastor what to do."

"That sounds democratic," Lola interjected, "but is it really a practical, workable system?"

"It works as long as the pastors have some kind of unity, but sometimes differences of opinion keep them from working as a team for the common good. I remember an instance when my grandfather had a disagreement with some of his fellow missionaries. One day I heard him say in frustration, 'If we only had a bishop to tell us what to do!' "

Doña Sabel changed the direction of the conversation. "All my life I have heard priests and ministers talk about being 'called' to church occupations—'vocations,' as they say. What does that mean?" Without waiting for a response, she offered her own opinion. "Most priests, pastors, and missionaries say they are 'God-called.' Well, you want to know what I think? I think they are 'mother-called.' "

While the others mulled over doña Sabel's pronouncement, Che quickly agreed with her. "I've noticed that, too, and let me tell you, it may very well be one way God works. My mother actually dedicated me to God while I was still in her womb. She was instrumental in my becoming a priest."

Dora had been sitting silently, but her patience had run out. Every eye in the room turned toward her when she pointed at Che and demanded, "What kind of herbs do you put in the 'holy water?' What is the secret of its magical power to heal the sick and frighten away evil spirits? And can you teach me the magical words of the prayers you say in the church?"

There was an awkward silence when no one offered Dora an answer, so Mona took the focus away from religious topics by remarking with a smile, "Chete seems to be spending a lot of time in the kitchen. Does he like to cook?"

"It's not the cooking. He's taken an interest in Leti," *doña* Sabel confided. "She's the handsome Mayan woman who works clean-up, a widow with two little children. Her husband was killed by a paramilitary raiding party last year. And Chete has been coming around quite often lately to see her. There just might be some *chispas* in the wind. Those sparks could burst into a flame one of these days."

Chip took advantage of the pen forum to inquire about the Crazy Viking, the previous occupant of his cottage.

Doña Sabel seemed eager to tell all she knew about the robust, blond, blue-eyed Scandinavian. "He always talked about a place called Valhalla—wherever that is."

Ollie helped her out. "Valhalla is a place in the legends of Norse mythology where the spirits of brave warriors go when they are killed in battle."

"He came here," *doña* Sabel continued, "believing he could find evidence that Vikings had found their way to Meso-America a thousand years ago. He was convinced they had a significant influence on Mayan culture."

"Their only influence on culture," Ollie said sarcastically, "was to destroy every civilization they came into contact with. They were bloody pirates who sailed up and down the European coastline raping, pillaging, and burning. It took Germanic barbarians to settle them down."

"I don't know anything about that," *Doña* Sabel said. "I just know that one day he started acting crazy. He told me he had found the 'Cave of Valhalla,' and he was going to go there—like he was going to heaven."

"Well, the Viking god Odin can have him," Ollie said, "because I'm sure Jesus wouldn't have him."

Doña Sabel ignored Ollie's caustic remark and said, "The last time anybody saw him was on a mountain trail. He was wearing only a loin cloth and leather sandals. And his skin was painted blue."

Hearing this, Chip could hardly wait for the social hour to break up. He wanted to go back to the cottage and look through the Old Viking's papers. *Every way I turn,* he said to himself, *I see a sign that says the answer is in a cave. But which cave?*

CHAPTER FIFTY-ONE

The next morning Chip got up early, went to the corner *tiendita*, a little store, bought some coffee grounds, went back to his cottage and brewed his own coffee. He had a strong desire to go in and see Mona, but since she had put a damper on his advances, and he didn't want to alienate her totally, he decided to go to La CIMA and see if there had been any new developments. Completely forgetting that there was a telephone in his kitchen, he locked his door and headed to the office.

Not seeing Chete, he parked his pickup and went directly to Ollie's office. Before he could greet Corina, she held up her hand, telling him that this was not a good time to interrupt Ollie. "The regional boss of the *sindicato*, the union, was in the office giving Ollie a hard time," she said. "He doesn't need the stress, but what can he do?"

"What's the problem now?" Chip asked curiously. "I thought the salary tables had already been ironed out and agreed upon."

"There's always a new problem. And the newest one involves you, Chip."

"Me? How can that be? I'm not even a union member."

"That's just the problem." Corina explained. "They are saying that since you are not a union member you should be removed from La CIMA, and replaced with someone who is. And that La CIMA should be fined for taking you here without membership initiation and monthly dues."

"If that's the only problem," Chip said. "I'll talk to the union representative and join up."

"I don't think it will be that easy," Corina informed him with a downward cast of her eyes.

"Why not?"

"Because Lydia the librarian is the union steward for La CIMA."

Suddenly Chip understood his predicament. "So what do I do now?" he asked.

Unexpectedly, Mona's voice came from behind him. "You go to the union meeting this evening at the Casa de Diego de Mazariegos and defend yourself. There may be some rational union members who will vote to accept you. But you may be fighting a losing battle."

Turning around to face Mona, he asked, "Why do you say that?"

"Because," Corina answered for her, "Lydia may not have been successful in seducing you, but she's been successful in bedding Pepe Rosales, the regional union president. He's come here to personally preside over this meeting. "

"Okay, so I'll go and put up a good fight," Chip said with more *machismo* than he felt and turned to go to his new office. But he was stopped in his tracks at what Mona's next words.

"You might also be interested to know that Lydia has been seen in the company of a Mr. Ted Cravens. Apparently she's found a way to tap into his expense account."

"*Maldita sea*! Curses!" Chip exclaimed. "He won't return my calls, but he sure has found a way to get under my skin." He banged his fist on the door jamb as he walked out.

Lola was waiting for Chip when he reached his office. It was obvious she had spent some time organizing things. "I made the right decision when I hired you," he told her gratefully.

On his desk, Chip found an old shoe box that he did not recognize. "What's this?" he asked.

"I'm not sure," she answered. "Mona brought it to me this morning and said *doña* Sabel gave it to her. She thinks it might have some of the Crazy Viking's papers in it."

Chip practically ripped the box open and sat down to read through the documents. Without even stopping for lunch he read on late into the afternoon. Finally, just before it was time to go to the union meeting, he jumped up and headed for Ollie's office. Corina waved him to go on in. The flow of visitors had finally stopped and Ollie was alone.

"Do me one favor, Corina," Chip ordered as he passed her desk. "Call Mona and ask her to come here immediately."

The urgency in Chip's voice convinced her to do as he asked without question. But Corina didn't have to make the call. Mona and her grandmother strolled in the door as if on cue. Chip motioned them to come into Ollie's office with him.

Ollie had been resting with his eyes closed, but sat up alertly when he heard Chip talking excitedly as he came through the door. "I think I have most of the puzzle put together," he said. Spreading out a series of hand drawn maps on Ollie's desk and pointed at various markings that apparently gave clues about prominent landmarks surrounding a 'hole in the earth.' "In other notes it was called the 'entrance to the underworld,'" Chip told them. "And still other documents refer to 'a treasure that must not fall into the hands of our enemies.'

"These are incredibly similar to the descriptions written by your husband, señora Dora. With these two sets of papers, I believe we have a very good diagram of the sacred cave." He could hardly contain himself as he gazed down at the papers laid out across the desktop, and Dora gave Chip a look that confirmed she knew exactly what he was talking about.

"But there's more," Chip went on. "In a related set of writings, an elder of the Ch'ol people, who live around the ruins of Palenque, describes another cave—a large cavern—that lies between Bonampak and Yaxchilan. He says the cave has always been an outlaw hideout and is known as 'snake pit.' Do any of you know of any place with that name today?"

"I know where those caves are," Dora stated excitedly. "My husband took me to the 'sacred cave' for the bloodletting ritual."

Chip glanced over at Ollie, his mind flashing back to the description of the bloodletting ritual to Chip when he was just a boy. Ollie nodded as if reading Chip's mind.

Mona was visibly tense. "Grandmother, can you tell us where the 'snake pit' is?"

Dora thought for a moment, then said, "I could probably tell you how to get there, but I don't understand why anyone would want to go there. Everybody knows it's a place where *banditos* flee to escape the law."

"There's something else about that place you told me once. Something about anyone going in there has to submit to being tattooed. Do you remember?"

Dora tried in vain to recall the details she had heard about the outlaw's identification body markings, but it was Ollie who supplied the information. "Actually, it's not a tattoo. Anyone who wants to go into that sanctuary, to be a part of that gang and receive its protection, must abide by its rules and must first submit to a tortuous branding—like a cattle brand—on the fleshy skin inside the left forearm. And the image of the brand is, appropriately, a snake head, a viper's triangular head. As I understand it, after the burn wound heals to an ugly scar, the proud owner of the brand is expected to fill in the outline of the snake head by means of a primitive tattoo needle made from the tail of a stingray. The scales are supposed to be green, the eyes red, and the forked tongue black."

Ollie paused for a moment, then practically jumped out of his chair, and shouted to his secretary, "Corina, get the governor on the line, please. I've got to talk to him." He didn't explain the urgency.

A minute later, the governor was on the line. Everyone quieted and listened to Ollie side of the conversation. "I'm sorry to bother you, but this is important. Did anyone locate the curandera who treated the old missionary? They did? Did they interrogate her? Was she able to give a description of the attackers? Did any of them have a brand or a tattoo of a snake head on his arm? They did? Yes, Governor, that's important information. I'll call you again in a few minutes. I think we might have a solid lead. Yes, thank you, Governor."

When Ollie hung up his phone, he had everyone's attention. "Well, I think we know who took the women from the Mission Station. Now, we just have to pinpoint the location of their hideout cave. There's a pretty good chance that they're keeping the women there." Everyone agreed with Ollie's conclusion.

Ollie fumbled through a desk drawer, pulled out a map of Chiapas and unfolded it on top of the papers Chip had just arranged. He motioned Dora to come and show him the location, but Dora hesitated and said, "I cannot read and write. I do not know how to read a map. I can only tell you what I saw on the path as we walked through the forest and jungle. If you want to write them on your paper, I will describe them to you."

When she had finished describing her walk, Chip whispered softly, "I know where it is. I went to a village near there several times with my grandfather." He walked to the desk and put his finger on the spot where Dora said the 'snake pit' should be.

There was a hush in the office for a few seconds, then Chip took charge. "Ollie, please call the governor and the regional military commander to have a unit of jungle fighters on standby near the Bonampak Ruins." He turned to Mona and said, "I don't care who you talk to, but send in some scouts to see if there are any indications that the hostage women are in the cave. If there are, then have the Zapatistas gather a mounted force on the far side of the river. Call your caver friend and ask if he wants to play soldier and lead a rappel party down from the cliffs above the cave entrance."

"Anything else, sir?" Mona smiled and gave him a mock salute.

"Yes, *mi comandante*," Chip said almost respectfully. "See if you can get hold of your father and ask him to get here tomorrow and put together a convoy of trucks and go to the area of operations to create a diversion. Ollie, call Luis and see how many fish trucks he can spare for this operation."

Chip paused a second to think, then added, "Mona, you'll have to be in command of this whole thing. Ollie, you've got to make it clear to the generals that Mona's the big cheese. And there's to be no conflict between the military and the Mayas. Understood?"

Mona looked at Chip and said, "That's rough terrain in the mountains. It'll take at least two days to get organized and put units into place." Then she asked, "And what are you going to do?"

Chip grinned and said, "Your grandmother and I are going to the union meeting. We're going to have a nice dinner and enjoy the show. Too bad you can't join us. By the way, where's Chete? I haven't seen him today."

"He got word this morning," Corina said, " that his mother is very close to death. He is out telling his aunts, uncles, brothers and sisters, and asking them if they want to go with him to be there when she dies, and to hold the traditional funeral ceremony. He'll be back here tonight and leave tomorrow morning for his village."

"Why don't you go with Chete—that is, if he'll let you go with him," Mona suggested. "You won't be able to do anything here except get in the way. If you're at the funeral, you'll be busy and won't have time to sit around and worry."

"That's right, *don* Chipotle. I'm taking you with me, whether you like it or not."

Everyone spun around to see Chete standing in the doorway

"How long have you been listening?" Mona asked.

"Long enough to know that I have to get *don* Chipotle out of here fast and bring him back when the fireworks are over. Call me when the union meeting is finished."

Before picking up the phone again, Ollie turned to Chip and asked curiously, "What was all that about a convoy of trucks?"

"Well," Chip said, "It would tip everybody off if a convoy of military trucks went to the area, so I think it's best if we send in the troops in civilian trucks. And then, after we get the women out and send in a mop-up crew, there will probably be a need to transport a good number of body bags out of there. I suspect the governor won't want to take too many prisoners."

Mona, who was now standing beside Chip, half-smiled at him and said in a low voice, "It's about time you started taking charge. You had me worried there for a while. I can't wait to see what you're going to do about Rainwater Pharms."

CHAPTER FIFTY-TWO

At the entrance of the building called Casa de Diego de Mazariegos, Chip paused for a moment to see if he could spot the mermaid carvings in the stone walls. Ollie had given him a brief history of the building. Imitating a cheap tour guide's monotone canned spiel, Ollie had rattled off some excerpts from a travel brochure. "Over there on the southeast corner of the main plaza is the Casa de Diego de Mazariegos. You will note that the coat of arms over the main entrance has been changed. Some historians believe that it was originally the house of a conquistador named Andrés de la Tovilla and was constructed in 1529, making it one of the oldest buildings in San Cristóbal. Now as we get closer you can see that there are a number of stone carvings on the walls and around the windows. Three of these carvings on the east wall are depictions of mermaids, the mythical sea nymphs who beguiled sailors with their lute-like voices and caused them to wreck their ships on the rocks. Since these mermaids—also known as serpent women—were called sirens, we still use the word 'siren' as a signal of danger." Then Ollie had dropped the act and become serious. "You are going to that 'house of sirens' this evening, Chip. Be on your guard. There will be a woman there whose sexual attraction could entice you into grave danger. And we all know who I'm talking about."

Ollie's warning echoed in his mind as he passed through the door into the "house of sirens." He paid little attention to the dirty looks he received as he escorted Dora into the assembly of university union workers in the convention hall. Although a jagged line of folding screens were in place to section off half the ballroom-sized salon, Chip saw that most of the tables were full and people were still coming in. *At this rate, those screens will have to be moved back*, Chip thought. *It's amazing how a free dinner and an open bar can draw a crowd.*

Chip stood looking for a pair of empty seats when a waiter came up and informed him that *señorita* Lydia Molina would like him to join her at a table near the speaker's microphone.

"Only if there's room for two," he told the waiter.

"I'll see that the two of you are seated at the same table," he assured Chip and led the way to Lydia's front row table. It was a round table for eight. Two men in suits stood and introduced themselves as union officials. From the number of snack trays and empty shot glasses on the table, they hadn't just arrived.

After taking their seats, Chip asked about Lydia's whereabouts and one man pointed to where Chip could now see her talking to Pepe Rosales, the regional union president. There was no need for them to speak in hushed tones because the noise level was steadily rising and it was becoming increasingly difficult to hear what even the person in the next chair was saying. Chip watched Lydia and Pepe for a moment and could almost read their lips when they spoke his last name, rounding their lips to form 'Oatley.'

Chip had never seen Pepe before and was surprised by the man's indescribable ugliness. *He must compensate*

by being unusually intelligent, ambitious and aggressive,
Chip figured. *Otherwise, how could he possibly score with
Lydia or any other female, for that matter?*

As if she could feel Chip staring at her, Lydia turned
and gave him a coy smile, fluttering her fingers. Making
a show the entire room seemed to watch, she half-waltzed
over to Chip, put her arms around his neck, pressed her
nose against his and slowly sat down on his knees.
"Aren't you going to order me a drink?" she cooed. Chip
leaned back, wanting to ask why Ted Cravens hadn't
already taken care of that chore, but let it pass. In his
head, he swore he heard a siren's lute playing in the
background. Chip ordered drinks for everyone at the
table. Even if the drinks hadn't been free, he still would
have treated. To Chip's relief, Lydia slid off his lap saying
she had to go to the ladies' room before the meeting
started. When Dora was certain that Lydia was out of
sight, she nudged Chip and said, "Pass me her drink."

Dora's old, weathered hands moved quickly as she
emptied a small vial of an odorless, colorless powder into
the drink and stirred it until the powder dissolved. The
two union officials on the other side of the table were
engrossed in an off-color joke and didn't notice Dora's
unobtrusive sleight of hand.

By the time Lydia returned, Pepe Rosales was at the
podium trying to quiet the crowd and call the meeting to
order. While he recognized the guests at the VIP table
and extolled the virtues of the *sindicado*, Lydia downed
her drink. And its effects were obvious when Pepe was
just about to bring up the main topic on the agenda, as
Lydia stood up beside Chip and began to sing in a low
sultry voice. Moving her hips suggestively, she began to
strip her clothing off, one piece at a time, striptease style.
Even Pepe went silent as all eyes went to Lydia. Chip
fought her off, disgusted, as she threw herself on him.

Pepe came running over, picked her up bodily, slung her over his shoulder and hauled her out the door where he hailed a taxi and disappeared into the night. Chip and Dora used the cover of chaos to make their exit.

In his mind's eye, Chip could just imagine the scene where Lydia probably woke up in bed with Pepe. *They're both nude and Pepe has a satisfied, lecherous grin on his face. Lydia looks at Pepe and feels nauseous.*

And the sound of the siren's lute slowly faded away from Chip's inner ear.

CHAPTER FIFTY-THREE

Outside the "house of sirens," Chip suddenly realized that Dora had slipped away into the darkness. It occurred to him that he had no idea where she stayed at night, now that Ollie was up and about. Pausing indecisively for a moment to consider whether to call Chete from the nearest phone or just walk back to La CIMA, he looked up and saw the object of his considerations pulling up to the curb in the research center's van a few feet away. "Get in," Chete called through his open window. "I'll take you by your house to get your travel bag. You gringos can't go anywhere without a shaving kit."

As Chip climbed into the passenger seat, he noticed Dora sitting in the seat behind Chete. Looking over his shoulder, he asked, "Where are we taking you?"

"I'm riding along with you to see Chete's mother," she explained. "She and I are of the same people and I have known her since she was a child. I want to see if there's anything I can do to relieve her suffering, and then, if it becomes necessary, I will help her family prepare her body and spirit for the journey into the afterlife."

As his eyes adjusted to the dimness of the van's interior, Chip saw that most of the seats and floor space were packed with foodstuffs, beverages, bedrolls, folding chairs, and flowers. Turning back around, he noticed, for the first time he could recall, a hint of emotion in the tenseness of Chete's countenance.

In normal times, the drive from San Cristóbal to Chete's village would have taken less than two hours. With the added obstacles of two military roadblocks, the trip took nearly three hours and six bottles of cheap tequila for the checkpoint guards.

It was well past midnight when they arrived in a sparsely populated spot called '*El Playon*,' on the banks of a river, not far from Oxchuc. Chete navigated the van through the *selva*, the rainforest, along dirt roads Chip could hardly make out, to a small cluster of cabins near the river. Although there was no electricity, Chete's family home was lit up like a Christmas tree. Lanterns, torches, candles, campfires, and a generator-powered string of naked light bulbs scattered prisms of light beams in all directions.

When they came to a stop in front of the cabin, Chete politely asked Chip to stay in the van while he and Dora went in to determine his mother's condition. Chip had expected as much and understood the customs and sympathetically assured Chete he would try to stay in the background as much as possible.

Chip relaxed in the van watching as Chete and Dora were met at the door and escorted into the cabin. A few minutes later, Dora came back to the van and told Chip the sad news. "She has already started her journey by closing her eyes to this world. Now we must prepare her body to be placed in the earth. But she will not totally leave us until we have said our prayers for her and spoken our goodbyes. She will speak to us no more, but she can hear us until we place the earth upon her grave.

"I will show the old women how to prepare the body for its final rites. When the body is ready, and Chete has dried his tears, he will stand guard with three other males at the four corners of the casket for one hour, when four others will take their places. This will continue until dawn, then we will have a ceremonial meal which the young women are cooking now. Chete would be honored if you will come and stand guard with him."

"I am honored to be asked," Chip replied. "Shall I go in now?"

"I think it would be best for you to stay here until I send for you," Dora said. "Try to get some sleep, if you can. In the morning, after we eat, you will be expected to help dig the grave. With only picks and shovels, that is backbreaking work. Then Chete will want you to help carry the casket to the grave, and after the burial, you will be asked to help cover the casket with earth. It will be a long, hard day for everyone."

"It will be my pleasure to assist Chete in this hour of sorrow," Chip said. "I'll wait until you call me in to stand guard."

Dora nodded solemnly, then suggested, "If you can focus your attention on what is happening here and on how you can help Chete, it will help keep you from worrying about the rescue of your mother and sister."

"I hope you are right. Do not let me keep you from doing what you need to do. I will be waiting."

Chip had no idea how long he had been sleeping when he was roused by Chete knocking on the van window. When Chip opened the door, Chete handed him a coffee mug filled with a clear liquid that looked like water. "This will calm your nerves and give you strength," he told Chip.

"What is it?" Chip asked. "Or would it be best if I don't know?"

"It's homemade *mescal*. Ollie says it's our version of 'white lightning.' Here we call it *café blanco*, white coffee.

Chip took one sip, feeling its warmth travel down to his stomach and turn to fire. "I hope you have some *sosa* ready for me. This stuff will burn a hole in my stomach."

"I'm sure Dora will have a remedy for that," Chete said with a faint smile.

"Are you okay, my friend?" Chip asked, embarrassed at his attempt at humor.

"My tears are drying, but my heart is heavy," Chete said, looking away. "This *café blanco* is helping me get through it. This is my third cup."

"Please be careful *mi hermano Indio*, my Indian brother. I have heard about your tendency to challenge the world with your machete when you have had too much *mescal*."

Chip followed Chete into the cabin and stood guard at the casket. By the time his relief came, Chip was sure that he had been give something more than mescal and he suspected that Dora was responsible.

Although he was mostly conscious and aware of what was happening, Chip's mind was fuzzy and events unfolded in slow motion. The room seemed to pulse in time with the marimba band that was accompanied by a reed pipe, a clarinet, a trumpet, an accordion, and a huge bass drum. Even as the meal was served and the grave was dug, he felt as though was floating through time. And Chip cried, too, when Chete knelt over the casket and to tell his mother how much he loved her and how much he was going to miss her.

It wasn't until the grave had been covered with earth that Chip began to regain a sense of normality. As the van was being reloaded, Chip shook his head in disbelief. *Where was I when they unloaded it?* he asked himself. Only after he recognized the outline of San Cristóbal coming into view, did Chip begin to believe he had returned to reality.

Turning toward the backseat, he saw Dora smiling at him. He started to ask what kind of mind-altering drug she had given him, but then thought better of it. Instead, he asked what she thought Mona would be doing. The answer was the last thing he would have expected.

"She has to be careful with her body," Dora said.

"Why? Is she injured or sick?" Chip asked with alarm.

"No, her condition is altogether different and more delicate than that. I have been observing her closely for these past few days." Dora said. Then, after a pause, she added, "She is with child."

CHAPTER FIFTY-FOUR

C hip woke to the beating of raindrops against the window near his bed. Sure that the pounding was inside his head, he dreaded facing a new day with the *cruda*, a hangover. But as he pulled himself from his bed and headed toward the bathroom, he realized his head was clear, his eyes focused, and he felt well rested and energetic. Only the dark, low-hanging clouds outside suggested gloom. The only thing fuzzy in Chip's mind was the whole spectrum of events that merged into yesterday. He wasn't entirely convinced that what he recalled was real, but confirmation would have to wait. Here and now, today, tomorrow and the future, were uppermost in his mind.

After his morning routine of cleansing and dressing, Chip went to his kitchen telephone and was gratified to learn that it had an expandable extension line that allowed him to move the phone over to the table. His first impulse was to call Mona and demand an explanation as to why she hadn't told him about her "condition," as well as let her know in no uncertain terms just how disappointed, disillusioned, and angry he was to find out about it from someone else. *And the father of her child is probably a priest, of all people,* he thought with indignation. His emotions bordered on rage.

Chip had heard that there was a thin line between love and hate. Now all those feelings of love and desire he had been harboring these past few days were fast dissolving into disgust and repulsion. He felt as though he had been kicked in the gut, with a resulting pain beyond the burn of acid reflux. It would take more than *sosa* to quench this fire. And he found himself thinking it would probably be best if he never saw Che again.

Controlling himself for the moment, Chip dialed Ollie and caught him before he left for the office. After satisfying Ollie's curiosity about the funeral, he demanded to know the latest developments concerning the rescue operation. Ollie assured him that everyone was on the same page and going according to plan. "Mona has some sophisticated communications equipment she somehow obtained through her contacts in Guatemala," he said, "so she keeps everything coordinated and all of us updated on the situation. The military special forces have been working closely with Zapatista scouts. They're positive the women are being held in the 'snake pit' cave."

"Then I better get to office and see how I can be the most help," Chip said.

"I think the best thing you can do is go to the *cacique's* birthday party," Ollie told him firmly. "The governor and the top generals will be there and everybody is going to act like nothing special is happening. Since you already accepted the invitation, it might look suspicious if you didn't attend. Besides, you'd be interested to know, Mona has ordered you to go to the fiesta. You did put her in charge, didn't you?"

There was no answering humor in Chip's voice when he asked flatly, "What time is Chete coming to pick me up?"

"You'll have to drive one of the La CIMA sedans yourself," Ollie informed him. "Chete has to be available as a messenger if he's needed—another of Mona's orders. I told her I'd keep him here on stand-by. So, whenever you're ready, stop by the office and Chete can give you instructions on how to get to El Tigre's *hacienda*. "

Just the mention of Mona's name brought Chip's foul mood back, but again he suppressed his feelings and consented to attend the *cacique's* fiesta.

"Good," Ollie said, sounding satisfied. "When you get here, I'll have Corina call and let them know your physical description, the kind of vehicle you'll be driving, the license plate number and your approximate time of arrival. The place will be well guarded and not just anyone will be allowed in."

"Just curious," Chip asked, "if Luis Mariscal, the seafood dealer and owner of the Delfilapa seafood restaurant will be there?"

"Of course," said Ollie. "He's catering the dinner. And you can bet he will have his truckers feeding him continuous reports. If you recall, Teresa the nurse is his fiancée."

"I remember," Chip answered. "That's why I'll keep a close watch on him. If he takes off for the jungle, I'm going with him."

"If that happens," Ollie said, "give me a quick call first. I might want to go with you."

****

Just as Ollie has predicted, a contingent of armed guards halted Chip on the narrow road leading into the *cacique's* estate. After a few quick questions, one of the guards climbed into the sedan's passenger seat and informed Chip that he would ride along to the parking area. When they arrived, the guard escorted Chip into the palatial, colonial-style home.

After a round of greeting and introductions, Chip noted that he was being shadowed by a voluptuous young woman who wasn't hiding her interest in him. *This woman could help me forget about Mona*, he thought vengefully, although he knew full well he had no claim on Mona. *Why do I feel as though I was betrayed? Was it because she didn't tell me from the beginning and let me make a fool of myself?*

When Chip was finally alone for a moment, the beautiful woman walked up to him and introduced herself as Bettina Bravo, a granddaughter of El Tigre. Chip was flattered by her attention, and it didn't take long for them to establish a first-name basis. Not many men could avoid an instant attraction to her natural beauty, and Chip was no exception. "That amber necklace and bracelet you're wearing are outshone only by your beauty," he told her sincerely. Leaning closer, he added, "Everything about you is beautiful. Your hair, your eyes, your skin, you've got it all. You remind me of a movie star." He lightly stroked her bare arm.

"It's always been my dream to be an actress," she informed him, responding with a subtle shiver at his touch, "and it hasn't hurt my career to have my grandfather's influence to open a few doors. People say that he and I are very much alike."

"In what way?" Chip asked idly, still intent on finding a way to touch her again.

"Well, we're both ambitious and strong willed. We want to succeed in everything we do and when we see something we want, we don't let anyone or anything stop us from getting it, she said, looking directly into his eyes, as if to make sure he understood her meaning. " I guess it's because we're so much alike that it's only natural that we fight once in a while."

"Did your grandfather give you the amber jewels?" Chip asked. "They're some of the most perfect specimens I've ever seen." Talking about the necklace gave him a natural-appearing opportunity to lower his eyes to her chest. She moved in closer to him and it was impossible to tell who was seducing whom.

"Not many people know that our family fortune started with an amber mine right here on this property by my great-great grandfather. The old abandoned mine is just a couple miles down the road. It was loaded with amber gems. It's kind of strange when you think that amber is not really stone, but drops and globules of pine resin that have hardened—almost petrified—over centuries in the ground. When they're polished like gems, they look like translucent stones. Although the amber supply ran out, it lasted long enough to make the family wealthy."

"Have you ever been in the mine? Is it still open to explore?" Chip asked, his interest in the mine momentarily distracting him from Beti's nearly overwhelming physical attraction.

"Oh, it's locked up now, but when I was a little girl, my grandfather used to take me there and show me the cave that was discovered one day when the miners dug through from the mine. It's a large grotto with ancient paintings on the walls." She leaned against the wall behind her, reaching to pull him next to her. "My grandfather found an old Mayan book—he called it a codex—and had a leatherworker make a special cover for it. It was inlaid with twelve perfect amber stones."

"What do you mean 'was'?" Chip asked, nearly jerking back in alarm, hoping the codex hadn't been lost or destroyed.

"I was just a little girl, but I knew I wanted those amber stones, so I begged and cried until granddad finally agreed to give them to me. He gave me one stone every year on my birthday, for twelve years. Then in the thirteenth year he had them all set in gold in this necklace you see around my neck." She patted the stones, drawing his attention once more to her smooth, bronze skin.

"It's fabulous!" Chip said, forcing his eyes back up to meet hers. He tried desperately to sound casual when he asked, "So what happened to the codex? Does he still have it?"

"Oh, it's still down there in the mine just gathering dust along with all those other Mayan things Grandpa collected."

"What other things?" Chip's voice nearly cracked with excitement.

"Lots of things," she answered with another shrug. Then her eyes brightened. "Want me to show you the mine and the cave and all that old junk in the mine shack?" But her interest slackened again as she remembered, "Oh, that's right—you're a college professor. You're an expert on Mayan things, aren't you?"

Now completely oblivious to her obvious disinterest in the treasure she had just described and her even more obvious interest in him as a man, Chip could hardly control his breathing. "If it wouldn't be too much trouble, I'd love to see the mine."

"Sure," she agreed. "I'll go change into jeans and tennis shoes. I'll get the keys from Granddad. I'll be right back."

While Beti made her way through the crowd to get the mine keys from her grandfather, Chip spotted Luis inspecting the display of shrimp cocktail that was being arranged on a side table. Luis greeted him warmly and thanked him for setting the rescue attempt in motion. Then he changed the subject. "Be careful with that fox you were talking to. She's *consentida*, a spoiled brat, and she will use you to get what she wants, then throw you to the dogs. And she will use all her feminine charms if she thinks she needs to."

"I could use a little feminine charm at this point," Chip said drily. "And she's well-endowed with feminine charms."

"Don't say I didn't warn you," Luis said as he headed back to the kitchen.

CHAPTER FIFTY-FIVE

Beti chose a four-wheel-drive Jeep from the fleet of vehicles behind the main building. Her hair blowing in the wind, she drove recklessly down the twisting road through the forested acreage, and braked into a sliding stop at the mine entrance. She jumped out, opened the lock, and unchained the heavy wooden sliding door. When she stepped inside with a flashlight in hand, Chip was right behind her.

With a broken broom handle in one hand to clear her way through spider webs and the flashlight in the other, Beti led Chip down a rotten wood stairway and into a dark, musky-smelling cavern. Pointing to a stack of torches, she asked Chip to light a few and place them at ten-yard intervals. By their light, Chip was able to make out the painting on the walls. Looking around, he saw the furnishings left by the miners. Near the stairs, he saw a desk, a table, some broken-down chairs, wooden boxes of various sizes, three suitcases, and two cots. Clearly, there had been enough activity down here at some point in the past to have not only an office, but also sleeping arrangement.

Everything was covered with a light coat of dust, and as Chip stood surveying his surroundings, Beti took the blankets and sheet off one of the cots and shook the dust out of them. Wondering why she felt the need to shake dust, Chip was caught off-guard when she pulled him over to the cot and began to unbutton his shirt. Before Chip fully realized what was happening, Beti not only had his shirt off, but hers as well. She drew him down to her side like a magnet.

Just as they embraced, his lips pressed against hers, his body ready to submit to her, a man wearing dark clothing and a black ski mask came crashing through the door from the mine and charged at them. Rushing up from behind, he grabbed a handful of Chip's hair, jerked him backward and threw him to the ground. Turning to Beti, the intruder spewed a string of obscenities, lifted a machete and began to swing it wildly in her direction. Beti screamed and jerked backwards. In desperation she grabbed an obsidian spear from the top of the desk. Thrusting the spear at the attacker, she missed and sent the razor-sharp spearhead gouging into Chip's groin. The attacker smashed his machete against the side of Beti's head and she collapsed to the floor. Not stopping to check how badly he'd been hurt, Chip grabbed a miner's pick leaning against the wall by the cot and prepared to fling himself at the attacker. But when Chip looked around, the masked assailant was gone.

Dropping the pick, Chip knelt down next to Beti. A pool of blood was spreading around her head. Ripping the sheet from the cot, he quickly tore off strips and made a bandage. After checking her breathing and pulse, which both seemed normal, he picked her up with an effort and laid her on the cot. Looking down at her, he suddenly realized that his own blood was dripping down the legs of his pants, over his shoes, and was being soaked up by the rags he had just torn. The pain roared into his consciousness, making him dizzy for a moment as he reached for the wall to steady himself.

Something in Chip's memory generated an unexpected inspiration. He stooped, carefully gathered up the bloody rags and stuffed them into an old metal can. Limping to the nearest the nearest torch, he set the rags on fire, watching them burn for a moment. As the smoke rose, he carefully fanned it toward his face and inhaled deeply through his nose. His mind's eye saw a serpent curling out of the smoldering can. He saw the 'vision serpent' Ollie had described to him years ago. And Chip remembered asking about "good snakes" and "evil snakes." The one he now saw had two heads.

Although weak from loss of blood, Chip checked Beti once more, then returned to the make-shift office and began rifling through the desk drawers, the boxes, and suitcases. One of the suitcases contained what he had been looking for. With trembling fingers he touched a stack of loose Mayan documents, then spotted the leather bound casing with empty settings where amber stones had once been. A quick glance inside the cover told him he had found, as he had suspected from Beti's description, an invaluable treasure. Closing it gently, he shut the suitcase and picked it up, but nearly dropped it when he felt a hand on his shoulder. Beti was conscious and standing by his side.

"Beti! Sit down. You've got a head wound and you've lost a lot of blood. Someone tried to kill you," Chip said in amazement. "Do you have any idea who it was?"

"I have no idea," Beti said shakily, "but we can worry about that later. You found what you wanted," she noted resentfully. "Now, let's get out of—" She suddenly noticed that Chip's pants and shoes were blood-soaked. "You've been hurt. Are you okay?"

"It's nothing much. I'll make it. Let's get out of here!"

Chip lugged the suitcase with one hand and helped Beti with the other. Somehow they managed to get to the Jeep. After a brief argument over who was to drive, Chip gave in when he realized how painful his wound would be if he tried to use the clutch pedal. When they arrived back at the house, Luis was outside checking a delivery of oysters. When he saw the blood and bandages, he demanded an explanation. After Chip briefly told him what happened, Luis ordered one of his drivers to put Chip and Beti into the La CIMA sedan and take them to a hospital in San Cristóbal. "I'll make up some story to tell El Tigre," he said. "If there's any news of the rescue operation, I'll come see you as soon as I can get away from this party. All the men inside are gathered around the military radio like they're listening to a soccer game. It sounds like all the units are in place. I've never prayed so much in all my life."

"Teri's going to be all right," Chip assured him.

"Well, if they've done any harm to her, I had my trucks take enough dynamite to blow those caves to hell. Now, get yourself to a doctor. I told you she was trouble, but you wouldn't listen."

CHAPTER FIFTY-SIX

C hip and Beti were semi-conscious when they arrived in San Cristóbal. The driver of the La CIMA sedan, one of Luis' truck drivers, was not surprised when police and military vehicles stopped them on the outskirts of the city. Beti was transferred to an ambulance and whisked to a waiting medevac helicopter and flown to Mexico City where she would receive the best of care. Chip was placed in a military ambulance and taken to a mobile field hospital. He still clutched the suitcase he had taken from the mine.

After receiving what seemed an unnecessarily brutal inspection of his wounded area, a minimal-treatment dressing and a field-expedient bandage of gauze and duct tape, Chip fully expected to be hauled to a recuperation tent and ignored. Instead he was taken to the 'head shed' tent, the office of the commander of the field hospital where he received VIP treatment and was seated next to the communication network radio that had been brought in to monitor the rescue operation in the jungle.

Chip sat in the folding canvas chair with clenched fists and pounding heart as he listened to the exchanges between Mona and the military commanders. He admired the way she positioned and combined the Zapatista foot soldiers with squads of horse-mounted cavalry, almost as if she directed military raids every day. And he wondered how she had managed to combine civilian rock climbers with military Special Forces units to be ready to rappel down the cliffs into the cave openings. Chip could hear the fatigue in the voice of the military field commander as he paraded troops and vehicles along the paved road ten miles from the caves. At the same time, a hundred of his soldiers in peasant clothing crept through the rainforest and positioned themselves within sight of the caves. Five miles away in a small, civilian airport, a squadron of Air Force helicopters warmed their engines.

After a while, there was a momentary lull in radio transmissions and it seemed as if everyone on the frequency simultaneously asked, "*Que pasa?* What's happening?" Chip leaned closer as he heard whispering on the airwaves. The scouts were reporting. *They're clearing off a brushy area. Hey, there's another entrance we didn't know about. How many more entrances are there that we don't know about? And what's this? Some guy is leading three horses into the cave. Are they getting ready to move the women? This could complicate the situation.*

After a few seconds of interminable complete silence, the unmistakable voice said clearly and firmly, the three words that prepare every warrior for that moment he or she has been trained for—to cross that line into deadly combat, "At my command."

It seemed to Chip that even the radio static ceased its crackling as his own breathing stopped and his heart jumped into his throat. Then Mona spoke the code words which set the operation into action, "Chili Chipotle... Chili Chipotle... Chili Chipotle." And Chip heard the world explode. The radio crackled and popped like a giant popcorn machine. He could only imagine the chaos at the 'snake pit.' He stood and gripped the table until his knuckles turned white, feeling no pain from his wound.

The rescue operation followed the agreed upon plan, focusing its attention on the main entrance. The peasant-looking soldiers yelled, blew whistles, and broke clay flower pots to create a distraction that would unsettle nerves for miles. Dozens of other soldiers fired randomly into the air. Machine gun fire added its flavor to the din. Helicopters circled overhead with power beam spotlights crisscrossing the entrance. As expected, a stream of *banditos* poured out of the cave like ants sprinting in all directions and firing automatic weapons at an enemy they could not see. Only when it appeared that no more defenders were coming out, the command was given for the climbers and cavers to rappel down to the entrance. With lanterns fastened to their plastic helmets, they led the exploration though the cavern and all its tunnels. Just before they reached the cave entrance, snipers began to pick off the bandits with deadly accuracy. Their fire was directed at those with firearms. When these were taken out of action and the sniper fire subsided, the sound of pounding hooves thundered toward the cave. The mounted Zapatistas descended upon those who stood braced with knives and machetes.

Suddenly all attention was diverted to the side entrance where the three horses had been led in. Now, the horses came crashing out at a full gallop, charging toward the tree line. Riding bareback, all three were clearly experienced riders. And all three riders were women. Listening to the description coming over the radio of the way the lead rider cut and turned around tree stumps and sandbag bunkers, Chip had no doubt that his mother, the rodeo barrel racing champion was breaking all her old records. Sis and Teri, her Mission Station protégés, were giving her a run for her money. Chip was on his feet and ready to give a rebel yell.

The roar of battle dropped noticeably and from a nearby clump of bushes a lone rider chased after the other three riders. It wasn't difficult to deduce that the three riders were the hostage women, and Mona was going after them. Shouting and waving a white scarf, Mona at last got the women to slow enough for her to explain that she was there to help. Instantly, they were surrounded by a cheering throng. Helicopters swooped down in a clearing close by and medics jumped out to gather up the women and give them a quick check.

At first, Chip's mother loudly insisted that they be taken to the Mission Station, but Mona and the military generals overruled her, ordering the pilot to fly them to San Cristóbal. Mona and the generals climbed in and flew with them.

From her command post in the air, Mona ordered Chip to stay where he was. The women would be arriving shortly and even though Teri, who was nurse, had assured them they were not seriously injured, all three would submit to a thorough medical examination. Chip felt as though he was dreaming, as if what he heard could hardly be true. But he was distracted by a commotion as someone rushed into the tent. He turned to see Luis who had tears of joy streaming down his cheeks.

With all the excitement at the cave, the mop-up units took longer than expected to do their job. After rounding up the banditos who were surrendering, a vocal contingent of Mayan soldiers were inclined to revive an ancient ritual of human sacrifice, but the military police units prevailed and took these prisoners-of-war and threw them into waiting fish truck to be hauled off and interrogated.

When the mop-up crew had their mission under control, a wave of pride swept over the entire rescue army. The scene resembled the end of a well-fought athletic competition as Zapatistas and government soldiers began to strip off their shirts like jerseys and exchange them with the other team. Before the field commanders readied their unit to assemble and move out, there was a good bit of souvenir-taking. More than one soldier made a quick search for a serpent-shaped branding iron to take home. The ecstasy of victory electrified the air.

CHAPTER FIFTY-SEVEN

At the Army Mobile Field Hospital at the edge of San Cristóbal, there were several emotional reunions. Before the military doctors could examine the newly-released hostages, Chip pushed his way in and huddled with his mother and sister, while Luis and Teri locked in a passionate embrace. When the medical staff finally separated the three women from their welcoming committees, Chip and Luis were escorted into a large briefing tent where a dozen folding tables were arranged with four folding chairs around each table.

On one side of the tent were tables with large pots of coffee and hot chocolate surrounded by an array of traditional Mexican *pan dulce*, "sweet bread" pastries. Chip suddenly realized he had not even sampled Luis' seafood delights at the *cacique*'s hacienda, and that he was now famished. His loss of blood must have added to his hunger, he thought. While he was helping himself to the refreshments, a parade of vehicles began to encircle the tent. With Chete at the wheel, the La CIMA van brought in an animated ensemble that included Ollie, Lola, and Dora. Before long, the tent had filled up with the same politicians and military brass who had been at the *cacique*'s hacienda. The governor made a grand entrance with his entourage. Most incredible to nearly everyone was the presence of Mona along with several known Zapatista "operatives." The archbishop and Che mingled with the festive crowd, but the *cacique* and his cohorts were conspicuously absent.

Limping through the crowded tent, Chip was continuously intercepted by congratulatory *abrazos* and handshakes. But before he could reach Ollie's table, Dora approached him and gently but firmly pushed him down. "You're injured in a very sensitive part of your body," she said. "What happened?"

Glancing around continuously, in as few words as possible, Chip told her the story. Dora carefully stood him up and pulled him to the van. "I have some ointment here that will ease your pain and help the wound heal quickly," she said.

"That's very kind of you," Chip replied, looking around for an escape, "and I know that you have special talents as a healer, but I'm a little shy about having you treat my—" his voice trailed off.

Dora nearly doubled over with laughter. "Oh my, you do have strange modesties, Chip, but I was telling you to apply the medicine yourself. You are not permanently disabled, young man. You will soon heal and then forget this pain, but you will never forget that you have undergone the bloodletting ritual of the Mayan people. And this sets you apart. This is a sign that you have been chosen by the gods for a special mission here on this earth." She turned and went back into the tent, leaving a very surprised and embarrassed Chip, who applied the ointment as she had directed. After wiping his hands on towel she had left, he saw that she had left a clean pair of white cotton peasant *pantalónes*, trousers, and a pair of leather *huaraches*, peasant sandals. He changed quickly

before returning to the tent, feeling better than he had
expected in such a short time.

Just as Chip entered, Ollie was busy pulling three
tables together and sitting his group down, making sure
to save chairs for Chip, his mother and his sister. His
timing was perfect; at that moment, the women were
being escorted into the tent by a cadre of doctors who
assured everyone that, except for some minor cuts and
bruises, they were in surprisingly good condition.

When the festive crowd quieted, Laurel Oatley,
Chip's mother, took the opportunity to explain why they
had been so well treated in the cave. "At first we were
treated badly, but then one of men assigned to guard us
began to sneak extra food and water to us. He even
brought us some first aid supplies and some personal
hygiene items. One day when the other guards were busy,
he told us that his wife had taken their infant girl to the
Mission Station and Teresa the nurse had given the child
some medicine that made her well. He felt he was
repaying a debt he owed. I have his name, General, so I
beg you to have mercy on him when he is questioned with
the other prisoners. Oh, and he was the one who brought
in the horses for us."

Teresa spent a few moments with her uncle, the
governor, before rushing into the waiting arms of her
fiancé, Luis. Chip came up and ushered his mother and
sister to Ollie's growing cluster of tables.

No one claimed responsibility, but from somewhere
six cases of champagne materialized and would have
added to the festivities, but there was no joy when Chip
felt it was time to tell the women about the old
missionary. While he told most of the story about the
curandera who had stolen the missionary away, taken
him to a cave, tended to his wounds, then brought him
back to the Mission Station, Chip anticipated a sadness

and weeping. To his surprise, the women, with tears standing in their eyes, gently told him that they had already heard the news and had spent days crying and mourning in the cave. Now, they had come to accept his death and believed he had joined his dear wife in heaven. Chip was even more astonished when his mother proposed a toast to her father. A round of champagne was quickly poured and the tired but smiling woman stood and said in a loud voice, "*Salud!* Cheers!" Her cry was echoed through the tent.

After surveying the crowd, Chip leaned over and whispered to Ollie for a moment, and then they both stood and began working their way through the crowd. Standing at last in front of the refreshment table, there were no objections when Ollie called out to the crowd that the missionary's memorial service was here and now. Everyone who really cared or mattered was here, so Chip stepped forward to take charge and called the archbishop up to give an invocation. Then he asked the governor to say a few words. Keeping the impromptu service brief, he asked his mother to speak for the family. For the occasion, he deliberately passed over the military and the Zapatistas, but when his mother finished, he heaped tribute and praise for their invaluable assistance in the rescue operation.

Chip would have said more, but roar of wave-after-wave of "*Salud!*" drowned him out and he returned to his seat, thinking he would relax for a moment. But as he sat down, his body went tense with alarm as he saw that Ted Cravens was sitting in the next chair.

"Relax," Ted said. "I'm here to help you." Looking at Chip's expression, he continued, "I know you find that hard to believe, and I understand why. You're probably aware that I set out to make your life difficult so that I could force you into cooperating with me. But these last few days have made me see things in a totally different light. I was supposed to be operating on my own down here, but I discovered that my boss from Rainwater Pharms was sending mercenaries to undercut my efforts. I caught one of them going through my hotel room and, with the aid of a .45 caliber pistol, persuaded him to talk. I'm here to warn you, I've learned from an informant that the *cacique* has put a bounty on your head. He holds you responsible for his granddaughter's injuries. I suggest you find a way to get out of Chiapas immediately. I'm sorry for any problem I may have caused you and I will do whatever I can to help you."

Amazed, Chip stared at the Rainwater Pharms rep for a long moment, but couldn't think of any reason for him to lie. When Ted put out his hand, Chip shook it firmly.

The others who were gathered around the table agreed it was best for Chip to leave Chiapas, at least for now. Chip, however, was not in such a hurry. He placed his arm around his mother's shoulder and whispered in her ear, "Mom, we have to talk. Grandpa told me some things before he died, and I found a diary you wrote about your first summer in Chiapas. I need to know if those things are true."

"Yes, Chip, it's all true." There were tears in her eyes. "I should have told you, but I didn't know how. I'm sorry you had to find out this way. I wish we had time to talk more now. I want to hear all about my granddaughter Honey Bee and the status of your doctoral research. We have so much to catch up on." She patted his hand. "But we can do that when you are safely out of here. So now, Gina and I will go back to the Mission Station and get it back into operation. I think Teri is going to be busy for a while making wedding plans. But I'm sure the governor will help us find a new nurse." She squeezed his hand and gave him a motherly peck on his cheek. "Go, now. Ollie will keep us informed."

"And just how am I supposed to sneak out of here?" Chip asked with genuine curiosity.

Chip nearly fell out of his chair when he felt a poke in his back and a familiar woman's voice behind him. "My father Mapache is waiting outside with some of his friends," Mona said. "You may remember Tom and Gerry. They can probably find a way to get you to the military airport in Terán, a suburb of Tuxtla," she said, then added, "I am sorry you were injured in the mine-cave. You were not supposed to get hurt."

"What? How do you know about the mine-cave?" Chip demanded. "And why do you care about me getting hurt?"

"Because I was there," she said, frowning. "I followed you to protect you. You dumb ox, you seemed oblivious to the trap that filthy tramp Beti was leading you into. I could have killed her with my bare hands—she was lucky I just knocked her out by hitting her with the flat side of the machete blade."

"Why do you care what happens to me?" Chip asked, angry and confused. "You're pregnant with Che's child, which pretty much eliminates me out of your life, doesn't it?"

Mona froze for a second, then grabbed his shirt collar with both hands and said, "Oh, no, Chip. Is that what you think? Yes, it's true—I'm pregnant, but Che is not the father. All I will tell you now is that if the child is a boy, I will name him Marcos."

"I think I'm beginning to understand why Marcos, the figurehead for the Zapatista movement, is called 'subcomandante,'" Ollie remarked from where he'd been listening on the other side of the table.

Chip was stunned and embarrassed. "I'm sorry, Mona. I jumped to conclusions. And I want to thank you for rescuing my mother and sister." Then he added, "And thanks for rescuing me from the mine-cave tramp."

"We've all made some mistakes," she said, then looked over at Dora the *curandera* and said, "I'm sorry Grandmother. I should have told you about my pregnancy."

"If I must leave Chiapas, there are some important things I need to take with me." Chip said.

"I've already prepared my father's papers for you to take," Mona informed him.

"I found some more manuscripts in the mine-cave," Chip said, not wanting to mention the codex yet. "I carried out a suitcase full of manuscripts and gave it to Luis to hold for me. Chete, can you come with me? We'll get it from him. I wanted to make copies and scan the documents, but it looks like we won't have time. If you all will excuse me for a moment, I want to go say hello to my old friends, Mapache, Tom, and Gerry. Then I'm going to use some of this sophisticated communications equipment here to call my daughter."

"I already copied and scanned my father's papers," Mona said. "They're safe."

As Chip stood up, he saw Lola sitting quietly beside Ollie. He started to speak, but she cut him off, grinning broadly. "Don't worry about having a job for me, Chip. Ollie and I are going to get married. I can see that taking care of him is going to be a full-time job."

"*Salud!*" Chip said. "Who's going to be the best man—the toucan?"

"Please hurry," Mona nudged him. "And don't worry, I'll pack up your things at the cottage and get Chete to store them at La CIMA. What do you want to do about your pickup truck?"

"I know a taxi driver who'd love to bring it to me in Oklahoma. He wants to practice his English."

CHAPTER FIFTY-EIGHT

After a few rounds of hearty abrazos with Mapache, Tom and Gerry, Chip noticed that Chete was about to toss the old suitcase into the back of Mapache's truck. Putting his hand on Chete's arm, chip told him, "I'd rather keep that where I can see and touch it." After Mapache helped him into the passenger's seat, Chete handed the suitcase to Chip, who placed it on the floorboard between his feet. "If I can ride with a toucan cage for hundreds of miles, I can ride with a suitcase," he said, looking around. "Where's everybody else? Do you think I'm safe with just these three trucks?"

"This is just for starters," Mapache told him. "We'll draw a lot less attention going through San Cristóbal this way. When we get out to the open road, some trucks will be out in front and others will fall in behind us. We won't be alone. So, buckle your seatbelt and enjoy the ride."

"Just like old times, huh?" Chip said with a trace of humor.

"*Vamanos*," Mapache sang out. "Let's go."

Tom pulled out into the lead, Mapache eased into second place, and Gerry flashed his light to signal that he was close behind and that the road to the rear was clear. They drove with caution through San Cristóbal, passing the bus station, and headed south with no sign of trouble.

"Why are you taking me to the military airport?" Chip asked. "Wouldn't it be easier for me to fly a civilian airline?"

"Under normal circumstances, that would probably be true," Mapache said, "but you seem to be involved in what you gringos call an 'international incident.' If I heard right, the governor of Chiapas has been in contact with the governor of Oklahoma. There's a rumor that the governor of Oklahoma is on his way here in his executive jet to fly you back to Oklahoma City."

"And I was trying to keep a low profile," Chip said drily.

Near the edge of town, Tom slowed just enough to allow three refrigerated fish trucks to slip in ahead of him. Three more pulled in behind Gerry. As the newly formed convoy came to a major intersection with a traffic signal, Mapache suddenly turned on his emergency blinker lights, turned sharply to the right and gunned the engine. Chip had never seen a large truck respond so quickly.

"What's happening?" Chip yelled over the roar of the engine as he held on to keep from being thrown from his seat.

Mapache yanked his CB microphone from its holder and called out to Tom and Gerry, "Banditos front and back. Take them out. I'll circle back at the next light. Those fish trucks are *falsos*, they're fake, they've been painted over."

Instantly, the tarps came off the stake beds of Tom's and Gerry's trucks, revealing a squad of infantry in each. Most soldiers held semi-automatic assault rifles, but on both sides men with .30 caliber M-60 machine guns stood at the ready. They heard the CB transmissions and clicked off their safeties. But just as they were about to open fire, six more fish trucks swarmed into the convoy. Suddenly there was mass confusion.

"Which ones are the real ones?" everyone was asking.

Mapache spoke as clearly as he could into his mike, "Do not shoot at the truck with big blue dolphins. Stop the trucks with three fish painted on the sides. I repeat. Save the dolphins!"

Within seconds, weapon muzzles flashed and fish trucks careened in all directions. Some exploded in place. Cars skidded and crashed. And while chaos ruled, Mapache circled around and took a side road to the highway, speeding down the mountainside to Tuxtla. Tom and Gerry emptied the soldiers from their trucks and raced after Mapache.

At the Chiapa de Corzo turnoff, a new convoy of Army trucks, city police and civilian taxis escorted the three trucks across the Grijalva River Bridge, around Tuxtla on the *Periferico Norte*, directly to the Terán airport. And Mapache had heard right—the governor of Oklahoma was there waiting to whisk Chip off in an executive jet. Chip did not relax the tight grip he had on the suitcase until the jet was in the air and safely headed north.

CHAPTER FIFTY-NINE

After a call to Xochi, Chip's flight back to Oklahoma seemed to be one long interrogation session with the FBI, CIA, and the Pottawatomie County Sheriff's Department. When they had finished with their questions, Chip was grateful that they were willing to attempt to answer some of his burning questions.

"We've been working closely with our Mexican counterparts and we think we have put most of the pieces of the puzzle together. We're pretty sure what happened, but it's still a mystery as to why. That means we don't have a motive."

"Please, just tell me what you know," Chip said wearily. "I just might have some information that will shed some light on the motive."

"All right," agreed the FBI agent sitting across from him. "You deserve to know that we've been investigating Rainwater Pharms for a some time. We've suspected they've been bribing foreign officials to get special treatment, and we've been authorized by the Justice Department to tap Rainwater's phone lines. We were surprised to learn that Dean Lambert was involved with Brandon Wesley."

"Who is that?" Chip asked.

"He's Ted Cravens' boss. But Cravens didn't know that Lambert and Wesley were old buddies. And Cravens didn't know that Wesley had other reps working for him in Chiapas. What we can't figure out is why Lambert persuaded Wesley to have the Mission Station attacked and the women kidnapped?"

"Well, I believe I can shed some light on that," Chip told him flatly. "I've learned some background information that might explain Dean Lambert's actions. I have to tell you, I have mixed emotions about the Dean because he has truly been like a father to me all my life. He was actually my father's best friend, but he also loved my mother. He was furious when my mother rejected him and married my father. And ever since my father was killed in Vietnam, he has been begging her to marry him. My theory is that, in his desperation, he had her kidnapped so that he could 'come to her rescue.' Then she would be grateful and feel obligated to marry him."

"That does make a credible motive," the agents agreed.

"But why would they attack me?" Chip asked.

"They were given orders to scare you and keep you away from the Mission Station, but they got carried away. They were not supposed to harm you—or your grandfather, for that matter."

"So what happens now? And why am I still being chased?"

"We're getting some details from the prisoners that were taken at the 'snake pit' cave. The Rainwater Pharms reps paid big money to the *cacique* to do the dirty work. The *cacique* was behind the actual raid on the Mission Station. And he has put a bounty on your head for the problems you caused his granddaughter, Beti Bravo."

The CIA agent spoke up, "We'll just send in a few of our own operatives to persuade him to retract his bounty offer."

About an hour before they reached Oklahoma City, the governor turned the controls of his plane over to the co-pilot and went back to talk to Chip. "I've been listening to the conversation on my headphones," he said. "You've had a bit of excitement these past few weeks and I'll bet you could use a bit of rest. So, I'm inviting you and your daughter to come and stay at my ranch up near Bartlesville for a few weeks and just take it easy. After that, I suspect that you're going to be a busy man."

"Yes, I found some old Mayan documents," Chip said, patting the suitcase, "that are going to astound the community of Mayan scholars, and you're right, this will keep me busy for a long time."

The CIA agent smiled and said, "Mr. Oatley, we pulled a fast one on you. We knew you valued the manuscripts and the codex that was in that suitcase, and we didn't want anyone to rob you of it."

"You knew about the codex?" Chip asked incredulously. "How did you know?"

"We didn't know," the agent said, "but we do now. You see, we switched your suitcase for an identical one. We wanted to make sure yours didn't fall into the wrong hands."

Chip opened the suitcase and rifled through its contents. It was full of old newspapers.

"There's more," the governor said. "I've had some lengthy conversations with the Chancellor of Sooner Institute and he knows the situation. The FBI is prepared to arrest Dean Lambert and an interim department chairperson will have to be appointed."

"I hope it will be someone I can work with," Chip commented.

"I took the liberty to tell the chancellor about the Mayan manuscripts and the codex you found," the governor went on, "and he seems to think that you'll finish up your doctorate and be publishing for a good, long while. He went so far as to say that he will personally nominate you to fill the Chair of the Language Department. So while an interim keeps thing going for a while, you might have to take your daughter to the Mission Station for the summer and finish your dissertation. Besides, the chancellor seems to think the department can run itself as long as Gretchen, that battle axe of a secretary, is in charge of the office. By the way, she's been most cooperative in this investigation and we have no reason to believe she knew anything about Dean Lambert's extracurricular activities."

The governor stood and shook Chip's hand. "I've got to get back to the controls," he said.

****

Chip's entrance into the department administrative office was no less stressful that his visits before going to Chiapas, but for different reasons. This was a confrontation he could not avoid and he just wanted to get it over with,Gretchen was there to usher him into the dean's office. "Go get him, tiger," she growled.

Chip did not smile as he replied, "Thanks, Princess."

Chip walked into the dean's office and went directly to the "hot seat' and sat down. "We need to talk," he said to the dean. The dean was looking in his direction, but his focus was somewhere else.

"I have only one question," Chip continued, although he wasn't sure the dean was even hearing him. "Why didn't you tell me you were my father? I read it all in Mom's diary. " Chip stood up and leaned into the dean's face. "Tell me!" he shouted. "Why couldn't you tell me who you are—and who I am?" Tears of anger and frustration streamed down his cheeks. "Don't you know that my mother loved you and wanted to marry you? But you wouldn't own-up to being my father and doing the right thing, so her love turned to loathing and disgust. She married Merle because he loved her and she didn't want me to be illegitimate. Somehow he found out the truth and went and got himself killed in Vietnam. Do you have any idea how much heartache and grief you have caused? Do you even care?!"

He would have gone on, but it was obvious the dean wasn't listening to him. He had retreated into a different world and totally lost touch with reality. Chip watched the dean's mouth and realized he was quoting scripture. Starting with Matthew 1:1 of the King James Bible, Dean Lambert was quoting every verse from memory, word-for-word.

Chip stood spellbound for a moment, remembering that the dean had once won a contest for quoting the first four books of the New Testament. Then with trembling lips and a broken heart, Chip whispered, "I'm sorry it turned out this way. You could have been a good father."

Before withdrawing from the dean's office, Chip went to the side wall and took down the faded photograph that had always captured his attention. It was the one where his mother smiled out between two young college students—Merle Oatley and Bertram Lambert, her arms around both of them.

When Chip walked sadly back into the administrative office, Gretchen was hiding her emotions in a file cabinet. "Do me a big favor, Princess. Before the law comes, see if you can find a good psychiatrist to come and take a look at the dean. He desperately needs the kind of help he probably won't get in the county jail."

EPILOGUE

Chip and his Xochi relaxed at the Oklahoma
Governor's ranch for a week. In bits and pieces, they
related to each other what they had experienced
during those few weeks of separation and both felt that it
seemed more like months, than weeks.

At first it was difficult for them to open up to each other.
Chip briefly told her about being mugged in Laredo, then
being rescued by a trucker who told him about some secret
manuscripts, and how the daughter of the trucker turned out
to be a Zapatista. In turn, Xochi gave her account of being
taken by her grandparent to El Paso and feeling like she was
a prisoner, then running away and coming back to
Oklahoma. But it wasn't long before they both felt
unsatisfied with superficial answers. To really know and
understand each other, they began to dig below the surface.
Gradually Xochi began to ask her father probing questions
about his reasons for his actions. "But why did you feel you
had to go to Chiapas in the first place?"

"I could give you a dozen reasons, Honey Bee. I'm
sorry, is it all right if I call you Honey Bee?"

"It's okay if *you* call that, but not for anybody else."

"Thanks," he said, then continued, "I think the real reason was because I had made such a mess of my life and I thought by going away to a different place, I could try to figure out where I went wrong, get myself together, and start all over again."

"Dad, it sounds like you were pretty busy down there. Did you have any time to think about yourself?"

"Not as much as I wanted," he answered, "but enough to make some important decisions about what direction I'd like my life to go in. Do you remember me telling you I was in a mine-cave and I was wounded and bleeding?"

"Yeah, you told me a little about that."

"Well, it was more than just a wound. In a way, it was a mystical experience much like the rite of passage that young Mayan boys go through. My blood was soaked up by rags, placed in a container and set afire. When I inhaled the smoke from those smoldering rags, I realized that there was copal incense and pungent herbs in that container. It put me in a trance for a while and I saw the vision serpent. It was an ugly, old serpent, but as it turned and twisted toward the ceiling, it shed its skin and became a new, beautiful creature and disappeared into the smoke."

"What did that mean to you, Dad?"

"I knew right then that I had the power to step out of my old life and start a new one. As I think more about that, I believe everyone can do that."

"That sounds like the sermon grandpa preached when he made me go to church. He said that people transform out of one life and become another person when they become a Christian. I wasn't sure what he was talking about, but now I'm starting to understand."

"Did you really hate being with your grandparents?"

"It wasn't so bad. I just wanted to be with you."

They talked about how they were going to adjust to the absence of her mother, Marlene. And they talked about what they were going to do when they could go together to the Mission Station for the summer.

"I've got an idea, Honey Bee," he said. "I'm going to call Ollie and see how things are going in Chiapas. If he thinks it's safe enough, would you like to go spend a year at the mission station with your other grandmother—my mother—and learn what it's like to live in the Garden of Eden? I'd come down to see you every now and then."

"I like the idea," she smiled. "Let me think about it."

On the governor's telephone, Chip talked to Ollie or Corina almost every day and kept up with the news of Chiapas. Ollie and Lola would wait until Chip returned to set their wedding date. Luis and Teresa were not going to wait. Mapache had planted an experimental acre or two of Okra to sell to Luis for Mexican gumbo. Mapache was going to try preserving Okra through a smoking process to see if it might be used as a chipotle chili substitute. There was a rumor that the Crazy Viking had returned to romance *doña* Sabel. Ollie had adopted the toucan. The governor of Chiapas promised to help Ollie obtain his doctorate that had been denied him years ago. There was a grainy picture in one of the newspaper of Mona astride a burro with a newborn child in her arms and there was speculation that the infant was fathered by *subcomandante* Marcos. Che had asked to be reassigned to a small village parish.

When the day came for Chip and Xochi to leave the ranch, they thanked the Oklahoma Governor for his hospitality and chatted for a while.

"Governor, I really appreciate all you done for me. And it was nice of you to talk to the chancellor of Sooner Institute on my behalf about saving the department chair for me. But I'm having second thoughts about accepting that position."

"What?" exclaimed the governor. "How could you possibly turn down a promotion like that?"

"When I was just a youngster," Chip explained, "I had a religious feeling—a sense that I was being called—that I wanted to be a missionary. And now I'm having those feelings again. So, I'm wondering if I should turn my life in a new direction and try to fill my grandfather's shoes at the Mission Station in the Lacandon Jungle."

The governor stared at Chip for a moment, the said, "Before you make that decision, there something I think you should consider. If you go to Chiapas, you'd be just one missionary. If you stay and become the Mayan scholar I know you can be, you'll be in a position to influence hundreds of young people who might be waiting for your example to hear their own call to a mission field. And who better than you could help them prepare for such a life?"

"I'll give you the same answer my daughter gave me—I'll think about it."

"Good," said the governor. "Now you better go see if your pickup is ready outside. I took the liberty of having it delivered here."

As they drove to Tecumseh, Honey Bee said, "Dad, I've learned a lot about myself. I'm not as grown up as I thought I was."

Chip chuckled and said, "It wasn't long ago that I told myself something very similar. I had to admit that I'm not as smart as I thought I was." Then he continued, "I'm going to give you the same advice your great-grandfather once gave me. When he gave me that Esterbrook fountain pen, he said 'Know thyself.' I wasn't sure what he was trying to tell me, but I have since come to believe that one of the smartest things we can do in this life is to find out who we are.